WICKED
HIGHLANDER

DONNA GRANT

St. Martin's Paperbacks

This is a work of fiction. All of the characters, organizations, and events portrayed in this novel are either products of the author's imagination or are used fictitiously.

WICKED HIGHLANDER

Copyright © 2010 by Donna Grant.
Excerpt from *Untamed Highlander* copyright © 2010 by Donna Grant.

All rights reserved.

For information address St. Martin's Press, 175 Fifth Avenue, New York, NY 10010.

ISBN: 978-0-312-38124-0

Printed in the United States of America

St. Martin's Paperbacks edition / November 2010

St. Martin's Paperbacks are published by St. Martin's Press, 175 Fifth Avenue, New York, NY 10010.

10 9 8 7 6 5 4 3 2 1

*To Melissa and Netti for being such great
advocates of the series.*

To the wonderful readers on the Dangerous loop.

A heartfelt thanks.

ACKNOWLEDGMENTS

My usual list of thanks: My husband for, well, everything. My kiddos, because they're young enough to think Mom is still special, and my biggest cheerleaders. To my parents and family, because y'all are the greatest! Thanks are due to my ever-wise editor, Monique Patterson, who has the best suggestions and greatest insights. To Holly and everyone else at St. Martin's working behind the scenes—you rock! And to my wonderful, supportive agent, Irene Goodman.

ONE

Deirdre stood on the balcony overlooking the cavern that made up her great hall. There were no lofty windows to let in the sunlight as they were deep in the mountain.

Instead, there were multiple large, oval candelabras hanging from the arched ceiling high above them shedding their light. In the yawning space, the glow from the candles couldn't reach everywhere. And that's just how she liked it.

Wyrran with their pale yellow skin mingled with her Warriors of every color imaginable. They looked like a rainbow below her, but she alone knew the sheer destructive power those Warriors had the potential to create. They were men with primeval gods inside them, each with a distinctive power that set them apart from the others. And these were hers to rule. The Warriors stared up at her, their attention rapt, as they waited to hear why she had convened them.

"Hear me. Feel me. Touch meeee . . ."

Powerless to ignore the call of the mountain, Deirdre closed her eyes and lost herself in the song of the stones. She forgot about the Warriors and why she had called them to her and placed her hand on the mound of rock next to her. She succumbed to the sweet oblivion the rocks gave her, had always given her. And always would give her.

It had been so since her tenth winter. She had woken to hear the mountain's call beckoning her. She walked out of her cottage and stared at the distant mountain, knowing that one day she would make the journey to the high peak.

That day was eons ago, but she could still smell the bread her mother baked, still feel the lash her father used on her bottom for not doing her spells correctly. And she could still see her sister's eyes watching her. Always watching.

Even at such a young age Deirdre had more power than any *drough* in their small community. She hid it well, for any *drough* whose power was that great was killed instantly. Because the *drough* aligned themselves with evil and created black magic, their power could be immense—and deadly.

Deirdre had plans. So she waited, and she learned.

The Druids had only been split into the two factions for a short time before they had called the gods from their prison in Hell, but in the time since, the *drough* did not mingle with the trusting *mie*. The *mie* with their talk of goodness and pure magic made Deirdre ill.

There were a few communities of *drough* who banded together. Deirdre's was one of the last. Their little group was mostly family and extended family, but the struggle for power went on daily.

In her eighteenth year Deirdre offered her blood in the ritual to become a *drough*. When her blood seeped from the cuts on her wrists, an excruciating pain sliced through her. In that instant she saw her future as the black magic and evil invaded her soul and claimed her for their own.

The very next day she began to hunt for the scrolls she knew her aunt kept hidden. She'd heard the elders whisper about them some nights, as if the very mention of the scrolls would have the *mie* descending upon them.

Once she found the scrolls taken from the *mie* she knew why the elders whispered, their gazes searching furtively around for listeners. Inside the rolled parchments were spells that were supposed to have been destroyed. Deirdre smiled as she tucked one particular scroll up her sleeve and turned to leave.

"How dare you!" her aunt screamed as she stared at Deirdre from the doorway.

Deirdre smiled to hide her surprise. She had expected to get caught, just not by her aunt. But any person would do for her purpose. "I dare many things, Aunt."

"You'll pay for snooping where you don't belong, you little viper," her aunt said, spittle flying from her thin lips. "You always did like to slink into belongings that weren't yours."

"And what do you think to do about it?"

Her aunt raised her hand to send a blast of magic. Deirdre flicked her wrist and her aunt slammed back against her cottage door, her eyes wide with dawning recognition of just how powerful Deirdre was.

Without hesitation Deirdre unsheathed the dagger she kept at her waist and plunged it into her aunt's heart.

It was the first time she had killed. But it wouldn't be the last.

Deirdre left the cottage and turned to stare at her mountain. That's when she felt her sister's eyes upon her once more. She turned to her twin, Laria. Both shared the blonde hair and sky-blue eyes of their mother, but that's where their similarities ended.

As her twin, Laria often knew when Deirdre had been into some mischief. Deirdre didn't expect to have an ally in her sister. In fact, Deirdre knew she would have to kill Laria.

"What have you done?" Laria asked calmly, but her shrewd eyes saw everything.

Deirdre looked into pale blue eyes that matched her own. She felt for her sister's magic, but just as always, there was nothing. Still, Laria was her twin. "The start of something wonderful, sister. Won't you join me?"

"You know I won't."

"A pity," Deirdre said and raised the dagger.

Laria glanced at the weapon as if it were a flower instead of a weapon with blood dripping from the end. "Will you kill us all?"

Deirdre began to laugh as a thought took root. She let loose a scream that had everyone running toward her. With her sister watching, Deirdre put on the performance of her life.

"Aunt has gained power," Deirdre shouted as she faked her tears and stumbled around. "She tried to kill me. She said she and Uncle would rule over all of us."

Just as Deirdre expected, chaos erupted. She watched as everyone turned on everyone else as accusations flew. A slaughter ensued. Deirdre backed away even though she couldn't take her eyes from the blood and death. The sight before her was gruesome . . . and awesome, feeding the evil inside her.

"Come to me."

The mountain. It called to her relentlessly, and she

would no longer ignore it. Deirdre turned her back on her tribe and looked at the mountain that was hers. It was time for her to embrace her destiny.

"You will pay for what you have done, Deirdre."

She looked over her shoulder at her twin. Blood dripped from a deep cut on Laria's arm and her lip was busted. "Do you think you can stop me? We both know I'm the one who received all the magic. Be glad I'm not slitting your throat, sister."

Deirdre had turned and walked to her mountain. There, in the cool stones, she found the first contentment of her life. Nothing else mattered but the mountain and the stones' call to her.

And she learned she had power over them. She could make the stones move and shift. It was how she created her palace within the huge mountain. The only real home she had ever known.

Sharp nails slid through her hair and brought her back to the present. Deirdre opened her eyes and looked down to find a wyrran staring up at her with its large yellow eyes as it reverently stroked her hair.

How long had she been lost in the past? How long had the stones pulled her under this time?

Deirdre petted the wyrran's smooth head. The wyrran was of her own making. She had used her black magic and created the creatures that served only her. They were her pets, though she heard some of the Warriors call them her children.

She glanced at William. His gaze was always on her, the desire in his eyes hard to miss. The royal-blue-skinned Warrior had shared her bed for a short time. Until he'd captured Quinn MacLeod.

Quinn. Finally, I have you for my own.

Once Quinn had healed from his injuries sustained in his capture, Deirdre had expected him to be grateful. She should have known he would be insolent, but that's why she wanted him so desperately.

The MacLeods had been the first Warriors she created. After centuries of the gods being bound, she had released them into Fallon, Lucan, and Quinn. Unfortunately, the MacLeod brothers had escaped before she could carry out her plans. A mistake she had made sure not to make again.

For three hundred years she had sought to have all three brothers back under her control. She had Quinn to start, and for now that was enough.

She regretted her hasty decision to have him thrown into the Pit, but he had to learn she was in control. She was his mistress, and he would obey her in *all* things.

For the last few weeks she had made herself stay away from him. She wanted him desperately in her bed, to give her the child that it had been foretold would rise—an evil unlike none other from Hell.

In order to have Quinn she had to break him. He held out hope of his brothers coming for him, but before they did, Deirdre had to force the god inside Quinn to take over completely. Only then could he be hers.

And once he was hers, his brothers would soon fall.

Deirdre thought of Fallon and Lucan MacLeod and the women they had claimed. Lucan had found a Druid, a Druid with *drough* blood in her veins thanks to her parents. The Druid would have given Deirdre much power, but the brothers had fought and won that skirmish.

Who would have thought there could be a female

Warrior? Yet that's exactly what Larena Monroe was. And Fallon had claimed her as his woman.

Deirdre rubbed her hands along the stones. When the brothers fell, their women would too. Everything Deirdre wanted was slowly coming to fruition. She just needed patience. It wasn't a virtue she had ever practiced before, but for her plans, she would do whatever she needed to see everything come together.

There was scuffling and a woman's angry hiss behind her. Deirdre turned and looked at the dark-haired, petite Druid being held between two Warriors. The Druid had sent her men on a wild chase through Scotland, but they had eventually caught her.

Deirdre studied her long nails a moment before she said, "It's a good thing it's buried deep in your mind, Marcail."

"It" was the spell to bind the gods in the Warriors. After all Deirdre had been through, after everything she had done, there was no way she would allow one little Druid to ruin everything.

The spell was supposed to have been destroyed when the gods were bound in the original Warriors who battled Rome for control of Britain. Just as with the enchantment to release the gods, the spell had been kept hidden. Until now.

It was by pure chance alone that Deirdre had come across the information about Marcail and her family history.

"How I wish it wasn't," the Druid said, her voice laced with repugnance. "I would bind all the gods in an instant if I could."

Deirdre grinned and looked over Marcail with new

eyes. She liked a show of spirit. Most Druids cowered in fear or begged her to spare them. But not this particular *mie*. Nay, Marcail had fought from the moment she was taken.

Maybe it had something to do with her family. Marcail was descended from some of the strongest Druids that hadn't survived centuries for nothing. Even if Deirdre didn't know Marcail's family, the fact the Druid wore the braids of a Holder told Deirdre everything.

"Ah, but if the spell wasn't hidden, I would kill everyone you had ever spoken with. Instead of just you. But . . . I might do it anyway just to be sure no one knows the spell. I cannot have you destroying my perfectly laid plans, now can I?"

Marcail's turquoise eyes blazed with hatred. She shook with anger, causing the gold bands that bound the tiny braids atop her head to bang together. "You will pay for your sins, Deirdre."

Deirdre stared at the Druid. Marcail had a classic beauty with her oval face and high cheekbones. Her curves obviously caught the attention of men by the looks of the Warriors watching Marcail.

But it was Marcail's magic that truly made her shine. It was one of the reasons Deirdre hated *mie* so. All that goodness just made her ill.

"You poor little *mie* with your thoughts of a reckoning. What you don't realize is that I'll be a goddess soon. There is no one who can defeat me now, and once I take over the world, no one will think of going against me."

Instead of whimpering, Marcail chuckled. "Such grand delusions you have. I may not be here to see you brought low, *drough*, but you will be destroyed."

For an instant, Deirdre knew real fear. Druids possessed powerful magic, and some could see into the future with alarming accuracy. She pushed the apprehension aside and raised a brow. Deirdre hadn't gained her power by giving into threads of panic. "Is that so, *mie*? And who might this savior of yours be?"

"The MacLeods, of course."

"The MacLeods?" Deirdre repeated. "Are you sure of that, little Marcail?"

Marcail nodded her head of wavy sable locks, rows upon rows of small braids falling around her face and over her shoulders and mixing with her hair. "It's spreading like wildfire across the Highlands. It's only a matter of time."

Deirdre looked at the Warriors holding Marcail and smiled. The Warriors began to laugh, their large muscular bodies shaking with mirth.

Deirdre turned to the crowd below her and raised her hand to gain their attention. "My prisoner says her saviors are the MacLeods."

Laughter erupted and filled the great cavern. She waited until it had quieted before she turned back to the Druid who had the potential to ruin everything.

"Do you not think the MacLeods have the power to best you?" Marcail asked, her unusual eyes narrowed on Deirdre.

Deirdre shrugged. "I have no idea. Why don't you ask one yourself?"

Marcail's eyes grew large as the Warriors hauled her down the stairs to the entrance of the Pit. Deirdre smiled and rubbed her hands together. She loved shocking people. Marcail had been too easy, though.

Deirdre leaned her hands on the rocks that lined the railing of her balcony and looked at the creatures below.

"Behold," she said and swept her arm toward Marcail and the Warriors leading her to the Pit.

The wyrran and the other Warriors parted to let them through. Marcail continued to struggle, even kicking the Warriors when she was able. She was a fighter to be sure. If Deirdre thought for a moment she could turn the *mie* to her side she would do it.

But what Marcail held in the darkest recess of her mind could undo everything Deirdre had put into place and then some. Deirdre couldn't even take the chance of killing the Druid herself, much as she wanted to.

Marcail came from a powerful line of Druids and there were enchantments and curses placed all around Marcail as well as in her blood. Whoever killed her was in for quite a surprise.

"We've captured another Druid," Deirdre continued. "A *mie* who would dare to defy me."

The Warriors throughout the cavern began to stomp their feet, banging them like a drum against the stones. Marcail raised her eyes to Deirdre as the two guards stopped in the middle of the cave.

There was a hint of fear in Marcail's gaze, but not the usual terror that Deirdre was used to. Marcail could be a problem, which is why she was being thrown into the Pit. Few Warriors survived in the shadows. There was no way a *mie* would last a day. Whether the Warriors raped Marcail or killed her, all that mattered was that the Druid would be dead—of course, those same Warriors would die for harming Marcail, but Deirdre didn't care. She wanted to focus on other things. Like Quinn.

With a nod, Deirdre bade the trapdoor open. Marcail screamed as the floor shifted and titled beneath her.

The Druid's feet slid out from underneath her. She clawed at the stones, looking for a way to keep herself from falling into the gaping darkness below her.

Deirdre wasn't worried that Marcail might get free. Her Warriors loved a good show, and they wouldn't be denied.

She wanted to watch what Quinn and the others would do to the Druid, but she knew the anticipation of seeing Quinn would make their joining that much better.

Deirdre turned her back on the Pit and the shouts and whistles of the Warriors. She headed toward her chamber so she could dream about Quinn. Already her body throbbed for his touch.

But it wouldn't be long now. He was succumbing to what the Pit was best for—beating away hope. Just a few more weeks and he would be hers.

Isla, hidden high above Deirdre in the shadows, gazed at the action below her with interest. As one of the few Druids who hadn't been killed, Isla was interested in what made Deirdre stay her hand with this newest Druid—Marcail.

It hadn't taken Isla long to discover that Marcail had buried in her mind the spell that would bind the gods in the Warriors.

That alone was what prompted Deirdre to have Dunmore, her mortal huntsman, seek out Marcail. It had taken Dunmore much longer than Deirdre had expected to bring Marcail to the mountain.

Isla had observed Druid after Druid die beneath Deirdre's magic. Deirdre enjoyed spilling a Druid's blood since it gave her magic added power, but she usually preferred to do it in her special chamber where she could be sure no magic escaped. Isla had sensed Marcail's potent magic as soon as the Druid had entered the mountain, so why then had Deirdre gathered everyone in the cavern?

No sooner had that thought crossed Isla's mind than the Warriors hauled Marcail to the entrance of the Pit. Isla's fingers dug into the stones, causing her nails to bend backward. She didn't feel the blood oozing from the sensitive skin beneath her nails as she watched Marcail fall into the Pit.

She gazed into the Pit, waiting for the Warriors to pounce on Marcail and tear her to shreds as they normally did anything that had the misfortune to be thrown into the darkness. Isla glanced at the place Deirdre had been only to find her gone.

When Isla turned her attention back to the Pit, she saw a black-skinned Warrior leap on top of Marcail. Isla had never figured Quinn MacLeod would give in to his god so easily. After everything she had heard of the MacLeod brothers, she was disappointed.

She began to turn away when she saw Quinn toss something out of the way, something that looked suspiciously like the body of a woman.

A slow smile spread on Isla's face.

TWO

The scream lodged in Marcail's throat as the floor slanted under her feet. She was falling. Into the Pit.

Stay strong. Focus. Think!

Her body hit the stone with a loud smack, and she scrambled to hold on to the sloping rock. She ignored the pain throughout her body and concentrated on not falling. Her fingers kept slipping on the smooth stone, the darkness rising up to meet her faster and faster with the lowering of the door.

Then, thank the saints, she found a handhold. She held on for dear life, her fingers aching with the effort. She wanted just a moment to get her bearings before she clawed her way back out.

But she should have known better.

She had forgotten the Warriors and wyrran surrounding her. Too late she saw the Warrior come at her out of the corner of her eye. His foot connected with her ribs, the pain sharp and terrible.

Her fingers released their hold at the same time her brain screamed at her not to let go.

And then she was falling.

She hit the ground on her side with a thud that left her dazed and her head spinning. She didn't move, afraid of the aches she would find. Seconds ticked by as the crowd above her shouted and roared their excitement. What did they know that she did not?

Then she heard it.

She wasn't alone in the darkness.

Marcail pushed past the hurt of her body and rose up on an elbow to peer into the shadows. Who was there? Or rather . . . *what*? She could feel them watching her. And waiting.

The hairs on the back of her neck lifted as she heard the first growl. Her stomach flipped then fell to her feet as fear took hold of her with a cold hand. She knew then what surrounded her. Warriors.

Her entire body hurt, and she feared her ribs might be cracked. There wasn't time to think about that, though, not when certain death faced her.

The first Warrior stepped out of the shadows at her feet. His skin was bright green, like the color of the first buds of spring. He crouched before her, his lips pulled back to bare his large fangs. His hair was matted and of indistinguishable color with all the filth in it as it hung in his face hiding everything but the blazing green eyes.

He was going to pounce on her and rip her flesh with his long, green claws. She had used all her courage with Deirdre. Now, all that was left was the terror that settled around her like a heavy cloak, preventing her from moving or even breathing.

Get up. You're a Druid. Act like it.

But she had no weapons, nothing to defend herself with other than some magic that would do no good against these Warriors. She wanted to curl in a ball and let the tears come.

What would Grandmother think?

Another Warrior joined the first. This one had skin the color of her favorite gray mare. The Warrior tilted his head to the side and licked his lips.

Please, God.

A Warrior of white stepped out of the shadows and regarded her with his pool of milky white eyes. He seemed almost uninterested in her, as if he cared more about what the other Warriors were doing.

A deep, feral growl filled with menace and death sounded to her left that made all the other Warriors look in that direction. A cold sweat broke out over Marcail's skin as dread overtook her.

It happened so fast. One moment the Warriors were looking in the darkness, the next the growling began in earnest. It grew and grew until her ears rang with it.

And then something large and black leapt out of the shadows to land on top of her.

Marcail swallowed a scream and braced herself for the pain she knew was coming. Only there was nothing.

Something grabbed her about the waist and tossed her into the shadows as if she weighed nothing more than a leaf. Marcail's already injured body shook with renewed pain as she landed against the stone walls. Her head banged against something hard.

She tried to focus her eyes, but all she saw was a mass of colored bodies flaying each other alive.

And then darkness took her.

Quinn waited until the other Warriors realized he would battle them forever if he had to. One by one, they drifted back to their caves. It wasn't until he was the only one left standing that he moved back into the shadows. It had taken him days to fight each one of the Warriors in the Pit to stamp his dominance on them after he'd first arrived.

They continued to test him, though. After all, they were Highlanders.

However, there were a few who sided with him and watched his back. Not that he fully trusted anyone in this Hell.

Quinn sighed and turned to where he had tossed the female. He had smelled her before Deirdre had thrown her into the Pit. Her scent was of sunshine and rain. He had known what Deirdre wanted of the Warriors as soon as the Druid had been brought to the trapdoor, and he'd given them a warning to stay away from the Druid.

He wasn't surprised when the other Warriors had gone toward her. Not that he blamed them. The woman was just what any man would want after being in the dark for so long, especially with the cravings, both physically and mentally, the Warriors dealt with constantly.

But Quinn knew he couldn't give in to the urges of Apodatoo, the god of revenge, who was inside him. Not now, not before his brothers came for him.

The gods had risen from the ravages of Hell all those centuries ago to take over the bodies of the strongest Celtic warriors to battle Rome and her great army.

The Druids hadn't realized what they had done when they released the gods, not that they'd had a choice. Rome had been destroying Britain bit by bit. The Celts did what they had to do to make sure the land stayed theirs.

Yet, when the Romans had been defeated, the Druids hadn't been able to coax the gods to leave the men.

The Celts had become Warriors, men with immortality and powers beyond their imagining. As powerful as the Druids were with their magic, they were no match for the Warriors.

The Druids, split into sects of good and evil, joined forces to bind the gods inside the men as a last resort. It worked, but none of them could have realized the gods would travel from generation to generation through the blood in the hopes of being loosened once more.

And then it had happened. Starting with Quinn and his brothers.

Quinn squeezed his eyes closed as he thought of that fateful day and the death and blood that had coated the land he loved. His life had been irrevocably altered in a split second, and there was nothing he could do to change it other than fight the god inside him. And hold onto the last shred of hope he possessed.

In order to keep his god from taking control, Quinn did what he knew his brothers would have done—save the woman.

He flexed his fingers, his long deadly claws clicking together, and winced at the wounds on his side and back. They would heal, but not fast enough, not if the other Warriors attacked again. And they would. They wanted the woman.

But so did he.

He walked into his cave where he had tossed her and stopped in front of her. He had sensed her magic as soon as she landed in the Pit. Just what was Deirdre doing tossing a Druid down here with Warriors? And more importantly, why wasn't the Druid moving?

Had he thrown her so hard that he knocked her unconscious? Or worse? Had he killed her? Quinn had tried to pull back his strength, but he forgot sometimes just how strong his god made him.

Quinn knelt beside the female and put his finger beneath her nose. Her breath washed warm and steady over his black skin, and he let out a sigh of relief.

"Is she hurt?"

Quinn looked over his shoulder to find Arran watching him. The white Warrior had recognized Quinn's name and had aligned with him just days after Quinn was thrown in the Pit.

"She breathes, but I fear I might have thrown her too hard," Quinn answered.

Arran walked toward him slowly, his gaze seeking the shadows where other Warriors waited and watched. In the Pit, none of the Warriors could afford to change out of their god form and risk being killed.

Quinn glanced at the woman. She had screamed when the stones had moved underneath her, but she hadn't made a sound since. Not even when one of Deirdre's Warriors kicked her, and he knew that had to have hurt by her wince.

"She fell hard," Arran said. "Many break bones on that plunge."

Quinn nodded. He would know since he had broken his arm and some ribs on his fall. If she had broken something he needed to discover where so he could see to it, but he prayed she hadn't. She was mortal and couldn't heal as they did.

"Shall I check?" Arran asked.

Quinn wanted to refuse Arran's aid since he didn't want anyone touching the female. He had claimed her when he saved her. She was his to watch over. Quinn shook his head and realized he was acting as Lucan had done when his brother had brought Cara into their castle. It was ridiculous for Quinn to want the Druid only for himself. Even knowing that didn't lesson his hunger for her, though.

A hunger that had begun the moment he saw her bravery, her beauty.

"You can help," he relented.

Together the men inspected her, and to Quinn's relief found nothing broken. There was a sizable knot on the back of her head, and he feared her ribs would bother her for some time. If they weren't cracked, they could be bruised, and even that would be painful and slow to mend.

"What are you going to do with her?" Arran asked as he stood.

Quinn shrugged and sat on a large rock next to the female. "I doona know."

"Deirdre obviously wants her dead."

"After the show we provided them, they'll think she is."

Arran snorted. "Deirdre wants you, in case you've forgotten. She's stayed away, but how much longer do you think that will last before she comes for you? And then finds the female?"

"I have no answers, Arran. I only know that I had to save the woman. I will continue to protect her as long as I'm in the Pit."

Arran raised his hands in front of himself, his white claws gleaming in the darkness and his long dark hair blending with the shadows. "Easy, Quinn. You know you have my loyalty. I just hope you know what you're doing. A female down here with Warriors who haven't seen—or smelled—a woman in years could be a terrible thing."

Quinn ran a hand down his face. What had he done? Aye, the Druid had smelled heavenly, and aye, she had brought out his protective instincts. But Arran was right. The other Warriors in the Pit would want her, and not to tear apart. They would want to slake their lust on her.

And, God help him, he couldn't blame them.

His cock had been hard since he'd gotten a whiff of her sunshine-and-rain scent. Despite the monster that he was and the evil place he was in, he couldn't stand by and not help her.

"Ian and Duncan have given you their loyalty," Arran said. "They will aid us in this."

"Aye." Quinn glanced at the two Warriors who stood on either side of the cave that Quinn used as his own. The twins. Just as with Quinn and his brothers, they were strong fighters, but when they fought together, they were lethal.

Ian and Duncan would watch his back. But how long would that last before lust took over?

Quinn's gaze caught that of a copper-skinned Warrior across the way. Charon kept to himself, neither fighting nor aligning with Quinn, but he watched Quinn often. Yet, he could see Charon's copper eyes on the woman, the lust filling his gaze.

Holy Hell.

Quinn blew out a long breath. Life was Hell in the Pit, and he had just added to his torment. He told himself he saved the woman because he was holding on to his humanity, but in truth, he did it because once he had smelled her, seen her, he had to have her.

What was wrong with him? He was supposed to be concentrating on keeping his god from taking over as he waited for Fallon and Lucan to rescue him. Quinn had no doubt his brothers would come for him. He both longed for it and feared it.

If Deirdre captured his brothers as well, they were doomed in ways he couldn't begin to fathom.

Quinn cursed himself as he had done many times since he had woken in Deirdre's hated mountain. He had run away from his brothers and the love they'd given because he couldn't stand to be around Lucan and his woman, Cara. The love they shared reminded Quinn of everything he had never had, and never would have.

But now all he wanted was to go back to their ruin of a castle and all the memories that were in the crumbling stones.

"We can hide her for a time."

Quinn jerked as Arran's voice penetrated his thoughts. "Maybe. There are at least twelve Warriors down here. Many we doona see because they keep to themselves."

"After you made it clear you ruled the Pit," Arran said with a hint of humor in his voice.

Quinn cut his eyes to Arran and snorted. The week it had taken him to dominate the Pit had been excruciating and not just because of his bodily injuries, but because he'd had to let his god loose in order to survive.

Only he, Arran, and the twins knew that when Quinn was in the shadows of his cave he transformed back into a man. It was a huge chance Quinn took each time, but he was already so close to allowing his god to take over that he couldn't take the possibility of it actually happening.

Not after surviving this mountain for these past weeks.

"Did you hear what Deirdre said?" Quinn asked to

turn his thoughts away from the hopelessness that took more of his soul every day.

Arran went down on his haunches next to him. "I was watching the others to see what they did when the woman fell. The female is a Druid, isn't she? I sense magic."

"You're correct, Arran. She's a Druid. Why not kill her like Deirdre has done other Druids, though?" Duncan asked.

Quinn glanced to his right to find the light blue skin of one of the twins. Behind Duncan was Ian, who moved closer to be able to hear. "That's what I've been thinking, Duncan. Every Druid she brings to the mountain she kills."

"There are a few who still live," Arran corrected him. "Isla is one Deirdre has kept alive."

"Aye." Quinn scratched his whiskered jaw, wishing he could shave. "Some she keeps. But not this one. Why?"

Ian crossed his arms over his chest and regarded the woman at his feet with a raised brow. "What is so special about her?"

Quinn motioned his men closer. He didn't want this getting any further. "There has to be a good reason for Deirdre not to have killed this Druid and used her blood for power. Do any of you have any idea what that could be?"

The twins exchanged a glance with each other before shaking their heads.

"We know next to nothing of Druids, Quinn. You know this," Duncan said.

Quinn looked at Arran to find the Warrior's brow furrowed, his gaze distant. "Arran?"

"I would say the Druid knew something, but if she

did, Deirdre would just kill her. It doesna make sense. There has to be a good reason for Deirdre not to have killed her to gain her magic."

"We need to find out what that reason is." Quinn rose to his feet and looked at his hands with his black claws still showing. The claws were long and sharp enough to cut through a tree. They weren't meant to handle the precious skin of a woman.

For three hundred years Quinn's rage at losing his wife and son in the massacre of his clan had allowed his god to gain much control over him. Now, he hated seeing the god shown in any form.

"We'll have to wait till she wakes. Until then, we keep watch. I doona want any of the other Warriors getting close to her," Quinn ordered them.

The three Warriors nodded and moved to take their positions at the entrance to his cave.

Quinn looked out into the Pit. In the center was a sizeable space where Deirdre would throw her victims and watch the battles take place. Off to each side of the area were caves the Warriors claimed as their homes.

Or prisons without bars, as Quinn thought of them.

His was the largest, but then that came with the territory he had claimed. He hadn't had to kill any Warriors for his bid for supremacy, and the cave was large enough that it allowed him and the other three Warriors to occupy it without it being crowded. Despite that, Arran and the twins had their own caves as well on either side of Quinn's.

The cave also had a slab in the back that Quinn used to lie on, not that he slept. Sleep had eluded him ever since he'd been in the mountain. It was for the best anyway. Whenever he closed his eyes he would either see his brothers' faces or dream about his god gaining control of him and aligning with Deirdre.

Quinn carried too much guilt over leaving his brothers and putting them in the predicament of freeing him to want to see their faces and open his memories of them.

They had spent almost three hundred years securing their castle and fighting any wyrran who dared to get too close to their home. More Warriors had come to them, ready to fight Deirdre in the coming war.

And what had he done? Quinn had ruined it all by running away.

How could he have done that to Fallon and Lucan? After everything they had done for him? Countless times his brothers had been there trying to coax him into controlling his god.

It had been Lucan who brought them back to the castle because he'd thought it would help Quinn. Quinn hadn't wanted to go, but Lucan had been right. Returning to their home had helped to calm Quinn in ways he couldn't explain.

With a sigh, Quinn gathered the Druid in his arms and stood. She weighed no more than a feather, but the feel of her soft body made Quinn realize how long he had been without a woman.

He held her pleasing body and curves longer than was necessary before he placed her on the slab he used for his bed. He yearned to lie beside her and feel her warmth, hungered to touch her skin. Longed to taste her lips. He brushed the dark locks of hair from her face, surprised to find rows of tiny braids on the crown of her head and her temples.

Quinn smiled as he fingered one of the plaits. She

was a child of the Celts. Her magic thrummed through her veins for all to feel. It was strong, very strong.

He wondered again why Deirdre hadn't killed her. Though the Pit was far below the space Deirdre used as her great hall, Quinn had heard Deirdre say the Druid thought the MacLeods could save her.

Was it because the woman knew of him and his brothers? Nay, he didn't think that would stop Deirdre. There had to be something else. If there was one thing Quinn knew about Deirdre it was her self-preservation. Deirdre thought of herself first and foremost on everything.

It was one of the many reasons she had lasted as long as she had. That and the black magic she used. Hatred for Deirdre swelled within Quinn, making his god growl and yearn to be free. The god promised vengeance against Deirdre, and for a heartbeat, Quinn nearly gave in.

He concentrated on battling the god and gaining control again. Each time became more difficult. Quinn didn't know how much longer he had before the god took over. He prayed his brothers reached him before that happened.

Quinn stilled when the female moaned. She was going to be in pain, but there was nothing he could do to help her. It was also chilly in the Pit. They were far below ground and water constantly ran down the walls, making the Pit damp as well.

He rubbed his hands along her bare arms and felt how cool her skin was. Quinn racked his mind for what Lucan or Fallon would do for the woman. He had no food, no blankets, and nothing to assist with her aches. Had he just prolonged her death?

Quinn sank onto the slab near her legs and allowed

himself to think of Lucan and the woman his brother loved. Cara was a perfect fit for his brother in all ways. He wondered if they had gotten married. He supposed they had, though the thought of the ceremony without him left an ache in Quinn's chest that made it difficult to breathe.

His thoughts then turned to Fallon. As eldest, Fallon had been taught since his birth the duties of a laird. None of them could have guessed an evil like Deirdre would wipe out their clan, leaving nothing behind.

Quinn had seen how difficult it had been for Fallon to deal with the god inside him, but Quinn hadn't been able to help his brother when he grieved so for his wife and son.

As always Lucan had been there to hold them together. Quinn hated himself for the jealousy he felt toward his brother. Lucan had shouldered so much with Quinn's rage and Fallon's drunken stupor that he deserved contentment.

Instead of sharing in the joy with Lucan, Quinn had resented him. Quinn envied Lucan because Lucan had what Quinn had always sought—love. The purest, truest form of love.

But Quinn would never know that kind of affection, of that he was certain.

He turned his eyes to the female beside him. She was petite and so slender she appeared no more than a child at first glance. Until one looked at her chest and saw the curves of breasts, full and pert.

Her gown was of common material, but the gold bands that held her braids told him she was much more than she seemed. As all Druids were.

Unable to help himself, he leaned forward and inhaled her scent again. She smelled so good he almost thought he was back at his castle standing on the cliffs with the sea wind ruffling his hair and the spray of the waves washing over him.

Quinn's gaze raked her face. Her long, sooty lashes rested against her cheeks, and dark brows arched softly above her eyes. He was curious to know what color her eyes were, to see if they were as exotic as the rest of her.

She had high cheekbones, a small, pert nose, and a mouth that begged to be kissed. His balls clenched, desire making his breathing harsh. He touched a finger to her lips before he could think better of it. They were so soft, so luscious he almost leaned down to taste them.

To savor. To enjoy. To claim.

Get a hold of yourself!

Quinn fisted his hand and moved it into his lap as his blood quickened and rushed to his cock. But he couldn't tear his gaze from her. The steady rise and fall of her chest drew his eyes. He wanted to tear her gown from her and see her body in all its naked glory.

To feast his gaze upon her creamy skin, her lush curves. To caress. To hold. To embrace.

"Holy Hell," he ground out as a wave of lust swallowed him.

It wasn't as if he had remained celibate like Fallon and Lucan. Nay, Quinn had given in to his body's urging when he could deny it no longer. His brothers never knew when he had left the castle. With some part of his god always showing, Quinn had left at night, keeping to the shadows and darkness.

But he had never wanted a woman like he wanted to touch, to taste . . . to *feel* the Druid beside him.

The woman issued a long, low moan that made Quinn

yank his gaze to her face and bite back a groan of his own. Out of the corner of his eye he saw Arran and the twins also glance her way.

She lifted a shaky hand and touched her forehead, her breath hitching as the pain registered in her mind.

"Don't move," he whispered in warning of the pain that was to come.

THREE

"You've got a rather nasty bump on the back of your head, and I think your ribs are bruised."

Marcail stilled at the sound of the deep, rich voice that sliced through her like the mist that came down from the mountains. A shiver raked her body that had nothing to do with the cool temperatures that surrounded her.

For that short moment, she forgot the throbbing of her head and how it hurt to breathe. All she could think about was who belonged to such a sensual, commanding voice.

And did she dare find out?

With each pounding inside her head she recalled everything that had happened over the past week, beginning with her running through the forest and being cornered by Dunmore and the wyrran. Then she had been brought to Deirdre and thrown into the Pit.

She remembered being surrounded by Warriors before something big and black leapt on top of her. She sucked in a sharp breath and instantly regretted it as the ache exploded in her chest.

"Easy."

The same seductive, smooth voice surrounded her once more; his tone left her feeling safe and protected.

It was a ruse, she knew, but in her current condition there was nothing she could do about it.

Marcail licked her lips, then bit back a moan as that simple movement caused pain to burst in her head once more. She laid there a moment thinking she heard what sounded like a chant. The more she tried to listen to it, the faster it faded until there was nothing.

Any moment she expected her head to explode from the pain. When nothing happened, she cracked open an eye to see she was surrounded by darkness. She hated the dark because of what it represented—evil. With a sigh, she closed her eyes and concentrated on alleviating the aches of her body.

She placed her hand on her forehead and felt a large, warm hand cover hers. "I have nothing to help with your pain."

Was there concern in his voice? She swallowed to wet her dry mouth. "I will be all right."

"You are a healer, then?"

She started to shake her head, but his hand held her still. Instead, she said, "Nay. I was taught how to speed the healing of my body."

Marcail wasn't sure why she told the stranger that. She shouldn't trust him, even if he had saved her. Or had he? Was it just another trick by Deirdre?

"You need to mend yourself, then," he said, his husky voice dropping even lower. "By saving you, I've put you in terrible danger. I will protect you, but with your injuries, it will make it more difficult."

She never liked being a burden to anyone, but there was something in his voice, a thread of despair and heartache that mirrored her own and caused emotions to stir within her. She had to have his name. "Who are you?"

"My name doesna matter. Rest and heal yourself, Druid."

The pain of her body began to drag her under, but she fought to stay awake, to learn more about the mysterious man beside her. "Marcail. My name is Marcail."

"You have my word I will protect you. Now sleep."

She could have sworn as she drifted off to sleep that he whispered her name.

Quinn lifted his hand from Marcail's forehead once he was sure she was asleep. He picked up her small hand and placed it on her stomach. Unable to help himself, he ran his fingers over the back of her hand, feeling her soft, supple skin. It wasn't until his claws touched her that he worried about her discerning what he was.

It had been Warriors, after all, who had thrown her into the Pit. She trusted him now, but how long would that last once she realized she was surrounded by more Warriors—most of whom wanted her for her body?

He told himself to leave her and let her sleep, but he couldn't make himself rise. He didn't fight the urge to stay near her. It seemed harmless enough. But when the desire to touch her rose within him, he fisted his hands on his thighs until he shook with the crushing need to lay his hands on her again. Was this how Lucan had felt when he'd had Cara in his arms?

Quinn knew in that instant he had made a fatal mistake. There was something about the female that moved a deep, dark primordial reaction inside him. That emotion could very well be the death of him.

With a curse Quinn leapt to his feet and stalked to the cave entrance. Marcail was too tempting, too sweet to be left alone with the likes of him. He would only bring her down as he had everything else in his life.

"She woke?" Arran asked.

Quinn almost didn't answer. "Briefly. She's in a tremendous amount of pain. However, she told me she knew how to help herself heal."

"Not surprising. Every Druid holds a special kind of magic. It's lucky for the female that she can mend herself."

Quinn grunted, not wishing to speak of Marcail any more since his body hungered for her so. "Any sign of trouble?"

Arran crossed his arms over his chest and jerked his chin to the left. "They smell her. God's blood, Quinn, we all smell her. She's like a feast to a starving man, in more ways than one. We're going to have our hands full."

"I'll be watching her myself." Quinn knew his voice came out more of a growl than anything, and Arran's narrowed white gaze let Quinn know the Warrior heard the challenge in it.

"Do you think I would fight you for her?" Arran asked, his voice hard with disbelief. "I gave you my word I would stand by your side. Do you doubt me?"

"What I question is the need within all of us—myself included."

Arran blew out a breath and raked a hand down his face. "None of us deserves to be here, the Druid especially because she doesn't stand a chance against us in a fight. Did she say anything else?"

"She told me her name. It's Marcail."

"Marcail," Arran repeated. "An unusual name. She

didn't happen to say why Deirdre didn't kill her, did she?"

Quinn shook his head. "Not yet."

"Let's hope she wakes soon so we can learn more about her." Arran turned and looked at Marcail over his shoulder.

Quinn watched Arran, waiting for the moment when he would have to battle one of the few men he gave his trust to.

"She reminds me of my sister," Arran said after a lengthy pause.

"You had a sister?"

Arran nodded and looked away from Marcail, his brow furrowed. "Two actually. One older and one younger. Marcail reminds me of my youngest sister. She was small and always into some kind of trouble. I used to call her my little sprite."

"What happened to her?" It was out of Quinn's mouth before he thought better of it.

"She died," Arran murmured absently.

Quinn didn't press for more. There wasn't a Warrior out there that hadn't suffered terribly when Deirdre found them. Quinn had discovered this the hard way.

With Arran lost in the memories of his past, Quinn walked to the twins. Both brothers were tall and thickly muscled. They stood similarly with their feet apart and their arms crossed over their chests as they stared at the other Warriors, waiting for someone to make a move against Quinn.

Duncan and Ian looked so much alike that they wore their hair differently to help people know who was who. Both had light brown hair that was streaked with gold, but Ian wore his shorn close to his head while Duncan preferred to let his grow down his back.

Ian turned his head to glance at him. "The Druid woke."

It wasn't a question. Quinn nodded. "She's healing herself now. I plan on questioning her more once she wakes again."

"Does she know where she's at?" Duncan asked.

Quinn shrugged. "If you two find any food, let me know. Marcail is going to be hungry."

They only got fed once a day, and then only some bread. But it was enough for them. Quinn planned on giving her most, if not all, his food if she needed it.

"I'll see to it," Ian said and walked away.

Duncan scratched his chin and watched his twin. "How long do you think it will take for Deirdre to realize the Druid isn't dead?"

"Not long enough," Quinn admitted. "Not nearly long enough."

FOUR

When Marcail next woke, she felt immensely better. There was still a dull ache in her head, but it would fade. She tried taking a deep breath and was rewarded with no pain.

In the distance she could hear the chanting again, as well as music. For an instant, Marcail thought she sensed magic in the tune, but just as before, it faded before she could discern more of it.

It was a heartbeat later that she realized she wasn't alone. Was it the man with the voice that made her stomach flutter? Or was it someone—or some*thing*—else?

Marcail opened her eyes to the darkness once more. She became aware of the steady dripping of water nearby, and with the cool air, she knew she was still in Deirdre's mountain.

"How are you feeling?"

She turned her head toward the now familiar voice. He wasn't sitting with her as before but stood off to the side. Try as she might she couldn't discern more than his silhouette in the gloom. She wanted to see his face, to know his name. "I'm better."

"Good."

Marcail sat up slowly, testing her body. When the

aches didn't scream in pain, she swung her legs to the ground. That's when she saw that what little light there was came from a torch on the outside of what looked like a cave. The Pit.

Across from the cave were even more caves, though they appeared smaller. And in between was the large open space where she had fallen.

Oh, God. Warriors.

She gripped the stone slab she sat on with both hands and tried to keep her breathing steady. She had never feared the Warriors before Deirdre had taken her prisoner. Mostly because, in her opinion, they weren't to blame for what was inside them.

Now that she had come in contact with those in Deirdre's control, she had a different opinion of the men.

"Are you the one who threw me after I fell?" she asked the man. He stood to her left, still as a statue.

There was a moment's pause and then, "Aye."

"Who are you?"

"What is so important about my name?"

She was taken aback by his hard tone and the anger. Why should he care about giving his name?

There was a loud sigh, then a shadow moved at the entrance of the cave. The torchlight glanced off his skin, but it was enough that she saw the milky expanse of his chest and the tattered breeches that hung on his hips.

She recalled looking into his white eyes, eyes of a Warrior. When the god was loosened and shown for everyone to see, the Warrior's skin turned whatever color the god had chosen. Added to the claws, their eyes changed as well, the color taking over the entire eye.

"You have nothing to fear from us," the white Warrior said. "I am Arran MacCarrick, held here by Deirdre until I either turn to her side or die."

"How many are you?" she asked hesitantly.

Another form moved at the entrance. This time, he jerked the torch out of its holder and brought it toward her. Marcail looked into two very similar faces, their skin a pale blue, with matching kilts, but one with long hair and the other short.

"We're Duncan and Ian Kerr," the long-haired one holding the torch said. "And that," he pointed across from him, "is Quinn MacLeod."

Marcail jerked her face to the Warrior hidden in the shadows. It all made sense now. Deirdre had flaunted that she held a MacLeod, but Marcail hadn't believed her. "You didn't want me to know you were a MacLeod?"

Quinn snorted. "Why would I want you to know that? After everyone heard you declare it would be the MacLeods who brought Deirdre down, yet one is captured in her mountain? It doesna exactly inspire confidence, does it?"

With the torch now close enough, she could see him standing tall and powerful with his fists clenched and looking as fierce as a Highlander about to enter battle.

She wanted to see his face clearly, to ingrain his image in her mind. The only thing she could see about him besides his plain red linen tunic and threadbare breeches was his hair. It was the color of caramel and hung in long thick waves past his shoulders and around his face.

It wasn't until she let her gaze fall to the ends of his hair that she spotted the gold torc around his neck. The wide metal was twisted into a braid as big around as her middle finger. And at each end of the torc was a wolf's head, its mouth opened on a snarl. The image of such a cunning and intelligent creature seemed to fit the youngest brother of the MacLeods.

Marcail rose and faced Quinn. She caught a glimpse of his skin as it faded from black to that of a man who had spent plenty of time in the sun.

She wondered why he didn't want her to see him in his Warrior form, but she would sooner or later. She had the most important part, though; his god color was midnight.

"Thank you for saving me."

He shook his head, his hair fanning over his brawny shoulders. "I'm not so sure I did. Every Warrior in the Pit wants you for his own now."

She wondered if he wanted her as well. His words caused her to glance over her shoulder to the three other Warriors. They watched her intently. One of the twins inhaled deeply, his nostrils flaring as if he were smelling her.

She rubbed her hand on her skirts, wishing she still had her dagger. Even if she had a dozen swords, nothing would help to keep the Warriors away if they wanted her.

"Why did you save me then?" she asked Quinn.

He shrugged away her words. "What do you know of Deirdre?"

"The usual. She has been alive for countless years and has more power than any Druid, *mie* or *drough*, has a right to. She has been capturing Druids for centuries and killing them. And everyone knows what she has done to the men who she thinks could be Warriors."

Arran shook his head and walked around to stand

beside Quinn. "Deirdre doesn't just kill the Druids, Marcail. She takes their blood and with it their magic. Deirdre kills them herself, careful to collect all the magic within their blood."

Marcail looked at Quinn for confirmation. He nodded and it made her blood turn to ice. How did none of the Druids in her village know this? Or had her grandmother known and not told her?

She gripped the fabric of her skirt in her hand to help steady herself. "Then why didn't she kill me?"

"That's the question we all want answered," Quinn said.

"I see." Marcail wrapped her arms around her waist and tried to not shiver. "Deirdre wants me dead. Why then throw me down here for you to do it?"

Duncan narrowed his dark eyes at her. "Why does she want you dead?"

Marcail licked her lips and wondered if she should tell them. She had kept her secret for so long she had begun to think her grandmother had spoken falsely. Until Dunmore had come hunting her.

"Most Druids can trace their family lineage to the very Druids who helped bind the gods inside you. My family was one of those."

Quinn's steady gaze held hers. "Why is that important?"

"Because one of my ancestors was the one who helped to come up with the binding spell."

The air grew thick with expectation. It was one of the reasons she hadn't wanted to tell them. It gave them hope. And she would have to kill it.

"The spell is passed down through each generation,"

Marcail continued. "My mother died when I was very young and didn't pass it on to me. My grandmother, however, did."

"What is it?" Arran asked anxiously. "Can you speak it now?"

Marcail shook her head and looked away from the Warriors. "My grandmother told me when I was but a child. She used her magic to push it so far back in my mind that I don't recall it."

"Not at all?" Ian asked.

"I'm sorry, nay." She wished she could help them. She would do it in a heartbeat. Anything to defeat an evil such as Deirdre.

Quinn shifted his feet. "How do you know you possess the spell, then?"

"I don't." She finally made herself look at Quinn. "The Druids I lived with all assumed I had the knowledge, just as I did. They helped to protect those of my family because we hoped that one day I would be able to use the spell."

It wasn't that Quinn didn't believe her. He knew first-hand that the Druids were capable of great magic, but something wasn't ringing true. "You say your grandmother gave you the spell?"

"Aye," she said.

"How?"

Marcail shrugged. "She told me."

"Do you recall when she gave you the spell?"

"I remember her sitting me down long after the sun set. It was just days after my brother had died. My grandmother was all I had left of family. She told me she had something important to tell me."

"And then she spoke the spell?" Duncan asked.

"Aye," Marcail whispered. "I can recall seeing her lips move, but I don't remember the words."

Quinn could see how agitated his men were becoming. He had felt that rush of anticipation at Marcail's words just as they had. "If you cannot remember the spell, how were you to pass it on to your daughter or son?"

"I don't know." She pushed her way between him and Arran and walked into the shadows.

Quinn didn't rush to follow her since she hadn't left the cave. She stood facing the wall, her back to him. She shivered in the cold and rubbed her hands along her arms for warmth.

He sighed and tried to think how best to approach Marcail. He wanted her to trust him, wanted her to look to him for everything. Quinn didn't know where the feelings had come from, but once he recognized them, he couldn't push them away.

It was the sound of her indrawn breath, unsteady and low, that made him close the distance between them. He drew in a deep breath of her scent and let it wash over him. It soothed him in ways he couldn't explain, just as her nearness sent his lust raging through his veins and his body shaking with need.

He had to get a hold of himself. Quinn mentally shook his head to clear it, but there was nothing he could do for his cockstand. As long as Marcail was near, he wanted her.

"We're just trying to discover why Deirdre didna kill you herself." Quinn spoke softly, wanting to draw her closer. "It's not like her, and she doesn't pass up a chance to gain power. Not unless there's a possibility she'll be harmed."

And that's when it hit him.

"What else did your grandmother do to you, Marcail?"

She slowly turned to face him, her body just a hands-width away. "She was a Druid, Quinn. She was always murmuring spells of some kind."

For the first time, Quinn allowed himself to look into her eyes. Thanks to the power of his god, he could see as well in the dark as he could in the light. And what he saw were eyes of turquoise, so enthralling he couldn't look away. Sleeping, she had been beautiful. Awake, she was stunning.

Every sensation she felt could be seen in her movements and her eyes. And right now she looked at him with such desperation and misery that he wanted to take her in his arms and tell her everything would be all right.

The last woman he had held in his arms had been his wife—a wife who had wanted nothing to do with him once they were married.

Quinn refused to think about Elspeth. Instead, he lost himself in the striking, petite Druid before him. "Is there a possibility that she could have protected you somehow?"

"If you knew my grandmother, you would know anything was possible. She always said my mother's death could have been prevented, just as my brother's could have."

"And your father?" Quinn asked.

She looked away, a small frown marking her brow. "My father, like my husband, was killed protecting our homes from wyrran."

Quinn felt as if he'd been punched in the kidneys. "You were married?"

"For a short time."

"How long ago?"

She lifted one slim shoulder. "Over a year. It was an arranged marriage. They wanted the best fighter we had to protect me."

It wasn't just what she said but the way she said it, with such resentment, that got Quinn's attention. "You didna care for your husband?"

"Rory was a good man. I tried to be happy in my marriage."

"And your people wanted to protect you?"

She nodded. "They've always sheltered my family."

Because she knew the spell to bind the gods? Or was it something else, something that Deirdre also knew and so didn't—or couldn't—kill Marcail?

Too damned many questions.

"What will happen now?" Marcail asked.

Quinn couldn't stop himself from reaching out and touching the flawless skin of her cheek. "You stay alive."

FIVE

Isla walked through the narrow corridors of the mountain alone. It was just as she preferred it. If she had her way, she would never see another face, human, Warrior, or wyrran, again for the rest of her days.

But her life wasn't her own. It hadn't been for so very long.

All too soon Deirdre would summon her. In the beginning, Isla had held out hope that not all of her summons would end in evil and death.

It hadn't taken her long to realize her hope had been false. Since then, she had lived each day as if it were her last. And in truth, she didn't expect to live much longer.

At least if she had her way she wouldn't.

"My lady."

Isla halted at the soft voice. She slowly turned her head to see one of the other Druids Deirdre kept in her mountain. These Druids, though, weren't confined to the dungeons or locked up awaiting death. Nay, these Druids had been turned to Deirdre's side, their magic removed.

Deirdre bade the Druids keep their heads covered with black sheer material at all times because she didn't want to look at their faces, faces Deirdre had deformed.

Even when the Druid slaves spoke, they spoke in a whisper so she couldn't distinguish their voices.

There were only three Druids who weren't made to wear the head covering. Those were Isla, her sister, and her niece.

Isla lifted an eyebrow at the servant. It was no secret she hated these Druids; they had been weak enough to give in to Deirdre because they feared death. "What is it you want?"

"You have been requested."

Isla tensed. She hadn't expected Deirdre to send for her for some time yet, but there was another who often sent for her. "By whom?"

The servant bowed her head. "Your niece, my lady."

That news should have relieved Isla, but it didn't. In fact, it made her more edgy. It had been over a month since she last saw Grania, and she could have gone the rest of her days without seeing her again.

Isla fell in behind the servant as she was led to Grania. Her niece was kept in a chamber locked by Deirdre's magic. In order to see Grania, Deirdre had to grant Isla permission, which was the only way someone could get through the barrier of magic.

By the time Isla arrived at her niece's chamber, her nerves were frayed. Nothing good could come of this meeting, of that she knew.

"Is there anything you require, my lady?" the servant asked as she stepped aside at the doorway.

Isla glanced inside the chamber to find her niece. "There is nothing. You may go now."

She waited until the servant shut the door before Isla turned to face Grania. She recalled the day Lavena had brought Grania into the world. The delivery had been long, and they had celebrated the birth of a healthy baby girl with much joy.

Lavena had promptly called the baby Grania, the name meaning love. It was a perfect finish to the day. Isla thought their happiness would never end. But just three short years later, Deirdre had come into their lives.

"Good day, Aunt," Grania said from her seat carved out of the wall.

Every time Isla saw Grania, it was like a dagger twisting in her heart. Deirdre had taken an instant liking to the child and used her magic to prevent Grania from aging. Ever.

But Isla knew that Deirdre's fondess wasn't the only reason she kept Grania a child. Isla would never do anything to put Grania in harm's way. An adult Grania who had turned to Deirdre's side, however, would be easier to go against. Deirdre knew Isla all too well.

"Grania. How do you fare?"

The child laughed and jumped to the floor. "You know I fare as well as a queen, Aunt."

Isla clasped her hands in front of her and waited. It did no good to try and prod Grania. The child was as manipulative as Deirdre, and nearly as evil. Where was the adorable, loving child who Isla used to rock to sleep?

"Tell me of the *mie* that Deirdre threw into the Pit."

Isla kept her features flat. She didn't like the interest Grania had in Marcail and nothing good could come of it either. "What is it you want to know?"

"Is it true the Druid knows how to bind the gods?"

"You know it is."

Grania laughed again, the laugh that Isla used to do anything to hear. "So it is. Once again, Mother and her foresight has helped Deirdre in her quest."

"It has."

The child resumed her seat on the rocks. "Now, I was told you saw the *mie* drop into the Pit. The servants didn't see what happened after that. I want to know what you saw."

"The Warriors attacked her."

"But she isn't dead, is she?"

Isla hesitated. There was something in the way Grania spoke that made the hairs on the back of her neck rise. "I didn't stay to see the body. Why?"

"The *mie* has been protected with a spell. Whoever spills her blood will die a horrible death. Since I've heard no screams of pain from the Pit, I assume the Druid isn't dead, only slightly injured."

At least Isla now knew why Deirdre hadn't claimed Marcail's blood for her own. However, it wouldn't take Deirdre long to realize Marcail wasn't dead. And then what?

"Now tell me," Grania demanded, "did all the Warriors attack the Druid?"

"Nearly. It was brutal. You would have loved it. Now, I must go. I have duties to see to."

Grania's blue eyes narrowed. "Don't make me summon you. You are my aunt, after all. You should visit me often. If I have to call for you again, you won't enjoy what I do to you."

"It is never my intention to ignore you, Grania. My duties take me away from the mountain as you well know."

But Grania was no longer paying attention. Isla took measured steps out of the chamber. Not until she was in the hallway did she breathe freely. Her once vivacious niece had been turned into a wicked monster with a thirst for blood and gore that would rival the Romans'.

* * *

Marcail missed the sun. It had only been hours since she last saw it, but already she yearned for it. There was no need for Deirdre to torture her or throw her into the Pit. Just deny her the warmth and light of the sun and Marcail would slowly go insane.

"I've brought you something," Quinn said as he squatted before her as she sat on the floor.

Marcail's eyes had grown accustomed to the dim light well enough that she was able to see Quinn's face clearly. Finally. He had pulled back his hair into a queue at the base of his neck, revealing a face women would die for.

Quinn's was perfection. His strong jawline was dusted with dark whiskers, giving him a lethal appearance and accentuating his firm lips and hollowed cheeks. The beard wasn't full, which told her he had shaved not too long ago. Though she didn't mind the beard, she wanted to see him without it.

His forehead was high with dark brows that slashed over eyes of the palest green. She had seen enough of his silhouette in her short time to know he was as tall and muscular as any man in the Pit. But there was a presence about him, an air of command, that got everyone's attention. Including her own.

"Marcail?"

She blinked and made herself look away from his spectacular eyes. "Forgive me. I've never seen eyes the color of yours."

One corner of his mouth lifted. "I could say the same for yours."

For a moment they stared at each other.

Finally, Quinn cleared his throat. "Your eyes have adjusted to the darkness, then?"

"They are better, aye. The light from the torch also helps. You said you brought me something?"

"Aye. Food. It isn't much, but it's something."

Marcail had been so wrapped up in being in the dark that she hadn't realized how hungry she was. Just then her stomach growled.

"Eat your fill," Quinn said as he handed her a loaf of bread. "I will get more if you need it."

Marcail placed her hand on his arm before he could leave. The feel of thick sinew bunching beneath her palm made her yearn to touch more. "Let me share with you."

"You need it more than I."

"Please, Quinn. I don't want anyone going hungry so that I may be fed." She broke the loaf in half and held it out. "Won't you eat with me?"

For a brief moment she thought he would refuse. He eventually took the bread and moved to sit beside her.

Maybe it was because he had saved her, maybe it was because he was a MacLeod, but she trusted Quinn. That trust might very well end her life, but she knew she would die in Deirdre's mountain one way or another.

"You see in the dark, don't you?" she asked.

He nodded slowly.

"Why then are there torches down here?"

"For Deirdre. She may be powerful and immortal, but she doesn't have the powers our gods have given us."

Marcail pulled a piece of bread apart and popped it into her mouth. "Interesting."

"How did Deirdre capture you?"

She was surprised by the question. She glanced at Quinn as she finished chewing. "Wyrran were spotted near our village. In the past, small groups of wyrran would roam the countryside looking for Druids. Those were the ones we always fought. But this time, they had a leader. A man."

"Dunmore," Quinn spat.

"Aye. I knew they had come looking for me. I couldn't stand the thought of anyone being killed so I made the decision to leave the village. By that time already half of the village had left to save themselves."

"That was foolish."

"It is the thought of every person on this earth to live another day. We all knew what awaited us if Deirdre captured us. I do not blame them for running."

"Then you left as well?"

"I did. It kept Dunmore and the wyrran from following the others. I stayed to the forest and led them about for nearly a week."

His brows rose. "A week? That's impressive."

"Only because I knew the land. Impressive would have been escaping."

"You couldna have escape'd the wyrran, Marcail. Magic aided them on their quest to find you."

"I know."

"What happened once you arrived here?"

Marcail took a deep breath. "I was immediately brought to Deirdre. She knew I have knowledge of the spell locked in my mind, but she didn't try to find it. Why?"

"I'm guessing it's because she's afraid to."

"I don't believe that."

Quinn shifted to his side so he faced her. "Deirdre is nothing if not intelligent. She hasn't gotten the power she has now by making costly decisions. I think she knew she couldna kill you or extract the spell the same way she knew you had the spell to begin with."

"And how is that?"

"Black magic."

Marcail shook her head. "As a Druid I know just how powerful magic can be, but to get the answers she somehow has . . . There has to be something else."

"You know *mie* magic. What you haven't encountered is *drough* magic. Black magic has much more power than yours. And as long as Deirdre's been alive and acquiring her power, her magic is nearly limitless."

"If that's so, why doesn't she have your brothers?"

Quinn found himself smiling again. Marcail's mind was quick. "Probably the same reason it took her three hundred years to capture me."

"Which is?"

"We fought her."

Marcail grinned, making Quinn forget to breathe. He would never tire of looking at her. She was exquisite. So pure in spirit and form that it boggled his mind that she was sitting next to him.

"There are Druids who fight her. The difference is our magic cannot touch hers," she said.

Quinn didn't want to talk about Deirdre any more. He reached out and touched one of the small braids that hung from Marcail's temple down to her breast. "Why do you braid your hair like this?"

"The holder of the spell always has bound her hair this way. It's a tradition that has been in my family since before Rome left Britain."

He glanced at the wealth of sable waves that fell down her back nearly to her hips and wanted to plunge his hands in the strands.

"I like it," he said.

"And your torc? That is also a tradition of the ancients."

"That it is. In my clan the laird's family always wore a torc. It was my mother who chose the animals that would grace mine and my brothers' torcs."

He stilled as her finger reached out to touch the wolf's head on his torc. His blood quickened when her hand brushed against his chest, sending currents of heat unfurling within him.

"Beautiful. The wolf suits you, I think."

"How can you say that? You doona know me."

She shrugged, her body leaning closer to look at the torc, teasing him with her scent and curves. Quinn forced his hands to stay as they were instead of reaching for her.

"Maybe," Marcail said. "Maybe not. However, I know the wolf is cunning and intelligent. I've seen those same traits in you."

Quinn dug his hands into the bread to keep from caressing her. It had been so long since he had kissed a woman that he'd forgotten how, but he wanted to taste her lips, to sweep his tongue into her mouth and learn her essence.

He wanted to drown in her scent of sunshine and rain, to feel her silky hair surround him and her soft skin bared to his touch.

Marcail suddenly sat back and lowered her hand. "And your brothers? What animal is on their torcs?"

Quinn opened his mouth to talk and had to clear his

throat before sound came out. "Fallon, the eldest, has a boar. Lucan has a griffin."

"Those are powerful animals your mother chose."

"My brothers are powerful men, and her choice fit each of them."

Marcail cocked her head to the side, her braids swinging with the movement. "Are you telling me you don't think your mother chose well for you?"

"Not at all." Quinn turned his head away and scratched his chin, ill at ease anytime he thought to compare himself with his brothers.

"Liar."

That one word brought his gaze back to her. "Why would you say that?"

"It's in your eyes," she whispered.

Quinn didn't know how to answer her. He should be angry that she called him a liar, but the truth was she was correct. He had lied.

He looked down to find she had eaten all her bread. "Are you thirsty? I can show you where to find the water."

"Arran already has, thank you."

No sooner had the words left her mouth than she yawned and wrapped her arms around herself.

"How much sleep did you get this past week while you were evading Dunmore?"

She lifted one shoulder. "Not much. It's one of the reasons he finally caught me."

"And food?"

"I ate what berries I could find as I ran."

Quinn put his bread in her hands. "Eat. No arguments, Marcail. You're going to need your strength down here."

"And you?"

"I've got a god inside me. Remember?"

She bit into the bread. "Tell me of your god."

Quinn would talk about anything as long as she ate. "He is Apodatoo, the god of revenge."

"It's true then, that the one god is in you and your brothers?"

"Aye. Each god chooses the strongest warrior of whatever bloodline he's in."

She swallowed and nodded. "Which means, you and your brothers were all three the strongest."

"Correct. We each are strong fighters, but when we battle together with the god unleashed, we are unstoppable."

Marcail's brow furrowed at his words. "Can you not fight Deirdre that way?"

"If only it were that easy. Maybe in the beginning we could have, but now she has too many wyrran and Warriors around her."

Quinn noticed how Marcail quickly ate the rest of the bread. She was probably starving for more, and she needed meat to help build her strength. Meat they didn't have.

"How long have you been down here?" she asked.

"I don't know. You lose track of time when you cannot see the sun."

"Have you been in the Pit the entire time?"

"Nay. I was chained in another dungeon for a while and beaten daily. Deirdre thought she could break me that way."

"But she didn't," Marcail said with a smile. "See? You and your brothers will save us."

Quinn wished it were that easy.

"How did you end up in here?"

Quinn grimaced as he thought of what Deirdre wanted from him. "She wants me to give her a child. I refused, so she put me here to change my mind."

Marcail's turquoise eyes grew wide. "Why does she want a child from you?"

"Something about a prophecy. She said I would give in to her demand one day."

"Why not just use magic to force you?"

"Probably the same reason she didna kill you—she canna."

Marcail leaned her head back at his words. Quinn had gone over in his mind a thousand times the incident with Deirdre. He had expected her to force him, but she hadn't. She needed him to come willing, and willing he would never be.

Just thinking of having sex with Deirdre made Quinn want to retch. He would kill himself before he ever agreed to give her his seed willingly.

Quinn looked over to find Marcail's eyes closed and her breathing evened in sleep. Her head tilted toward his shoulder. He reached up and leaned her against him so she wouldn't harm herself on the jagged rocks on the walls.

The Pit was not a noisy place. The Warriors kept to themselves for the most part. Few spoke, and when they did it was in whispers. When Quinn had first been thrown in the Pit, the constant dripping of water had nearly made him daft, but now, he didn't notice it.

What he did notice was a conversation going on between a couple of Warriors. It was quickly escalating, which meant a fight was brewing. A battle between Warriors could get loud. Quinn reached up and covered

Marcail's ear with his hand to help drown out the noise he knew would come.

From his position he could see movement near the entrance to his cave. Other Warriors moved closer to the action to discover what was going on.

Quinn spotted Duncan and knew the Warrior would report all he discovered. Quinn wished the others would stop fighting amongst themselves and learn to band together to battle Deirdre, but nothing he said could convince them.

He also had a suspicion that Deirdre had a spy in the Pit. That notion would be tested soon enough, because if there was a spy, he would report Marcail to Deirdre as soon as he could.

Quinn knew once Deirdre discovered Marcail there was nothing he could do to save her. Deirdre might not kill Marcail herself, but she would do whatever it took to see the Druid dead because of the spell she carried.

If only Quinn could get the spell out of Marcail then they could use it against Deirdre and bind all the gods once more. Without her Warriors, Deirdre only had her wyrran. Though the wyrran were tough, they could be killed easily enough.

Quinn found his eyes closing. He should be up and seeing about stopping the fight between the Warriors, but it felt so good to have Marcail next to him, her head leaning on his shoulder as she slept.

He rubbed his cheek against the top of her head and felt her braids. He couldn't imagine how long it took her to plait her hair, but he would enjoy watching.

It had been three hundred years since he had let a woman touch him as Marcail was. The women he had taken his ease with had been in the dark where they couldn't see him, and he had never wanted to hold them.

With Marcail it was different. But then much had changed since Deirdre had captured him. He was able to manage his god now, something he hadn't been able to do in hundreds of years. Quinn couldn't wait to tell his brothers.

Marcail nestled more comfortably against him. Quinn smiled and let himself enjoy the small moment. By the growls, the fight between the Warriors had broken out. Soon, the smell of blood and death would fill the Pit.

The ever present rats were moving closer to the brawl, hoping to find something to eat. Quinn sensed when one reached the entry to his cave and began to move inside.

"Out. Now," Quinn told the animal. *"You will not enter here or come near me or the woman."*

The rat immediately moved away from the cave. Quinn had learned of his power only when he had awakened in Deirdre's dungeon. All those years and he'd had no idea of the power he'd held. For three centuries he hadn't developed that power or learned to use it.

How he regretted the fury that had run his life. He would do so many things differently if he could. But there was no going back and reliving the past. There was only the future.

And that looked bleak.

SIX

Quinn snapped his eyes open. He hadn't let himself drift off that deeply since being thrown in the Pit. Anything could have happened to him . . . or to Marcail.

He looked down to find the Druid half lying in his arms. Her head must have slid off his shoulder while he dozed. Thankfully, he had fit her in his arms and her face against his chest.

Her lips were parted as she slept, his arm supporting her head while her hair draped over his arm and legs. Quinn could honestly say he had never seen a more beautiful woman in all his days.

There was a purity about Marcail that shone for everyone to see. But there was strength there as well. Marcail had been intelligent enough to run and lead Dunmore and the wyrran from her village. She had saved countless lives by doing so. It had taken much courage, courage Quinn hadn't expected from a woman.

Unable to stop himself, Quinn lifted his free hand and ran the back of his fingers over the smooth skin of Marcail's cheek. His hand shook with the need, the hunger, to touch more of her.

Even knowing he wasn't good enough for her didn't stop the yearning to know her as only a man could. He wanted to kiss, to lick every inch of her body.

His rod throbbed. It was made worse by the feel of her in his arms. Three hundred years was a long time not to feel the softness of a woman as he was now.

Quinn's gaze fastened on Marcail's mouth. Such a luscious, decadent mouth. Her lips were full, wide, and delectable. He knew they would taste heavenly, and that one kiss would never be enough.

He lowered his head before he realized what he was doing. Just before his lips touched hers, he managed to stop himself. What would she think when she woke to find him kissing her?

Quinn didn't want to find out. She looked at him with trust in her gorgeous turquoise eyes. He didn't want that to change.

His free hand brought a lock of her hair to his nose. Quinn breathed in the scent that was hers alone. But it wasn't enough. He wanted more. With a tilt of his head, he fit his face against her neck and drowned in the sunshine and rain fragrance. He could still smell the sun on her skin.

Slowly, he lifted his head, afraid she would wake. And afraid she wouldn't.

Her eyelids lifted, and he found himself gazing into her eyes. For several heartbeats they didn't move, didn't speak. Quinn realized he still held a lock of her hair in his grasp, but he couldn't seem to let go.

"I didn't mean for you to become my bed." Her voice was barely above a whisper, soft and seductive.

Quinn's balls tightened in response. "It was my pleasure."

Her lips tilted into a smile. "You don't stay in your god form as the others do. Why?"

"Because it's what Deirdre wants. I'm very close to

my god taking control of me. If that happens, I'm hers."

Marcail's hand cupped his cheek and her brow furrowed. "You take a grave chance by allowing your god loose."

"I owe it to my brothers."

"And to yourself?" she asked.

He began to shake his head no when her thumb brushed his lips.

"Don't you dare tell me nay." She sat up and put her face close to his. "You can beat whatever Deirdre tries to use to lure you or trap you. I've heard tales of you and your brothers my entire life, Quinn. You were the three who have outwitted her for hundreds of years."

Quinn closed his eyes against her words. He couldn't move, not with her hand on him, but he didn't want to hear her words. She didn't know the true him, the person who had disgraced his brothers and put their plan in jeopardy.

No one wanted to know that person—not even Quinn.

"You doona know what you're saying," Quinn finally said. "There are things about me you doona know."

"No one is perfect, Quinn MacLeod. You need to realize that before it's too late."

Before he could respond, she was gone. Her touch, her heat . . . vanished. Quinn felt bereft, as if he had been shown a glimpse of heaven for those few moments she was in his arms.

But when he opened his eyes, he was still in Hell.

He found Marcail at the water that collected in a hollowed-out stone. She drank her fill, then splashed the water on her face.

Quinn wanted to go to her, but he had nothing to

say. He wasn't about to tell her who he really was. She was one of the few people who saw him as he wanted to be.

Odd that he had recognized that so quickly. Maybe it was because she claimed the MacLeods would save her, and he wanted to be the one who did it. For whatever reason, when she was near, she made him want to be the man he saw in her eyes.

Lucan MacLeod washed the blood from his tunic in the loch and draped the tunic over a tree limb to dry. For the third time in two days they had been attacked by wyrran.

"There will be more attacks," Ramsey said.

Lucan looked to the calm, reserved Warrior. Ramsey was the one who listened, formed his opinions, and then spoke. So, when he stated something, it was to everyone's benefit to take notice.

Fallon blew out a breath and rubbed the back of his neck. "Of course there will be more. Deirdre knows we would come for Quinn. I'm not going to let my brother rot in her mountain to do with as she wants."

Lucan glanced from his brother to Larena. Fallon's wife was the only female Warrior they knew of, and her power to become invisible was a huge asset they planned to use once they reached Deirdre's mountain.

Ever since Quinn had been taken, Lucan had worried for his younger brother. Quinn had always been rash, allowing his temper to rule him instead of listening to reason.

The fury that rode Quinn was understandable. Lucan didn't know how he would deal with losing Cara, much less a child along with her. It was one of the reasons

Cara and Larena took a special brew that prevented them from becoming pregnant, just in case. There was no record of a Warrior getting a woman with child, but Lucan didn't want to take any chances until Deirdre was dead.

Quinn had every right to want his vengeance against Deirdre, but he hadn't learned to control the rage. It was that anger that worried Lucan the most.

"You doona think he'll survive, do you?" Galen asked him.

Lucan had stopped wondering how Galen always knew what he was thinking. Galen said he could read people's expressions and how they held their bodies, but Lucan was beginning to suspect it was much more than that.

"It's the truth I'm concerned," Lucan admitted.

Galen raised a dark blond brow. He was still in Warrior form, his dark green skin cloaking him in the forest. Galen flexed the claws of his right hand and gazed at the ground. "Quinn is burdened by the deaths of his wife and son, as you know. But there is more."

"I know." Lucan ran a hand down his face and lowered himself to a fallen log. He longed to dive into the cool waters of the loch, but there wasn't time for small enjoyments such as that. "Fallon told me all that Quinn had admitted to him about his relationship with Elspeth."

Lucan had thought Quinn and Elspeth had loved each other. True, it wasn't the love like their parents, but Lucan had thought his brother was happy. None of them had known just how wretched Quinn had been.

"Do you think Quinn is lost to us?" Lucan asked

Galen. The question lodged in his throat, but it was one he asked himself every hour of every day.

In a blink Galen's dark green skin, claws, and fangs vanished. He looked at Lucan with knowing blue eyes and shrugged. "We willna know that until we arrive. There is one thing you can never doubt, Lucan."

"What's that?"

"You and Fallon are all Quinn has in this world. The bond that holds the three of you together is stronger than all of Deirdre's magic."

Lucan thought over his words as Galen walked away. Lucan's gaze shifted to the other six who traveled with him. There was Fallon who had finally taken his place as leader, and his wife Larena. Then there was Galen, Ramsey, Logan who kept them all laughing with his jests, and Hayden who had a hatred for *drough* that consumed him.

Quinn's life rested on the fate of seven Warriors who were coming to free him.

"I wish we could get there sooner as well," Fallon said as he walked up.

Lucan had been angry at first that Fallon couldn't use his power to jump them from the castle to Cairn Toul Mountain in a blink. It had been too many years since any of them had been to the mountain, and if Fallon jumped and landed them in the middle of a rock, they would all be dead. They had to be safe, and that meant traveling on foot.

"We'll get there," Lucan answered. "We run faster than horses and can maneuver quickly if need be."

Fallon nodded, but Lucan saw the weariness on his brother's face.

"Galen told me something I hadn't considered."

Fallon chuckled and pushed his long dark brown hair away from his face. "I'm not surprised. Tell me."

"He said that the bond between us brothers is stronger than any of Deirdre's magic."

"Do you think he's right?"

Lucan considered it a moment and nodded. "Aye, brother, I do. Quinn might be many things, but he will fight against Deirdre."

"A man can only last so long in her mountain, Lucan."

"Then we best hurry."

Fallon jumped to his feet, his brow furrowed. It was a look Lucan knew well. His brother's mind was spinning with a plan.

"Let's split up," Fallon said. "The wyrran can only attack one group at a time."

"And the other?"

Fallon smiled, the gleam of battle shining in his dark green eyes. "The other forges ahead."

Lucan clapped his brother on the back. "Let's get moving then. Quinn has waited long enough for us." He grabbed his still-damp tunic and pulled it over his head.

With a nod to Fallon, Lucan motioned for Hayden, Logan, and Galen to come to him and continued on the path. Fallon took Larena and Ramsey by a different route to Deirdre's mountain.

SEVEN

Marcail found herself watching Quinn as her mind turned from the chanting and music she had sworn she heard yet again. Every time Quinn walked about the cave or spoke to his men, her gaze tracked him. His movements were fluid and powerful.

She noticed the way he and his men would search the Pit with their eyes relentlessly. It didn't take her long to understand what Quinn had meant when he said he had put her in greater danger by saving her.

Even in the shadows of Quinn's cave she could feel the eyes of other Warriors on her. There was no privacy for her, but as long as she stayed in the cave, she was safe.

Safe, however, was a relative word at the moment. As long as Deirdre held her, Marcail would never be secure. Despite knowing this, she couldn't make herself leave Quinn. Deirdre might not kill her, but Deirdre would make sure she was dead.

The thought of never looking into Quinn's pale green gaze again left Marcail feeling ill to her stomach. Every Druid in Britain knew how important the MacLeods were to their survival. Was it the idea, as Quinn had said, of him and his brothers in the tales she heard that made her look at him as her savior?

It's more than that. I know it is.

Marcail had seen into Quinn's eyes. She had glimpsed for herself the shadows that haunted him, but she had also seen him take command. Every Warrior in the Pit regarded him as a leader. They might not all side with him, but they knew better than to question his authority.

Quinn turned and caught her staring at him. He frowned and asked her with just a shift of his head if everything was all right. She nodded and looked away. But it was too late. She saw him approach out of the corner of her eye.

"What is it?" he asked.

Marcail drew her legs up to her chest and rested her chin on her knees. She had been sitting on the slab Quinn used for his bed ever since she had left him that morning. Her bottom was numb, but she was scared to move, terrified to bring more attention to herself.

"Marcail?"

"It's nothing. I was just watching you with your men."

He sat beside her and leaned his elbows on his knees. "None of the Warriors would dare to come inside my cave. You can move around freely."

"And if Deirdre discovers me?"

"In truth, it's only a matter of time before she does."

Marcail licked her lips as her skin rippled with trepidation. "Why put off the inevitable then? I'm putting you, Arran, and the twins in danger by hiding here."

Quinn straightened and turned his head to look at her. "Do you think we care what Deirdre will do to us? Marcail, she puts people she wants to break in the Pit. We will either turn to her side or die. It's the only way any of us will be released."

"So you think she will leave me in here?"

"It's crossed my mind. You said yourself she wants you dead."

Marcail hoped Quinn was right. She had a better chance of survival with Quinn than anywhere else. "I hope you're right."

"I am. My brothers are coming for me, and when they do, I'm taking you out of here."

"Are you sure your brothers know you are here?"

Quinn smiled wryly. "Oh, aye. Deirdre told me she left them a missive. They know she has me."

"How did Deirdre capture you?"

By the way Quinn frowned she wished she hadn't asked. "Never mind," she said. "It doesn't matter."

"What did the stories tell you about me and my brothers?"

She hesitated, unsure of where to begin. "We were told you three were the first Warriors Deirdre found, that she killed your entire clan to get to you three."

"That's truth. Deirdre killed everything from livestock to children and babies. Anything that was on MacLeod land died."

The way he said it made her soul ache. She heard the horror and acceptance in his voice, and it saddened her. "I'm sorry, Quinn."

"My wife and son died in the slaughter along with my parents. I was with Fallon and Lucan and a handful of clansmen as we went to meet Fallon's intended. Deirdre must have attacked right after we left."

Marcail's stomach rolled. She'd had no idea Quinn had been married and a father. She placed her hand atop his on his leg. "There is nothing I can say that will lessen the pain of losing a wife and child."

"What else did you hear?"

She removed her hand and cleared her throat. It was obvious he didn't like talking about his wife and son, not that she could blame him. She had always heard time heals all wounds. It might diminish the pain, but one never forgot the dead.

"The stories say you went looking for Deirdre."

"Nay," Quinn said with a shake of his head. "She sent us a note saying she knew who had attacked us. My brothers and I never realized the trap for what it was. As soon as we stepped foot in this mountain she chained us and unleashed the god."

"What was it like having the god unbound?"

"More painful than you can imagine." He blew out a breath and leaned back against the stones. "It felt as if every bone in my body snapped in two and then melded back together. My blood was like fire in my veins as the power of the god flowed through me. My body shook from the pain, but the power the god gave us overcame even that. We shattered the chains she had put us in and escaped before she realized what had happened."

"You three were lucky."

"Extremely so. Though at the time we didna think it. What do the stories say happened to us?"

Marcail tucked her legs underneath her. "Once you escaped Deirdre you disappeared, always fighting her."

"Disappeared." Quinn chuckled. "We lived for fifty years like animals in the mountains, fighting each other. We were too afraid to go into villages. It was Lucan who took us back to our castle."

"MacLeod Castle?"

"Aye."

Marcail couldn't believe it. "No one ever thought to

look there. The MacLeod lands were divided between clans and everyone assumed the castle was empty."

"There was a village near the castle that made it interesting for us. We led them to believe the castle was haunted."

"And you never left the castle?"

Quinn shrugged. "Occasionally I would, but my brothers didn't. We wanted to stay hidden from Deirdre, and any time we spotted a wyrran we would kill it."

"Is that how you got captured?"

Quinn hung his head. Marcail was full of questions. He might not have wanted her to know the real him, but it would come out eventually. He never cared to lie, and he didn't want to lie to her, even if the trust disappeared from her turquoise eyes.

"Nay, Marcail. I got captured because Lucan fell in love with Cara, and I couldn't bear to see them together."

"Because you missed your wife?"

If only it were that simple. "In a way. Deirdre attacked the castle in an effort to capture Cara, who is a Druid. We beat back the Warriors and wyrran to save her, and despite Cara being mortal and Lucan immortal, their love knew no bounds. So, I ran away to have some time to myself. I spotted a wyrran and gave chase only to fall into a trap. Again."

"So Deirdre discovered where you and your brothers were?"

"She did. I'm sure she's attacked again since that time, and if I know my brothers and the other Warriors with them, Deirdre wouldna have stood a chance."

"There are other Warriors with your brothers?" she asked, shock in her voice.

Quinn paused in his story. Marcail hadn't turned from him when he confessed to running away from his brothers. He was curious as to why. "Aye, there are others. When I left, four had joined us to fight Deirdre."

"Does she know this?"

"She does."

Marcail's eyes were wide with disbelief and hope. "Do you expect more Warriors to join you?"

"My brothers expect more, and Arran, Duncan, and Ian have joined me."

"Will that be enough to defeat Deirdre?"

"It will have to be."

Marcail put her hand on his arm and scooted closer to him. Quinn's heart raced every time she touched him. He wanted to drag her into his arms and kiss her until they were both breathless and lay her down so he could cover her body with his own. To press into her softness, to hear her soft moans of desire.

"Another Druid can help," she said. "May I join with you?"

Quinn's mouth suddenly went dry. Marcail's face was breaths away, her breast brushing against his arm. His body was ablaze and the only thing that would quench him was the woman beseeching him with her exotic turquoise eyes.

"Of course," he answered. "Cara will enjoy having another Druid in the castle."

Marcail's smile was blinding. "Thank you."

It was Quinn who should be thanking her. Marcail was special, and not just because she was a Druid. She was extraordinary because she made him feel like a man again.

The desire flooding his veins must have shown in his eyes because the smile slowly dropped from her face. She didn't move away from him, though.

And that was all Quinn needed to give in to the urge to kiss her.

EIGHT

"Quinn."

Arran's voice broke whatever held Marcail and Quinn. Marcail looked away so Quinn wouldn't see how desperately she had wanted his kiss.

It was a startling sensation to want him to touch her. During her brief marriage, Marcail hadn't enjoyed Rory's touch or his unfeeling, chaste kisses.

But with Quinn everything was different. Her heart raced, her breath quickened, and her body burned. She didn't understand how one man could do such things to her, but she enjoyed it too much to question it.

Marcail licked her lips as Quinn rose to his feet. There were no more words between the men. Whatever Arran had wanted Quinn to know, just saying his name had conveyed the information.

Quinn gave a brief nod to Arran before he turned to her. "Stay in the shadows. Doona move, and for God's sake, doona make a sound."

"Is it Deirdre?" she asked.

"I doona think so, but whoever it is, I doona want them to know of you."

Marcail squared her shoulders. "I'll do as you ask."

Quinn gave her a wink and freed his hair from the queue before he doused the torch. He hesitated a moment, but it was enough that she realized he had transformed into a Warrior.

The cave was blanketed in darkness, leaving Marcail feeling alone. She huddled against the cool stones. She didn't think there was time for her to move to one of the darker corners.

With the light of the few other torches Marcail could see Quinn and Arran take places at the entrance to Quinn's cave. She also spotted the twin with short hair, Ian, moving near them.

"Stay where you are," Duncan said as he came to stand in front of her. "I will shield you."

When Marcail tilted her head to the side she could see Quinn and his midnight skin fading into the shadows that surrounded him. Her curiosity was too great not to want to know what was going on. Her heart pounded in her ears as her anxiety rose.

"Easy," Duncan whispered to her. "All will be well."

Marcail wanted to believe the light blue Warrior, but nothing had been "well" for her in weeks, years even.

"It's not Deirdre."

She looked up at the big Warrior. Only his silhouette could be seen, but even that little bit showed her his gaze was riveted on Quinn.

"How do you know?" she asked.

"The other Warriors. If it was Deirdre, they would hide."

The only Warrior she could catch a glimpse of besides Quinn, Arran, and Ian was the one across from them. The Warrior leaned one shoulder casually against the stones, his arms crossed over his thick chest.

The torchlight flickered, revealing his copper skin and chin-length brown hair that parted in the middle and hung on either side of his face. His kilt was in better condition than the twins', but she didn't recognize the tartan. On either side of the Warrior's temples were two thick horns that curved around his forehead.

If the Warrior was any indication, Duncan was correct and it wasn't Deirdre who was coming into the Pit. But if it wasn't Deirdre, then who was it?

"Quinn," a deep voice echoed through the Pit.

Quinn wasn't surprised to find Broc beckoning him. What did the flying Warrior want, though? Quinn had the urge to look back at Marcail, but he kept his head forward and trusted Duncan to watch over her.

"Do you want me to come with you?" Arran asked.

"Nay. I'll deal with Broc on my own."

Quinn hadn't understood Broc's need to torment him while he had been in the mountain, but the indigo Warrior made sure to look in on Quinn often enough.

Whatever Broc wanted, he didn't wish for the others to hear it. Broc wasn't afraid of anything, not even being attacked in the Pit. It had been Quinn's plan. Attack the Warrior, and he would get free. Though Arran and the twins were up for the task, the other Warriors refused to commit to the plan.

Quinn took his time walking to the door that locked them in the Pit. As with everything, the door was made of stone, with a square large enough for food to be passed through but too small for anyone to escape through. Besides, Deirdre had used her magic, and no matter the power of a Warrior, he wouldn't be able to flee the Pit without the door being opened.

And even then it was risky.

"What do you want?" Quinn demanded when he reached the door.

Broc flexed his great wings that loomed over his head and folded his arms over his chest. "Your time is running out."

"Does Deirdre send you here to annoy me, because you aren't telling me anything I don't already know?"

Broc rolled his eyes. "You may be the smart one of the brothers, but sometimes, Quinn MacLeod, you are dense."

Now that got Quinn's attention. He moved closer to the door and lowered his voice. "What are you talking about?"

"Do you really believe Fallon and Lucan will come for you?"

"Without a doubt." Though he'd had his reservations a time or two. After all, he hadn't been the best of brothers.

Broc glanced at the guard to his left and lowered his voice. "She will make it difficult for them and you. She wants you, Quinn, wants you enough to make sure you never leave."

"Why are you telling me this?"

"I think you need to understand where you stand. You've been in the Pit for a few weeks. You've stated your authority with the Warriors, which just proved to Deirdre that you are the one she needs."

Quinn narrowed his gaze on Broc. "It doesna matter what she threatens me with, I will never succumb to her."

"Be careful what you say," Broc warned and backed up a step. "Your time is running out."

Quinn wanted to call Broc back and ask why he had repeated that last statement. Just what did Broc know? Quinn knew better than to ask the Warrior, though he longed to call him back. If Broc had wanted him to know, the Warrior would have said.

Quinn turned and walked back to his cave. He didn't stop at the entrance but continued inside to Marcail. As soon as she saw him, she stood, once Duncan had moved aside.

"Who was that?" she asked.

"One of Deirdre's Warriors, named Broc. He's the only Warrior I know that has wings."

"Wings?" she repeated, her eyes wide.

Quinn nodded and glanced down to the torch that Duncan grabbed to relight. "Every Warrior is different."

"I'm beginning to realize that," she murmured. "What did Broc want?"

"To warn me." Quinn looked from Arran to the twins. "Broc asked if I was sure my brothers would come."

Arran snorted. "Of course they will come."

Quinn began to wonder, though. Maybe Deirdre hadn't told his brothers where he was, as he had been led to believe. Maybe she'd told Lucan and Fallon that he had joined her.

He should never have run from his brothers no matter how painful it was to see Lucan and Cara together. If, no, *when*, he escaped the mountain, Quinn was going straight to his brothers and begging their forgiveness for being such an arse for three centuries.

"What else did Broc say?" Ian asked.

Quinn shrugged. "He just wanted to remind me that Deirdre has noticed how I've taken over down here."

"I assume that has pleased her," Arran said dryly.

"Unfortunately." Quinn looked down at his black claws. They were long and sharp and had seen much blood since his god had been unbound. How much more blood would have to be spilled before he found some peace?

Marcail's hand touched his arm. In a heartbeat he tamped his god down. He didn't like her being around him when he was transformed. It was silly, he knew. She saw the others in their Warrior form, but he had spent so many years with some part of his god showing that he wanted to prove to himself he was in complete control.

It took a moment for him to realize the others had left him and Marcail alone.

"They are never far from you," she said of his men.

Quinn looked back at her hand on his arm. "You touch me more freely than anyone ever has."

"And that bothers you?" She let her arm drop to her side.

"It should."

"My grandmother taught us that sometimes a touch can do more for a person than any amount of words."

Quinn clenched his hand in an effort not to wrap his fingers around her wrist and pull her against him. "Your grandmother was very wise."

"Why is it my touch disturbs you so?"

"I told you. It's because I'm not used to it."

She shook her head, the rows of braids falling into her eyes. "That's very sad."

"My wife didn't like my touch."

Quinn wasn't sure what made him share such a secret

with Marcail. It could be because the Druid hadn't judged him in any way, or it could be that he just wanted to talk about Elspeth.

Marcail grabbed his fist with both of her hands and gently pried open his fingers. She sat on the slab and tugged him down beside her. "What kind of woman wouldn't want your touch? You're a handsome man who comes from a powerful family. You had your pick of women, didn't you?"

"I did," Quinn confessed. "My wife and I grew up together. She was always following me around. As a lad she was an annoyance. When I got older we became friends."

"She must have loved you very much."

"I thought so." And that had been his downfall. His mother had cautioned him on marrying Elspeth before looking around at other women, but Quinn hadn't listened. He had paid dearly for his mistake.

"Were you married long?"

"Nearly four years." It had felt like four lifetimes.

Marcail sighed, her hands still wrapped around his. "Do you want to tell me what happened?"

Quinn didn't want to do any such thing. But his mouth opened, and the words spilled out. "Elspeth became pregnant almost immediately. I was so happy, and she seemed to be as well. She had a difficult time, though. She was sick most of her term and could rarely leave the bed. Any time I got near her she asked me to leave."

"Some women's bodies don't have an easy time of it. None of that was your fault."

He knew that now, but at the time he hadn't. "When my son finally came I thought everything would be all right, but he was turned. She was in labor for hours. At one point, the midwife didna believe Elspeth would live. It was nearly two days after she went into labor that our son was born."

"A joyous moment to be sure."

Quinn smiled, recalling how Lucan, Fallon, and their parents had celebrated. "Oh, aye. It was a grand celebration, I was told later. I didn't join in because I wanted to be with Elspeth."

Marcail's lips lifted in a smile. "As you should have been."

"The midwife told Elspeth that she shouldna chance having any more children. She gave Elspeth some herbs to take daily so she wouldn't swell with my child again."

Marcail inwardly cringed. She knew what Quinn would say next, but she didn't stop him. He needed to share this.

"Elspeth refused to take the herbs for fear they wouldn't work, and I didn't want to risk her life again. She wouldn't even allow me to sleep in the bed with her because she thought I would force her."

Marcail couldn't believe Quinn's wife had been so selfish. If she had really known Quinn, Elspeth would have realized he would never harm her.

"Did you never speak to her about it?" she asked.

Quinn shook his head. "I tried a few times in the beginning, but she wouldn't listen to reason. I stopped trying after that."

"No one knew, did they? Your family? They thought you were happy?"

The way Quinn looked at her, as if it was strange that she understood him, made her heart catch. The stories she had heard about the MacLeods didn't tell much about the brothers. They certainly never told her how handsome Quinn was or how he would make her wish she had the magic to give him all the happiness he wanted.

"Nay," he answered after a long stretch of silence. "My family never knew. I wanted it that way. And yours? Did your grandmother know you were unhappy?"

Marcail released his hand and turned her head away. It was always easier listening to others than revealing anything about herself, especially a part she wished had never existed.

To her surprise, Quinn took her hand in one of his large ones. A finger from his other gently turned her face back to his.

"Is it too painful?"

"Only because I wish it had never happened. Rory wasn't abusive, but he feared the magic that ran in my family's blood."

Quinn's brows drew together at her words. "How powerful?"

"Powerful enough that my grandmother can hide the spell somewhere in my mind."

"And your magic?"

She swallowed and lowered her eyes. "My mother and grandmother did not have an easy relationship. My mother thought we should forget the Druid ways. Because of that, I was not taught the spells, and my mother refused to allow my grandmother near me so I could be taught."

"You don't know magic?"

"I do, just not as I should. When my father was

killed defending our village from wyrran, I think my
mother realized how wrong she had been. Yet the grief
she felt for my father's death made her forget me and
my brother. It wasn't long afterward that she died.
When my grandmother came, she began teaching me
as much as she could, but too many years had gone by
already."

Quinn's thumb rubbed over the back of her hand.
"You know how to heal yourself."

"Aye, and I can sense people's moods. My grandmother said that was my greatest power that could have
been much more had my mother done as she should
have. You see, not every Druid has special magic."

"Why is that?" He leaned back against the rocks and
brought a knee up to place his arm on.

"My grandmother says it's because they have either
begun to drift from the Druid way or their magic wasn't
very strong to begin with."

Quinn shook his head. "I doona understand. Either
you have power or you doona. Cara, my brother's woman,
had no idea she was a Druid. We all discovered it by
chance when she was trying to grow the garden."

"Ah. It is a part of every *mie* to want to see something grow. We have that power."

"As we discovered with Cara. It was when she got
angry and the plant took it into itself and began to die
that we realized the magic she had."

"Is she learning of her magic? Is there a Druid to
teach her?"

Quinn lifted a shoulder. "When I left, Lucan was
talking about trying to search out a Druid for Cara, but
I don't know what has happened since I was taken."

"If there isn't a Druid to help Cara, then I will."

"You are a good woman, Marcail."

She smiled, at ease once more.

"Now, tell me of Rory."

NINE

Quinn hated to say her husband's name, to know that another man had tasted her lips and felt her skin on his. It made Quinn's rage bubble forth all too quickly from unwanted jealousy. He fought to keep his god under control, praying Marcail didn't notice how stiff he had become.

"There's nothing to tell. I didn't want to be married. It's as simple as that."

"Nothing is that straightforward," Quinn said. "You might not have loved him, but you two could have been friends."

"I don't think that was ever a possibility," she whispered. "He didn't want to marry me any more than I wanted to marry him. Neither of us had a choice. We did what was best for the village."

"What was best?" Quinn knew what it was like being married to someone he wished he weren't. But at least he and Elspeth had been friends once upon a time. Marcail and Rory apparently couldn't even say that.

Marcail leaned her head against the rocks and sighed. "I wasn't happy when he died, but I was pleased to be free. He made me question everything about myself. He didn't like my hair, he didn't like my magic but hated when I didn't know everything a Druid should know."

"He might have been the best fighter your village had, but he was the wrong man for you."

She chuckled. "Thank you. No one would admit that in the village."

"They're idiots."

Her smile was infectious as she turned it on him. "You've made me laugh despite my situation."

Just as he had earlier, he found himself drowning in her turquoise eyes, his body demanding he pull her against him and kiss her. To claim her lips and her body as his. He wanted nothing more than to have her arms wrap around his neck and hear her sigh as her body sank into his.

But then he thought of his conversation with Broc and the Warrior's words of warning.

"You're frowning," Marcail said.

"Broc told me I was running out of time."

"What does that mean?"

Quinn leaned forward and put his elbows on his knees. His head dropped down as he blew out a deep breath. "I have no idea. I'm assuming it has something to do with Deirdre. Everything in this cursed place has to do with that bitch."

"Lucan and Fallon will come, Quinn. I know they will."

Quinn wished he had her confidence.

Charon tapped his copper claw against the rocks at the entrance to his cave. He hated the Pit, hated the mountain, but just as with the rest of them, he wouldn't be leaving any time soon.

He would depart before many of them, though. Deirdre had made him an offer he couldn't refuse. Everyone suspected there was a spy in the Pit, but no one had realized it was him.

Though he was interested in what Quinn MacLeod did, Charon didn't enjoy spying when he was forced into it. He liked to choose his own vices, and he had many.

He was surprised at how quickly Quinn had stamped his domination over the Warriors in the Pit. Charon hadn't fought him. Yet. It would come to that eventually. But Charon was biding his time.

Everyone had a weakness, including the great Quinn MacLeod. Charon would find that weak spot and use it to his advantage against Quinn and Deirdre. It was all a matter of time before Charon put this heap of stone behind him and got back to the pursuits he enjoyed.

Charon smiled at Arran, the white Warrior who always stood near Quinn. Arran didn't trust Charon, as well he shouldn't. What was interesting was Quinn saving the woman. Not that Charon wouldn't have helped her.

He was a man after all. It had been a terribly long time since he had slaked his lust between a woman's thighs. And the wee Druid was certainly delectable enough.

Quinn, however, had reached her first. And now Quinn sheltered her as if she were the answer to his prayers. Arran and the twins were never far from the woman either.

Fascinating, very fascinating.

Charon wasn't surprised when Arran walked across the space to him. "More protective than usual, aren't you?"

Arran stopped in front of him. "Tell me, Charon,

why haven't you sided with us? You don't help Deirdre. The more Warriors on Quinn's side, the better our chances of escaping."

"It's been many decades since anyone has escaped from this mountain. I doona expect to be seeing someone do it anytime soon."

"Why not help?"

"Why should I?" Charon asked.

A muscle in Arran's jaw jumped. "Because we're put in here to either die or convert. Personally, I would rather do neither. Quinn is our best hope."

"He's *your* best hope. For me, I look to myself."

"One day you're going to need my help, and I'm going to be in the position to tell you nay."

Charon laughed. "That day will never come."

"We shall see," Arran said before he turned on his heel and strode away.

He kept the smile in place even as Arran disappeared into Quinn's cave. Charon didn't like predictions of any kind, because he had learned early on just how far a foretelling could go.

Marcail tried to pass the time by thinking of the spells her grandmother had taught her instead of gazing at Quinn like a girl who had never seen a handsome man before.

She had seen handsome men, but none of them had been Quinn MacLeod.

For all her words to Quinn, Marcail had kept much of her mother's ideas throughout her learning. The Druid ways hadn't been part of Marcail's upbringing, so to hear her grandmother spout words such as "war to end all wars" and "the end of all that is good in this world" hadn't meant much to Marcail.

They hadn't until Dunmore and the wyrran had shown up at her village. All the while Marcail had run through the forest she had tried to recall every word her grandmother had ever told her. But it was too late.

The magic she should have held easily within her body didn't respond when she called it forth. She could heal herself, aye, but only because her grandmother had made her do it every day while she had been alive.

Her grandmother had made Marcail practice it so often that it had become second nature to her, unlike any of her other magic. Marcail's one great power, discerning people's feelings, came to her at unexpected times. And other times, like now, when she wanted to discover what kept Quinn so reserved, her magic ignored her call.

It was beyond frustrating. And she hated herself at that moment. Her grandmother had tried to warn her, tried to prepare her for what was to come. Maybe it was because Marcail hadn't paid attention as she should have that her grandmother had buried the spell to bind the gods in Marcail's mind.

Marcail held out her hands. The flickering light of the torch cast her hands in a red-orange glow. She had the hands of a Druid, with strong Druid blood in her veins, but she couldn't help the men around her fight a relentless evil.

At one time the *mie* could have stood against Deirdre, but Deirdre had kept her growing power to herself, quietly hunting along the countryside for any Druids and stealing their power. By the time that the *mie* realized what she was about, Deirdre's magic was too strong. It would have taken many *mie* standing against Deirdre, and the Druids, both *mie* and *drough* alike, were too afraid of her.

Marcail sighed and clenched her hands. She could focus her power and make a flower bloom, but she had nothing with which to fight Deirdre or aid Quinn and his brothers on their quest. She was useless as a Druid.

No wonder Deirdre hadn't taken the time to kill her herself. There wasn't enough magic in her blood to do Deirdre any good.

A shadow moved and came towards her. Marcail spotted the pale blue skin and long brown hair of Duncan.

He regarded her for a moment in silence. "You are quiet, lady."

"The gloom makes me reflect on the past, which is never a good thing."

"We cannot outrun our pasts, no matter how much we want to."

Wise words. "Is it always this still down here?"

"Sometimes. Sometimes there are fights between Warriors like there was the other night."

Marcail frowned. Had there been a fight? She didn't remember hearing one, but she was a heavy sleeper. There was a distinct chance she slept right through it. "Do you ever get involved in a fight?"

"Only if I have to," he said with a shrug of his thick shoulder. "My loyalty is to my brother, Quinn, and Arran. I will always side with them in battle."

"How long have you been down here?"

"Much longer than Quinn, but not as long as Arran." Which told her nothing, but then again, a person could lose track of time in the darkness. "Were you and Arran friends before Quinn came?"

"We didn't fight each other if that's what you mean."

Marcail glanced at Quinn again. He hadn't moved from his spot just inside the entrance to his cave. He stood in the shadows, but she felt his presence. "And Quinn? Did you fight him?"

"As soon as he was captured, Deirdre's Warriors couldna stop bragging that they'd caught one of the MacLeods. I had hoped to meet Quinn, but I never expected Deirdre to toss him in the Pit."

"But she did."

"Aye, she did. Ian and I knew by the way she spoke to Quinn that he could be the MacLeod we'd heard so much aboot. Deirdre was careful never to speak his name. It didn't take us long to discover it, though."

"I gather the others fought him?"

Duncan scratched his chin. "The way to survive down here is to prove that you cannot be beaten, that you are the strongest, the most powerful. When someone new is thrown in, a fight is the first thing that happens. It was so with Quinn. Ian and I stayed back and watched. All the stories we had heard telling what great fighters the MacLeods were did not lie."

Marcail was fascinated, but then she had always been captivated by the MacLeod story. Her grandmother would tell her the story every night, never deviating from a single word.

"Did Arran fight him?"

"Arran did as we did, he watched. Quinn didn't need our help even when six Warriors attacked him at once."

Marcail's mouth parted in shock. "Six? Six and you didn't help him?"

Duncan chuckled and shifted his feet. "You havena seen him fight yet. Once you do, you will understand why it was so easy for him to be the leader here."

"You didn't want his position?"

"Before Quinn there were battles every day, nearly all day. Each of us was trying to best the others."

"But you're Warriors. Each of you is powerful, or at least that is what we were told in our stories."

Duncan crossed his arms over his chest. "We each have a god unbound within us, aye, but Quinn is the oldest of us. He has lived with his god the longest. Also, there are some gods that are stronger than others."

"What is your god?"

"Ian and I have the god Farmire. He is the god of battle, or father of battle as he likes to be known."

"Both of you have the same god?"

"Aye," Duncan answered. "We are twins, so we share everything, even the god. Quinn and his brothers have the same god."

She nodded. "Quinn told me. How is that possible? I thought only one god in one man?"

"You'll have to ask the gods," Duncan said before he walked away.

Marcail was now, more than ever, curious about Quinn. In none of the stories had it said the brothers shared the same god.

If Marcail believed Duncan, it made the MacLeod brothers stronger. She wished now she had been able to see him battle the other Warriors when she was tossed into the Pit. There had been very few times that she saw men fight, and never had she found it intriguing.

But then again, none of them had been Quinn Mac-Leod.

TEN

No matter how hard Quinn tried to forget there was a very alluring, very beautiful female just steps away from him, he couldn't.

He tried to think of Deirdre and a plan of escape, but all his mind could concentrate on was the shape of Marcail's plump lips and her delectable scent. Every drop of blood was now centered in his groin, and by the ache that had settled there, it wasn't going away anytime soon.

The other Warriors in the Pit had begun to grow restless as well. They smelled her, they heard her. No matter what, Quinn would never be able to leave the Pit or one of them would take her. That thought sent his rage to rising.

Quinn turned that rage to his advantage and channeled it into communicating with the rats. Though he hadn't mastered his power in human form yet as Lucan had, Quinn was getting stronger with each use.

He had already transformed into his god as he did each time he wanted to be seen. His power swirled within him, growing larger and potent with each beat of his heart.

"Find the other Warriors. Bite them, attack them, annoy them. Keep them occupied," Quinn commanded the rats.

His sharp hearing picked up the scratch of the rats' claws as they hurried to carry out his orders. Quinn didn't hide his smile when he heard the first growl of a Warrior being bitten.

The distraction wasn't much, but the rats would keep the Warriors occupied for a long time. Quinn couldn't wait to leave the mountain and try his power out on other animals, like horses.

He had used to love to ride. His favorite mount had been a bay stallion. Quinn missed that horse. Ever since he'd become immortal, he hadn't ridden. There wasn't a reason to when he could move as fast, or faster, than any horse could run.

Still, he longed to feel a horse beneath him and see the ground blurred under the animal's hooves as it moved across the land. Three hundred years ago, racing his mount had made him feel like a god. How naïve he had been.

Quinn felt a presence beside him and looked over to find Arran. The Warrior glared across the way into Charon's cave. For some reason, Arran hated Charon, but Quinn hadn't figured out why.

"You have claimed the female as your own, yet you doona want to be near her," Arran said before turning his gaze to Quinn.

Just the mention of Marcail made Quinn's blood heat. "It's not a question of wanting, it's a question of deserving. I'm not the man for her."

"But you want her."

"More than I've wanted anything in a long time. She's a good person who got caught in Deirdre's web. I've evil inside me, Arran."

"The evil inside us doesn't make us wicked. We have that choice."

Quinn smiled and shook his head. "You sound just like Lucan. He said the same thing to me once."

"Then your brother is obviously the clever one, not you, as they say."

Quinn rolled his eyes. "I'll admit Lucan and Fallon are better men, and at times, Lucan has shown himself to be nearly as clever as me, but never has he outwitted me."

Arran's grin, weak though it was, dropped from his lips. "If you want Marcail then take her. I've seen the way she looks at you, my friend. Doona be a fool and allow this moment to pass you by. I live daily with regrets. Learn from me."

Quinn lived with his own regrets. "I canna chance it, Arran. Deirdre will discover Marcail soon enough. Already I've endangered her by saving her. If I take her as I long to do, Deirdre's wrath will be fierce."

"And you worry for Marcail?"

"I do. Deirdre wants her dead. I believe Deirdre will leave Marcail down here to die unless Deirdre discovers I've taken Marcail as mine. You can be certain to see Deirdre's wrath then."

Arran ran a hand down his face. "You may be right. Who knows how much longer you have before Deirdre takes you? She does want your child."

When Quinn was first dropped into the Pit he fully expected to stay there until he was either rescued or died. But the longer he was in and the more times Broc and Isla visited him, Quinn knew that one day Deirdre would tire of her game and summon him.

Was that what Broc meant when he said Quinn's time was running out?

"Holy Hell," Quinn murmured. He trusted Arran and the twins, but how long would their honor last when faced with Marcail's beauty on a daily basis without Quinn there?

Not long.

Arran slapped him on the back. "Exactly."

Quinn yawned and rubbed his eyes. When he glanced behind him he found Marcail stretched out on the slab with her arms wrapped around herself, shivering.

"Go to her," Arran said. "You've kept watch long enough."

Quinn didn't argue, not when he yearned to be close to Marcail again. He walked to her and stared down at her form as she rested on her side, facing him. Her eyes were closed, but she wasn't asleep. Yet.

He kept his vigil until her breathing slowed. Then he lowered himself beside her. The slab was large, but not large enough to fit two people on their backs comfortably. Thankfully, with Marcail on her side, Quinn was able to lie on his back and scoot close to her.

Quinn raised his arm closest to Marcail and tucked his hand beneath his head. As if she sensed his warmth, she shifted closer to him.

The moments ticked by as Quinn studied her face. She was beauty personified. Her skin was flawless except for a small mole on the left side of her upper lip. But even that didn't distract from her loveliness.

Unable to help himself, Quinn traced her cheek and jaw with his fingers. Her skin was as smooth as ermine. To his surprise, Marcail's head moved until she rested against his chest.

Quinn's heart pounded in his chest. No woman, not even his wife, had ever lain on him so. He slowly lowered the arm he had behind his head and wrapped it around Marcail. Her shivers had lessened with the addition of his body heat.

At first he was afraid to move, afraid he might wake her. He liked her draped on his chest as she was, and if she never moved it would be too soon.

He forced himself to relax and take the time his body needed to rest.

Deirdre paced her chamber. She didn't like being denied. For any reason. She had told herself holding out for Quinn would make finally having him that much more enjoyable, but she was beginning to doubt that.

It seemed that no matter how long Quinn remained in the Pit, it wasn't weakening him. She had been overjoyed to see him take over as he had. It had proven to her that he was, indeed, the Warrior to rule by her side. Or as much as she would allow him to rule.

"Maybe he needs some incentive."

Deirdre halted and swiveled her head to William, who lounged naked on her bed. She had forgotten he was still in her chamber. Though he had occupied her bed for some weeks now, she didn't find the satisfaction she knew awaited her in Quinn's arms.

William's royal blue skin still shone with sweat from their recent lovemaking. Deirdre found it exciting to have the Warriors with their fangs and claws in her bed. She forbade any of them to convert to their human forms once they pledged their loyalty to her. They had no idea that the longer they stayed in their god form, the more hold the god had over them.

As enticing as William was, she knew he loathed Quinn. She understood it. William wanted to be the one to give her a child and rule. But he never would.

"What do you have in mind?" she asked the Warrior.

"The more you ask—or even demand—that Quinn come to your bed, he will deny you. Take something from him. That's the only way you'll break him."

Deirdre flipped her long white hair over her shoulder and considered William's words. She knew from Charon's reports that the twins, Duncan and Ian, as well as Arran, had sided with Quinn. Charon had reported no other Warriors, but that didn't mean there weren't more. She didn't trust Charon, though he was proving more reliable than she had first thought.

"Take something from Quinn," she murmured to herself. She smiled at William. "I think you might have something there."

William rose from his position on the bed and walked to her. "Let me do it. Let me be the one to take from Quinn."

"Wasn't it enough that you were the one to capture him?"

"Nay. I want to prove to you that he isn't the man you think he is."

Deirdre tilted her head to look at the Warrior. William had served her faithfully for over two centuries, ever since she had unbound his god. She knew he was in love with her, or as in love as a Warrior could feel, and she had always used it to her advantage.

"Just because I plan to take Quinn to my bed doesn't mean that you will no longer be welcome, William."

His royal blue eyes narrowed. "You would still want me?"

"I will always want you."

"So I can be the one to hurt Quinn?"

She nodded. "Aye, my lover. But first, I want more of your body."

William growled and wrapped his hands around her waist, his claws scraping her skin. He turned and threw her onto the bed. She kicked out at him, striking him in the chin.

He bared his teeth with a growl and grabbed her ankle before she could kick him again. With one jerk, he pulled her to the end of the massive bed and onto his cock.

Deirdre gasped at the feeling of being impaled on his shaft so suddenly. He pulled out only to thrust hard and fast into her, just as she liked it. She clawed at his back with her long nails as her legs wrapped around his waist. He fisted one hand in her floor-length hair and tugged.

It was too bad William wasn't the one to give her the child of destiny. She could control him easily enough, and he was a great lover.

But it was Quinn who held her attention.

As if sensing her thoughts, William dug his claws into her hips and pounded into her violently. She screamed as her climax came upon her without warning.

William wrenched every last tremor from her before turning her onto her stomach and sliding into her from behind. Their night of sex had just begun, and by the time he was finished with her, Deirdre would be as sated as she could get.

Quinn woke to the most delicious feel of a woman snuggled against him. He smiled as he realized Marcail's legs were intertwined with his and her arm was thrown over his chest.

It was the smell of bread that alerted him he had slept, and slept deeply. Even on the hard rock beneath him, he had slumbered like he was in a feather bed. And it was all because of Marcail.

Somehow being around the Druid relaxed him as well as bringing him desire unlike he had ever known. It took everything he had not to ground his aching rod into her leg. It would be so simple to turn her onto her back and cover her body with his. ·

Holly Hell.

He needed to keep his distance from Marcail before he gave in to this yearning that consumed him. And though every fiber of his being told him to get up, he couldn't.

Marcail trusted him, a Warrior, with her life. She molded her body to his for warmth and safety as she slept. That meant more to him than anything she could have done. His own wife hadn't trusted him that way, a wife who had known him for nearly his entire life.

Marcail had known him for such a short time. What was the difference? Why did Marcail understand him when Elspeth had not?

Quinn smoothed the braids that had fallen in Marcail's face as she'd slept. She blinked and opened her eyes. For a heartbeat she didn't move. Then she tilted her face to his.

"I would say good morn, but I'm not sure what time of day it is."

He smiled. "We usually get bread in the mornings, and since there is some waiting for us, I think it's safe to say good morn."

"You kept me warm while I slept."

Quinn glanced away. "You were freezing. I had no blanket to offer. Only myself."

"Thank you," she whispered.

"It was my pleasure." And he meant every word.

With a shy grin, Marcail rose and moved to the water behind Quinn's head. He sat up and tracked her with his eyes. Just as on the previous morning, she drank her fill before splashing water on her face and neck.

Quinn reached for the bread to break it in half when he saw three other pieces beside it. He glanced at his men. He hadn't asked, or expected, them to share their food with Marcail, yet they had. He gave them a nod of thanks before tearing off a piece of his to add to the pile.

When Marcail walked back to him and saw the bread she shook her head with a smile. "You and your men?"

"We want to make sure you're fed."

"I don't need all of this."

Quinn stopped her with a hand on her arm before she could give the bread back. "If you return the bread, you will offend them. I didna ask them to share with you. They've done it on their own."

"I see," she said. "I'm . . . touched."

"You are one to be protected, Marcail. And not just because you are a Druid. You're a woman first and foremost."

She laughed. "Weak, you mean."

"That's not what I meant at all. As men, we are raised to protect women and children, to give our lives if necessary. It is what a Highlander is."

Marcail tore off a piece of bread and squished it between her fingers. "Things were different in my village.

The men did look out for the women and children, but not as you say. My father gave his life for us, but I would not expect any other man to die for me."

"Then you obviously haven't encountered a true Highlander."

Her smile warmed his heart.

"So it seems, Quinn MacLeod. You are the first Highlander I've met, and I must say, I'm duly impressed."

ELEVEN

Quinn didn't know what to think of the warm feeling in his chest at waking up with Marcail in his arms. The way she looked at him, so open and honest, and the way she spoke to him, as if she didn't fear him, only made him want to be around her more.

He loved to see her many smiles, from her shy grins to the open-mouthed smiles that lit her up from the inside out.

They talked nonsense through their meal, and it had been too easy, too comfortable to suit Quinn. He was used to rarely speaking to anyone about anything. Hell, half the time he didn't even eat with his brothers.

Why then couldn't he stay away from Marcail? What was it about her that made him feel at ease, as if he could tell her anything?

Quinn squatted beside the water and jerked off his tunic. He tossed the dark red tunic aside, hating it because it had come from Deirdre. But it was either wear it or go naked since he would have to remove his breeches and boots as well.

Since the collection of water was also where they drank, Duncan had managed to secure a small bucket. Quinn used the bucket to scoop out some water. Then he splashed the water on his arms, chest, and face in an effort to keep clean before dumping the rest over his head.

He tossed his head side to side to remove the excess water before he ran his hands down his face. Quinn had taken the sea he loved for granted. He missed fishing and hunting as he never thought he would.

But more than that, he missed his home, his brothers, and the land that was in his soul. He wanted out of Deirdre's mountain, and he would see that it was done if he had to claw his way through the rocks himself.

A change in the atmosphere of the Pit alerted Quinn that someone was coming, and it wasn't Broc. Quinn released his god as he rose to his feet. He turned to find Arran hurrying toward him.

"Who is it?" Quinn asked.

Arran hesitated, but it was all the answer Quinn needed.

Deirdre.

"Why won't the bitch leave me alone," Quinn growled.

"We don't know if it is her. It could be Isla."

Quinn shook his head and walked around Arran to the entrance. "I know the feel of that magic, Arran. Isla's is strong, but this . . . this is Deirdre."

The rest of the Warriors in the Pit must have realized it as well because they hurried to their caves and hid in the darkness. Quinn didn't blame them. He would have liked to do the same. Not from fear but because he couldn't stand to look at Deirdre.

Arran stood at Quinn's right while Ian took Quinn's left. He had warned the Warriors to stay away from him when Deirdre visited, but they had never listened before. He doubted they would now.

Quinn turned his head, his eyes seeking Marcail. She was walking toward him when Duncan stopped her. Quinn gave a small shake of his head. Thankfully, it was enough that Marcail went with Duncan.

The Warrior tucked her into a corner and stood in front of her. Quinn knew Duncan wanted to be closer but none of them could risk having Marcail near Deirdre.

Duncan crossed his big arms over his chest and slowly nodded to Quinn. He would protect Marcail with his life. Quinn returned the nod and faced the doorway Deirdre would enter.

They didn't have long to wait.

Quinn spotted Deirdre through the square in the door. His skin prickled with the need to sink his claws into Deirdre's white eyes. The evil that surrounded her could be felt through the stones, but when she was near, it was like the evil was choking the life from Quinn.

He curled his fingers, his claws growing even longer. Blood filled his mouth as his tongue scraped across his fangs. He'd never felt such hatred for another person before. Every time he saw Deirdre he pictured the massacre of his clan and the death of his son.

With just a wave of Deirdre's hand the door swung open with a few creaks as the rocks scraped against each other. Quinn wasn't surprised to see the royal blue Warrior he had come to despise almost as much as Deirdre.

William.

He had dared to attack the castle twice, and it had been he who had nearly made off with Cara. It had only been because Fallon finally released his god that Lucan had time to reach his woman.

Quinn was going to kill William as well. The Warrior's death would bring him much delight, but not nearly the pleasure that Deirdre's death would give Quinn.

Deirdre and William strolled into the Pit as if they were walking down the streets of Edinburgh. They were a perfect pair, Deirdre and William. Both had submerged themselves in evil and craved power like a body craved breath.

"Quinn," Deirdre said as she stopped in front of him. "You are looking well. Or as well as can be expected living in the Pit."

He didn't bother answering her.

She glanced from Arran to Ian, then looked into the cave for Duncan. "I see that you've taken over."

"Stop," Quinn demanded. "You've known from the day I was dropped in here."

She laughed, the sound like a banshee's scream. "So I have, Quinn. Are you ready to come with me and take your place by my side? And in my bed? To give me the child I need?"

"I'd rather eat my own eyeballs."

The smile dropped from her thin face. Her nostrils flared and anger poured off her in waves. "That can be arranged."

"As long as I wouldn't have to see you," Quinn taunted. He knew he shouldn't, but he couldn't help himself.

As suddenly as her anger came, it left. She took a

deep breath and raised her chin. "Why do you fight me? We are destined to be together. I have the prophecy to prove it."

"I doona believe in destiny. I make my own decisions, and my answer to you will always be *never.*"

William growled from next to Deirdre. Quinn peeled back his lips and bared his fangs. He'd been itching for another fight with the bastard. Now was as good a time as any.

"William," Deirdre barked.

Instantly the royal blue Warrior was silenced. He turned his gaze to Deirdre with reverence. It made Quinn want to gag.

"Tell me," Deirdre said as a strand of her white hair lifted from the ground to caress Quinn's chest. "What is it you care about most in this world?"

Quinn bit his tongue to keep from saying a snide remark aimed at her. He wanted to brush aside her hair, which she liked to use as a weapon.

"That would be your brothers. I suppose that Cara is now added to that as well, since she is Lucan's."

It took every effort not to swipe away her hair. Quinn clenched his jaw and tried to think of the sound of the waves crashing into the cliffs, anything other than the rage rising within him.

Deirdre's knowing grin grew. "You've been away from your brothers for over a month now. Many things could have changed. Fallon mayhap has found his own woman."

Think of the waves. Think of the waves.

"Better yet," Deirdre continued, "let us talk about the men around you now. What would you do in order to save them?"

Quinn's control snapped. "You touch them, any of them, and I will make your death as painful as I can."

"I don't think so. In fact, I know that will never happen. You will be mine, Quinn. Will you make this easy or difficult?"

He would slit his own throat before he became hers, but there was no need to alert her to his last resort. "As I said, my answer is never."

"William," Deirdre said with a snap of her fingers.

In the next heartbeat, chaos rained. William launched himself at Ian as Deirdre used her hair to bind Quinn. Arran tried to help but was flung backward with a blast of magic from Deirdre.

Quinn used his claws to slice Deirdre's hair. As soon as a strand was severed, it mended itself instantly. There was a great roar behind Quinn as Ian was dragged away.

There was a blur of pale blue as Duncan attacked William in order to save his brother. Before Duncan could reach Ian, Broc and six other Warriors raced into the Pit.

Quinn bellowed his rage as Duncan was knocked unconscious and Ian was hauled away. Deirdre's hair coiled around Quinn's neck, choking him.

"You're beginning to make me angry," Deirdre told him. "Ian is mine now. I will torture him, kill him, and bring him back to life to do it all over again until he turns to my side."

"Nay."

"Aye," she yelled. "I will do it to each one of your men. If that still doesn't make you willingly come to my bed, I will make you watch as I torture the young Druids I've captured."

She walked toward him and placed her hands on his chest. "I will leave you to think about what I've said. The next time I come for you, I suggest you take my offer."

The moment her hair released him, Quinn staggered backward. Ian was gone, perhaps forever. Duncan's wrath would know no boundaries, and it was all Quinn's fault. He shouldn't have mocked Deirdre.

Across the way Quinn caught sight of Charon watching him. Arran had already reached Duncan and dragged the big Warrior into his and Ian's cave.

Quinn had never hated himself more than at that moment. Was his own future worth more than the lives of his friends? And God forbid if Deirdre discovered Marcail. What she would do to Marcail would be worse than what she would do to any of the Warriors.

He turned and made his way into the cave, but the crushing weight of what had just happened brought him to his knees. Quinn curled his arms around his head and let out the bellow he'd been holding in.

All the anger, frustration, and resentment came out in his roar. But even that didn't make him feel better.

When he sensed Marcail's presense, felt her magic, he doubled over. "Leave me be."

Marcail could no more walk away from Quinn than she could stop the magic of her ancestors. Her own magic vibrated with the feelings that rolled off Quinn.

She wanted to help him, nay, she *had* to help him. It was apparent he blamed himself, but the blame lay only on one person—Deirdre.

Marcail's heart bled for the heartache that still echoed in Quinn's roar. She had never seen someone hurt so much before. It would only get worse once Duncan woke. Just thinking of his angry growl when they had taken Ian made her shiver with dread.

Deirdre thought she was breaking Quinn and the others, but all she was doing was strengthening their resolve to fight her.

Marcail slowly knelt in front of Quinn. Her hand shook as she reached out to him, but not in fear. She shook from the depth of his feelings. She could make him feel better. All she had to do was touch him.

"Quinn," she whispered and ran her hands over his bare back.

His muscles jerked at her touch, but he didn't move away. Marcail began to take in his anger and frustration. Whenever she had done this in the past it left her feeling dizzy and sick to her stomach. But now, all she felt was Quinn's warm black skin and thick muscles beneath her palms.

She closed her eyes when his arms wrapped around her hips and his head rested on her legs. His hair was still damp, and she longed to run her fingers through the wavy strands.

When Quinn's fingers threaded through her hair she didn't pull away. He lifted his shoulders and began to straighten, all the while his head touching her stomach, her breasts, and then her chest. Her breathing grew ragged as his hands crept up her back. But it was her heart that threatened to jump from her chest when he pulled her against him. They were pressed together from knees to chest.

Her lips parted of their own accord when she found his face mere breaths from hers. One brawny arm wrapped around her tightly, molding her to his chest that rippled with sinew.

With her body on fire with a need she had never felt before, Marcail thrust her fingers into the cool locks of his hair. The damp, silky strands helped to anchor her against a tide of desire that threatened to engulf her.

That desire drowned out the raging emotions she was taking from Quinn. She watched, fascinated, as his eyes that had been swamped in black instantly changed to pale green.

She didn't need to look at his skin or hands to know the black had faded and the claws were no longer visible. But the yearning she saw in his eyes only fueled her own.

Marcail whispered his name when his hand cupped the back of her head. As his head lowered, she let her eyes close.

The first brush of his lips on hers stole her breath. She shivered and he brought her tighter against him, if that were possible. She could feel the beating of his heart, hear his harsh breathing.

And then he kissed her again. This time longer, his lips learning hers. She sighed when he licked her, and then his tongue swept into her mouth.

Marcail moaned, her body flooded with heat that centered between her legs at the taste of him. He deepened the kiss until she was clinging to him. Desperate for more. Desperate for him.

Her body was no longer her own. Every touch, every sweep of his tongue against hers made her yearning grow until her body trembled with it.

"My God," Quinn said.

She blinked up at him, unsure she could use her voice. But he slanted his mouth over hers again. The arm he had locked around her moved to her lower back. He pressed against her and she felt the thick shaft of his arousal.

And God help her, she wanted him. She wanted to feel him, see him, and experience him. Nothing else mattered at the moment but Quinn and the need they shared.

TWELVE

Quinn had never tasted anything so sweet as Marcail's kisses. He hadn't wanted her near him, but at the first touch of her hand on his back, he had been powerless to push her away.

Now, with her pliant body against him and her soft moans filling his ears as he kissed her, all he wanted to do was make love to her. To sink into her softness, to have her legs wrap around his waist. To hear her scream his name. He ran his hands down her body to her small waist and over her hips that flared ever so invitingly.

But he couldn't stop kissing her. It had been hundreds of years since he kissed, and he had never had a woman kiss him with as much fervor and need as Marcail.

His cock throbbed with need, and his hands shook as he cupped her buttocks and drew her against him, pressing her breasts to his chest. She groaned, making his already heated blood boil with need. Desire. Longing.

With the hunger to taste more of her hounding him, he forgot everything but the wildly beautiful woman in his arms.

Quinn didn't stop kissing her as he lifted her off the ground and wrapped her legs around his waist. Only then did he lower her onto her back.

"I love to feel you," she whispered in his ear when his weight settled on her.

He groaned and kissed her again. He could kiss her for an eternity and it would never be enough. With her hands roaming over his back and shoulders, Quinn cupped her breast. Her nails dug into his back when his finger circled her nipple through her gown and he felt the peak grow.

Her startled gasp told him she had never known that kind of enjoyment, and he was determined to give her even more.

She didn't stop him when he bunched up her skirt until he could touch her inner thigh. For a moment he let his hands rest on the smooth skin of her leg before he moved to her sex. His balls tightened when he felt the wetness between her legs.

Unable to hold back, Quinn placed his hand over her sex before sliding a finger inside her.

"Quinn. By the saints," she whispered into his shoulder. "What are you doing to me?"

"I'm giving you pleasure."

He kissed her again while his finger circled her clitoris. Marcail's body shook in his arms. He had barely begun to touch her, yet he knew she was close to peaking.

Quinn slid another finger deep inside her and began to move within her while letting his thumb tease her clitoris, slowly and lightly.

He altered the tempo of his fingers. First plunging inside her hard and fast, then soft and unhurried. Her hips shifted and rose in time with his thrusts, her breathing coming in ragged gasps. Quinn had never seen anything so beautiful.

Until she came apart in his arms.

He stared transfixed at her face and the pleasure that consumed her. He knew in that instant, once would never be enough when it came to Marcail.

Quinn removed his hand and pushed down her skirts before he could plunge his aching cock deep within her. He would have her, but the reality of where they were descended upon him all too soon.

Marcail's eyes opened and she smiled at him with a look of pure contentment. "What did you do to me?"

"Have you never climaxed before?"

She shook her head. "Does it happen often?"

"It will every time I touch you," he vowed.

She cupped his face with both hands before she kissed him. Slowly, leisurely. "You didn't take me. As a man does," she finished softly.

Quinn wanted to dig her husband out of the ground and tear off his head for being so insensitive to a woman such as Marcail.

"I want to. More than anything, I want you, Marcail." He took her hand and placed it over his shaft. "I want to kiss you again, to taste you again."

"I hope you do."

He sighed and lowered his forehead to hers. He hadn't realized how much he needed to hear those words until she'd said them.

"How do you feel?" she asked.

It was then Quinn realized all the emotions that had consumed him with the taking of Ian were gone. He lifted his head and looked into her eyes. "What did you do?"

Marcail shrugged. "It is my magic. It doesn't always work. Remember when I told you that I could sense people's emotions? I can also take those feelings away."

Quinn blinked. The thought of all that rage inside Marcail made his heart drop to his feet. "You took them into yourself?"

"I have in the past, but this time . . . this time with you was different."

"Different how?"

"The few times I've used my magic that way, I became ill. But not with you. You gave me pleasure beyond anything I knew existed."

Quinn gazed at her a moment before he kissed her again.

And then everything shattered with Duncan's bellow.

It had taken Duncan all of a heartbeat to recall that Deirdre had taken his twin.

Ian!

In all their years, they had never been apart. They were connected in ways that most people couldn't understand, and that was before their god was unbound. With the added power from their god, their bond had only strengthened.

Duncan couldn't control the fury inside him. He had to let it out some way or explode.

"Easy, Duncan."

He ignored Arran and tried to rise to his feet, but the crushing weight of the loss of Ian was too much. Duncan's claws tore into his palms and his vision swam with the anger churning inside him.

The roar rose up in him, and he was powerless to stop it. But that small release did nothing to staunch the loss of his twin.

Quinn raced into the cave and came to a stop before Duncan. "If I had known what she would do—"

"Don't," Duncan stopped him. "None of us could have known. You did what any of us would have done. I do not fault you for that."

"You should," his leader said. "I do."

If there was anyone who could begin to understand what Duncan was going through, it was Quinn. Duncan climbed to his feet until he looked Quinn in the eye. A part of him wanted to blame Quinn, but the blame lay squarely with Deirdre.

"Hit me," Quinn said. "Take your rage out on me before it consumes you."

Duncan lowered his gaze and shook his head. "I willna, Quinn. She could have taken any one of us."

"I'll get him back," Quinn said as he clasped Duncan's shoulder. "I swear it."

Duncan nodded, though he knew the chances were slim that his brother would be returned to him the man that he had been. They had all seen what Deirdre was capable of, and they all knew their time in the mountain was limited.

But it had never occurred to Duncan that his twin might be taken.

Duncan took a deep breath. "Did Deirdre see Marcail?"

"Nay," Arran said. "She would have taken her instead of Ian, I'm sure."

"Go to Marcail," Duncan told Quinn.

"I will make this right," Quinn vowed again. "I will get Ian back."

With one last look, Quinn left the cave. Duncan lowered himself onto one of the small boulders they used for seats and put his head in his hands.

What the others didn't know was that Duncan would

feel every cut, every punch that was dealt to Ian. Whatever Ian suffered, so would Duncan.

Marcail stretched lazily, her body still pleasured beyond her wildest dreams. She sat up and hugged her legs to her chest. She found herself smiling dreamily, her thoughts centered on a handsome, immortal Highlander.

In those precious moments with Quinn, Marcail had forgotten where they were, had forgotten about Deirdre and her evil plan, had even forgotten that her very life hung in the balance. All that had mattered was the exquisite way Quinn had touched her body.

Reality, however, had crashed down upon them all too soon. Marcail rubbed her hands over her arms through the sleeves of her gown. The only time she was warm was when she was with Quinn. Any other time, the cool temperatures sucked every last bit of heat from her body.

The first notes of a melody floated through her mind, a tune that she recognized instantly. A heartbeat later and the chanting began. As suddenly as it had come, it vanished, leaving Marcail feeling bereft and wishing she could hear the music again.

She rose to her feet in an effort to stay warm when she caught sight of the copper Warrior across the way. Charon's gaze, like always, was riveted on Quinn.

Marcail didn't need to be in Duncan's cave to know that was who Charon stared at. Why the copper Warrior was so intrigued by Quinn she didn't know.

Duncan had told her he hadn't sided with Quinn. Why, then, was Charon so interested in everything Quinn did?

Marcail took a step toward Charon to ask him when Quinn strode back into his cave. Her gaze fastened on

Quinn, and the smile she had worn just moments ago reappeared.

Quinn's steps slowed when he caught sight of her. His tunic was still gone, and he had once again transformed into his god.

She met him in the middle of the cave. She lifted his hand in hers, examining the black skin and claws. Just as she touched one of those deadly long claws he began to shift back.

"Nay," she begged. "Let me feel you. All of you."

He hesitated for a moment, and when he didn't move, she again touched his claw. His claws were longer than her fingers and, she imagined, sharper than any blade.

It was amazing to watch him change from man to Warrior and back again. She didn't know where the claws and fangs went, and she didn't care.

Before her stood the very reason Rome didn't rule Britain, and for that she was grateful.

"What do you see?" Quinn asked.

She glanced into his black eyes. That was the one part of a Warrior she would never become accustomed to. She missed seeing Quinn's green eyes, but more than that, when the entire eye changed, removing any iris and the whites of the eyes, it was . . . disturbing.

"I see strength and power," she whispered. "The evidence of magic is standing before me in all its stunning ebony glory."

"Magic?"

She nodded and lifted his hand so that his palm faced her. "You need no sword or dagger to defend yourself. You have your weapons right here. Ten, in fact. Is that not magic?"

"It's evil."

"Is it?" She dropped his hand and reached up to touch one of his fangs. "Do you not feel the magic coursing through your blood each time you allow your god to show? Are you not reminded how the Druids and Celts sacrificed so much just to save this land?"

"I'm reminded every damned day, Marcail. How can you look at me and not be repulsed? I have fangs and claws like a beast," he said with a growl.

She understood in that moment that there was nothing she could say to Quinn to prove to him that, even in his Warrior form, he was magnificent to her.

Maybe it was because she had just had the most wondrous experience of her life, but Marcail felt daring. She rose up on her toes and kissed Quinn.

The tips of his fangs snagged her lips but she didn't care. At the first contact of his mouth against hers, the heat that had filled her body a short while before surged through her once more.

Quinn's arms wound around her as he slanted his mouth over hers. He was careful not to cut her lips, and no matter how hard she tried to deepen the kiss, he wouldn't let her.

"My God," he whispered when he ended the kiss. "What are you trying to do to me?"

Marcail smiled. "I wanted to show you what I think of you as either the man Quinn MacLeod or the legendary Warrior all of Scotland is talking about."

"If you keep this up, I'll have you on your back again."

She loved how he teased her, but she also knew he was deadly serious. And it thrilled her beyond reason. "Really?"

He sighed and pulled her against him as he wrapped

his arms around her. "You are like the first rays of sun after a hard winter. You shouldn't be in this dark, evil place, Marcail."

"Neither should you, Quinn."

THIRTEEN

Isla shouldn't have been surprised to find Deirdre had taken steps to turn Quinn to her side. Deirdre was known to use whatever tactic she had to ensure she got what she wanted, and she wanted Quinn, regardless of everything else.

Isla was one of the few who knew that Quinn was supposed to give Deirdre a child, a child that would house all the evil of Hell. Just thinking about it made Isla shudder.

"Where shall we start?" William asked Deirdre.

Isla looked around the small chamber. Besides Deirdre, William, and the two Warriors who held their prisoner, Broc was also in the chamber.

Isla knew why Deirdre wanted her there, but why was Broc present? Broc usually kept to himself. Lately, however, he had been called more and more to Deirdre's side.

"Not just yet," Deirdre said, interrupting Isla's musings.

Isla turned her attention back to the prisoner. He was one of the twins from the Pit. Why Deirdre had taken him, though, was a mystery.

Deirdre moved in front of Ian, who was held on his

knees. She bent and put her face near his pale blue one. "I will ask you this only once. Will you turn to my side?"

"Never, bitch."

Deirdre stepped out of the way and William sliced open Ian's chest with his claws before punching him in the face. Isla had learned long ago how to keep her feelings from her face. Even so, she wasn't shocked to find Deirdre watching her.

"I'm very disappointed in you, Ian," Deirdre said and turned to face the Warrior. "I had thought you would understand the situation. Quinn has refused me, and so someone has to experience my wrath."

Ian spit a mouthful of blood on the hem of Deirdre's gown and smiled up at her. "Do your worst, *drough*."

Instead of killing Ian as Isla had thought she would, Deirdre merely took a step back. Isla had been around Deirdre long enough to know that no good could come out of Deirdre when she was as calm in her anger as she was now.

"You are very close to your twin, are you not, Ian? I wonder just how close the two of you are joined through your god?"

"I'm a Highlander. I will withstand any amount of pain you give me," Ian retorted, his lips raised in a sneer.

Isla was impressed with the Warrior, but with his comments, he wouldn't live long at all.

"I will make sure you withstand all of the pain I give you," Deirdre said. "I wonder, though, have you thought about how Duncan will endure the pain, knowing you are suffering as you will?"

In a flash Ian jerked out of the guards' hold and launched himself at Deirdre. "I'll kill you," he bellowed.

Deirdre's primary weapon, her hair, halted Ian before he could reach her. The white locks squeezed his neck until he passed out from lack of air. Once Deirdre released him and Ian fell to the floor, the pale blue tint of his skin faded away.

Lying just steps away from Isla was a man with short, light brown hair and a kilt so frayed and faded that she could barely make out the colors.

William and the two guards lifted Ian and carried him from the chamber, leaving Isla alone with Deirdre and Broc. Isla at one time had thought Broc might betray Deirdre, but the dark blue Warrior was as faithful as ever.

"Quinn is holding out hope of his brothers' arrival," Deirdre said. "I want to be able to give him proof that Lucan and Fallon have either been caught or won't be coming for him."

Broc lifted a shoulder. "You've sent wyrran to stop the brothers."

"Ah, but Lucan and Fallon have outsmarted my pets. For the moment."

"Then let me find the MacLeods," Broc said. "You know I can track anything anywhere. I will find them for you."

Deirdre considered his words. "Can you trap them?"

"That will take more planning. If you want something done now, I can ensure that they are . . . occupied with wyrran until Quinn agrees to your terms."

Isla didn't like the feeling that swirled cacophonously in her stomach at Broc's words. For years Isla hated the MacLeods because the scroll Deirdre had found had named them. Because of that one surname, Isla's life had been taken away from her.

She hated the MacLeods, hated all Warriors, in truth, but more than anything she wanted her freedom. She was tired of being used as Deirdre's puppet.

"I have another weapon," Deirdre said, her white eyes flashing dangerously, and turned to Isla.

Isla met Deirdre's gaze without blinking. To show any fear or weakness would ensure her doom.

"Nay," Broc said into the silence. "Not yet, mistress. Let me detain Fallon and Lucan. Once Quinn breaks, we can capture the brothers. They'll see Quinn has chosen you and they will no longer deny you rule them."

Isla's eyes jerked to Broc, but the Warrior refused to look at her. Why didn't he want Deirdre to send her? They could capture the brothers, but why then did Broc want to wait? Was he thinking of siding with the Mac-Leods?

She wanted to talk to him, but Isla knew she couldn't chance it, and neither could Broc. If Deirdre suspected anything, they would be killed instantly.

"I will agree for the moment, Broc," Deirdre said and ran her hand down the black material of her gown. "But only because I want to keep the brothers from reaching Quinn just yet. I do want all three MacLeod brothers under my rule before the moon has finished its cycle this month."

Broc bowed his head. "I will see it done, mistress."

"You may leave us."

Isla waited as Broc left the chamber before she turned to Deirdre. There was no use asking the *drough* what she wanted. Deirdre would tell all when she felt like it.

"It's time for you to visit him again."

Isla jerked even though she tried hard not to. Every time she saw Phelan she remembered she had been the one to deceive him, the one to chain him in the mountain as a child.

To fight Deirdre or try to talk her way out of it would only let Deirdre know how much Isla hated visiting Phelan in any fashion. Instead, Isla merely gave a nod of her head.

"I'm told you are the only one that can approach him."

Isla lifted a brow. "No one can approach him, which is why he is chained." *Constantly.*

"He is going to be one of my greatest Warriors. I still celebrate the day your sister discovered him. And let's not forget how you captured him."

Isla fisted her hand in her skirt as her stomach rolled. She would never forget that day. She relived it every night in her nightmares.

Deirdre walked to the door and paused. "Stay with him longer this time. It won't be long now before I will have need of him. He has to be tamed."

To say Quinn was worried was putting it mildly. It wasn't just Duncan and Ian or Marcail, either, it was his brothers.

It was true Quinn had lost track of time in the mountain, but he knew a considerable amount had passed. Where were Lucan and Fallon? Why hadn't they come for him?

Or worse, had they tried to rescue him and Deirdre had them?

That thought made Quinn want to kill something. He breathed through his mouth to calm his rage while ignoring his god.

It just took one look at Marcail for his fury to disappear while his desire flared to life. She sat on the floor, her head to the side as all her hair draped over one shoulder, and combed out the back of her hair with her fingers.

He could sit and watch her for hours. The way she moved and spoke and did everything fascinated him. The fact she was not only unafraid of him but seemed to like his Warrior form by the way she kissed him earlier had made him want her all the more.

She amazed him at every turn. Marcail had courage and spirit and strength that rivaled his brothers'. She was what every Highlander looked for in a mate.

Quinn's view of Marcail was blocked by Arran when he walked into the cave. Quinn turned his attention to Arran, who paced in front of him.

"What are they going to do to Ian?" Arran asked.

Quinn ran a hand through his hair and grimaced. "Deirdre told you what they would do. They will make him suffer."

"Will she kill him?"

"Only so she can bring him back."

Arran halted and turned a concerned face to Quinn. "Can she really do that?"

"I have no idea, but with the power she holds, it wouldna surprise me."

Arran blew out a long breath. "How long will she keep it up?"

"I can end it before it begins, Arran. It's what I should do. She is only hurting Ian to hurt me."

"You canna, Quinn. We need you."

"And Duncan needs his brother."

"Quinn—"

Quinn held up a hand to stop him. "I know what you would say, and I thank you for it. The simple truth is

my brothers are better men than I am. They can—and
will—destroy Deirdre with or without me."

"You've already made up your mind, haven't you?
You're going to go to that bitch."

"I am."

"And Marcail?"

Quinn tried, and failed, not to look at the Druid in
question. He was going to miss her. He wanted one
night of loving her, of tasting her kisses and feeling her
heated touch, but it was one night he couldn't allow
himself.

There was a man going through torture because of
him. Quinn couldn't live with himself if he allowed
that.

"Take care of her for me," Quinn said.

"You arna going to tell her farewell?"

He should, he knew it. "I canna."

Quinn moved past Arran before he could stop him
and walked to the doorway of the Pit. Though Deirdre
warded the door with her spells and magic, there were
always Warriors standing guard.

Quinn stopped at the door and whistled to get the
guards' attention. "Take me to Deirdre."

The Warrior on the left began to laugh. "She said you
would want to see her. We're to relay a message to you."

"And what would that message be?"

"That she's busy torturing Ian, and that you shouldn't
have refused her."

Quinn cursed and turned on his heel. He hadn't expected that move from Deirdre. She wanted him, aye,
but he had infuriated her. Now Ian would pay for it
with torture that would likely last for days if not weeks.

Once back in his cave Ian leaned against the stone

wall and stared up into the darkness. "Holy Hell," he ground out.

"She wouldna see you?" Arran asked.

"Nay. She said she's too busy torturing Ian."

"Shite. What are you going to do now?"

Quinn shrugged. "I canna do anything but wait. She knew I would give in after she took Ian. She did it to make a statement. There's nothing I can do for Ian now, but I will see everything put to rights as soon as I can."

"As much as I don't like Ian or anyone tortured, I think that's a very bad idea," said a feminine voice.

Quinn jerked his head around to find Marcail standing two steps away from him. "What choice do I have?"

"You and your brothers are the key, Quinn," she argued. "You have to continue to reject her."

He pushed off from the wall and faced her. "Then what? She takes Arran or you? Am I supposed to stand by while the people who have befriended me are tormented or killed? You canna ask that of me."

"I am, and I will," she said calmly. "I know exactly what it means to say that I've sided with the MacLeods. I'm sure if you ask Ian he will say the same."

Arran nodded. "As do I. If I have to die, then I will die."

"You're very noble now, my friend," Quinn said to Arran. "You willna be quite so noble once Deirdre begins to torture you."

"I'm a Highlander, Quinn. Doona insult me."

Quinn bowed his head. "Forgive me. I know the courage that's within you, and it's going to be Warriors like you who will help end Deirdre."

"I'm ready for that battle."

"As am I," Quinn murmured. "I've been ready for it since I first laid eyes on her."

Marcail put her hand on his arm. "The time will come. Until then, you need to prepare yourselves for whatever is to come next."

"And do you have an idea of what that will be?" Arran asked.

Marcail bit her bottom lip as she hesitated. "Deirdre has already told us. She'll start with Ian and work her way through all of us."

Quinn stalked around them, the anger at his situation rising within him. "You two are asking too much of me."

"Deirdre held that you have a destiny," Marcail said as she trailed after him. "I believe she is right."

Quinn stopped and spun to face her. "You mean to give her a child?"

"Nay, to kill her. The prophecy about the child could very well be truth, I don't know. What I do think is that Deirdre knows how important you and your brothers are to us, to the world. She knows if she can have you on her side, the battle is over before it has begun."

Quinn wanted to believe her, but he couldn't. The idea that the Druids and other Warriors were putting all their hope on the MacLeods was humbling and overwhelming. Too overwhelming, especially for a man who had lost everything once already.

FOURTEEN

Hours had slowly ticked by since Marcail had told Quinn she believed it was his destiny to kill Deirdre. He hadn't bolted, but he wasn't comfortable with the news either. Not that she could blame him. She certainly wouldn't want to have that responsibility on her shoulders.

From what she had learned from Quinn, there was much of his past he was ashamed of. She was apt to forgive him because he had been acting on losing his wife and child. That in itself had broken many a man.

Quinn hadn't broken, though, thanks to his brothers. Marcail wanted to meet them. She was curious as to the sort of men they were. Quinn spoke highly of them, which said a lot for the bond they shared, a bond that could never be broken.

Marcail huddled in Quinn's tunic against the chill. He had tossed it to her before he had set up to keep watch. With Ian gone and Duncan lost in his misery, Marcail didn't expect to see Quinn for several more hours yet.

But she longed to.

She yearned to wrap her arms around him and kiss his lips. She wanted to feel his hard body against hers, to know the skilled caress of his hands. He had told her he would take her, and God help her, she wanted it to be tonight. She wanted to feel again that utter bliss when she had peaked by Quinn's hands and mouth.

Not knowing what the morrow brought made her want to grasp the here and now with both hands and never let go, especially of Quinn.

Marcail knew she was foolish to latch on to Quinn as she had, but not only had he saved her, he protected her. And he showed her the pleasures of being a woman.

Her body heated just thinking of being touched and held by Quinn again. She squeezed her legs together as a bolt of desire speared her, but the pressure only increased her longing.

She hadn't bothered to lie down on the slab. After waking in Quinn's arms that morning surrounded by his heat and scent, Marcail preferred to doze as she sat.

It wasn't until she had met Quinn, had felt his desire, and had experienced the need within herself that she realized how lonely she had been.

Marcail's gaze shifted to the cave's entrance when a shadow moved. Quinn had taken the torch from his cave, which left her bathed in darkness. She was learning the Pit, though. Since she couldn't see as well as the Warriors in the dark, she relied on her hearing.

The shadow that moved stood tall, and she could just make out the torc around his neck.

Quinn.

She hadn't realized he had been so close to her all this time. Her heart leapt in her chest as he took a step toward her.

Marcail rose to her feet, her hands clutching his tunic. When he didn't make another move to come to her, she decided to go to him instead. For too long she had sat through life and waited to see what would come her way. It was time for her to take charge.

She had crossed half the distance when Quinn took two long strides and grabbed her before he spun her toward the wall. She gasped as his hard, hot body pressed her against the cool stones of the mountain. She was so surprised that her hands released their hold on his tunic.

"You should have pretended to be asleep," he murmured in her ear.

"Impossible when all I think about is you."

He growled and took her mouth in a kiss that stole her breath. She didn't need magic to feel his desire. Each stroke of his tongue against hers told her all she needed to know.

And she couldn't wait to feel more. She wanted all of it—all of *him*—and she would have it tonight.

Quinn's body had never hungered for a woman the way it did for Marcail. She might have been married, but her body was still innocent to the ways of the flesh. But she learned quickly.

Already, she held him captive with just her amazing turquoise eyes. He had known the entire time he kept watch that she was awake. He prayed she would sleep so that he could keep his distance, but he should have known better. His body craved another taste of her.

Right now, he would move heaven and earth to ensure he had her.

His fingers dug into her hips in an effort to keep her still. He had such slim control over his desire that he feared he would lose all of it if she ground against him.

Control or not, he had to touch more of her. He let his hands move up to the indent of her small waist, then up farther still. He paused and let his thumbs rest against the bottom swell of her breasts.

Quinn wanted to slice her gown from her body so he could feast upon her with his own eyes. He stopped himself at the last moment when he realized she didn't have anything else to wear.

She arched her back when he deepened the kiss, pushing her breasts against his chest. He cupped the mounds, marveling at the fullness that filled his hands.

He lightly skimmed her breasts with his thumbs and heard her sharp intake of breath when he touched her nipples. Instantly, he could feel the hard little buds as they pushed against the fabric that held them.

"Quinn," she moaned.

"I'm going to have you, Marcail."

Her fingers slid into his hair and pulled his head back down to hers. "Aye, you are."

Holy Hell, she stirred his blood.

Quinn released her breasts and tugged her skirts up until they were bunched in his hands. Marcail took over from there and hastily removed her clothing.

He knelt down in front of her and kissed her bare stomach while his hands removed her shoes and woolen stockings. Her legs were lithe and her skin smooth to the touch. He kissed each knee before he stood and pulled her into his arms.

"I'm without clothes," she said.

Quinn grinned. "I can see that."

"You aren't."

"Hmm," he said against her neck. "That's because if I remove my boots and breeches, I willna stop to do this."

She whispered his name when he bent and closed

his mouth around one pert nipple. Quinn smiled against the creamy smoothness of her breast and suckled harder.

He wrapped an arm around her to keep her upright when she sagged against him. Her breathing was ragged, and her moans music to his ears.

But he wasn't nearly done with her.

Quinn spread her gown and his tunic out as best he could with his foot before he lifted Marcail in his arms and laid her on the clothes. It wasn't a bed, but it was the closest thing he had.

Marcail smiled at him, her half-closed eyes watching his every movement. Quinn knew he should wait to remove his clothes, but he wanted to feel his skin against her. Without another thought, he pulled off his boots and jerked out of his breeches.

"Oh," Marcail murmured and sat up on her forearm. "You're . . . stunning, Quinn."

"Nay, my Druid. You are the one that is stunning." He knelt at her feet and crawled over her. "You have skin softer than silk and eyes more exotic than any treasure on earth. You," he licked her navel, "make me," he nipped her breast, "burn."

Her arms wrapped around his neck. "I've been burning too, Quinn. Don't make me wait. Please."

There was so much he wanted to do to her, but he felt her need and it matched his own. Hungry. Yearning. Aching.

As soon as his body touched hers, he was lost. He had loved holding her before, but skin to skin, he craved to get closer to her.

Quinn claimed her lips again because he couldn't get enough of her taste. How he had gone three hundred years without kissing was beyond him, but he knew as long as Marcail was near him, he would kiss her at least once an hour.

He groaned when her hands roamed over his back to his buttocks. She squeezed and raised her hips to grind into his already aching rod.

The feel of her wet heat against him shredded the last bit of control. With just a shift of his hips, the head of his shaft slid against her sex.

He had felt the heated folds of her sex, knew how sensitive she was. Quinn rotated his hips so that his cock circled her clitoris. Marcail groaned his name as she arched her back and wrapped her legs around his waist.

Quinn wanted to tease her body more, but the need to feel her slick heat surrounding him won out. He shifted his hand between them and guided his cock to her entrance.

He paused before he pushed inside her. He wanted Marcail with an intensity that frightened him, but more than that, he wanted her to want him as well.

"Quinn?"

"I want you," he said. "I want you desperately, but—"

She placed a finger over his lips. "No one, *no one*, has ever touched me as you have. If you stop now, I think I might die."

It was all the answer he needed. Quinn clenched his teeth together when her wet heat surrounded him and he eased his way into her sex. She was so tight, so hot that he shook with need. He tried to be gentle, but his desire—and his god—pushed him for more.

Quinn thrust once, seating himself to the hilt. Marcail's nails dug in his back, her breath hitching. He glanced down at her to find her eyes closed, her head thrown back, and her mouth parted in bliss.

He kissed her neck and began to move within her, slowly at first and then gradually increasing his tempo. The friction of his shaft in her nearly made him spill his seed right then. It was only the way her body began to move with his that kept him from giving in to the climax.

Quinn felt her stiffen and knew Marcail was close to peaking. He bent his head and fastened his lips around her nipple. He laved and suckled the tiny nub until she was trembling. And then he bit down gently.

He watched, amazed, as she shattered in his arms. It was the most beautiful thing he had ever witnessed. He continued to move, prolonging her orgasm. When the last tremor ran through her body, his climax burst from him.

With his face buried in Marcail's neck, Quinn experienced the most glorious, most moving orgasm of his very long life.

Marcail didn't want to move. She loved the feel of Quinn on top of her, but more than that, she loved the feel of him inside her.

The few times she and Rory had mated, it had been quick and, though not painful, it hadn't been pleasant either. But those memories shouldn't mar what had just taken place.

"Are you all right?" Quinn asked.

Marcail nodded and let her feet run over his tight buttocks and firm legs to his calves. She couldn't get enough of touching him. The way his muscles moved and bunched beneath her hands was mesmerizing.

And his body. She sighed. He was so gloriously beautiful that she couldn't look her fill enough. Not only was he finely sculpted with muscles across his shoulders and arms, but also down his chest, which narrowed to his waist and firm bottom and legs. He was perfection in every way.

"I didn't hurt you, did I?"

She heard the worry in his voice and gave him a quick kiss. "Nay, Quinn MacLeod, you did not. The one thing you did do was pleasure me so well I don't think I can move."

He chuckled. "Is that so?"

"It is. Tell me something."

"Anything."

"What just happened between us? Is it normal?"

He hesitated for a moment, and Marcail was afraid he either wouldn't answer, or she wouldn't like what he had to say.

"Nay, it isna normal. A man will usually always experience pleasure, but not a woman. For a woman to peak, a man must stimulate her."

Just as she thought. Rory hadn't cared enough about her to give her any pleasure. "Then I'm glad to share this with you."

"Aye, Marcail. I agree."

He pulled out of her and rolled to his back before he tucked her against his side. She enjoyed resting her head on his shoulder. It was an intimacy she had never had before, and one that she wouldn't be able to live without now.

If it weren't for his fingers caressing her back she would have thought he was asleep by how quiet he was. She was not known for her patience, and even though she told herself it was none of her business, she wanted to know where his thoughts were.

"What are you thinking?" she asked.

He blew out a breath. "My clan and the day they all died."

Marcail put her hand over his heart, wishing her magic would work instantly so she could take away his pain. "Time has not dulled that day, has it?"

"Nay. The smell of rotting and burning flesh was so great I kept gagging. That is a smell I hope you never have to suffer."

"If Deirdre has her way, everyone will know that odor."

"Do you know what I remember most about that day?" he asked. "The silence. MacLeod Castle had always been full of people. Amid the conversations were men training, children laughing, the blacksmith at work, and the animals. So many sounds."

Marcail kissed his shoulder. "I cannot imagine."

"The first sound I heard was that of a crow. The next thing I knew they were everywhere."

"The stories never say what you did with everyone. Did you bury them?"

He wrapped a lock of her sable hair around his finger. "We wanted to, but there were just too many. We had to burn them."

"You said that you returned to the castle."

"For two hundred and fifty years we've lived in the castle of our birth. We could not repair it as we wanted because we didn't wish anyone to know we were there. People feared what had happened to our clan, so they stayed away from the castle."

Marcail rose up on her elbow to look into his face. She smoothed a lock of his light brown hair from his brow. "You've had a very hard life."

"Nay," he said with a shake of his head. "It's been Hell, but others have had it worse. I realized that after I've been in here. I wish you could have seen the castle before it was ruined. It was majestic."

"Will you show it to me?"

That brought a grin to his face. "Oh, aye. I will surely do that. Lucan has a gift for shaping wood to whatever he wants. He made us a new table and chairs and even repaired our beds."

"And Fallon? What is his talent?"

"Leading," Quinn answered without hesitation. "He was born to be the laird, and a better man God couldn't have chosen. He will lead Hayden, Ramsey, Galen, and Logan well."

"Who are these other Warriors?"

Quinn put a hand behind his head, his brow furrowed. "Galen found Cara first. Cara had run away from Lucan because everyone around her was killed by Deirdre, and she didn't want Lucan to die."

"I gather Lucan went after her?"

"He did. In the process, Galen found Cara in the woods. Galen recognized what the Demon's Kiss was around Cara's neck."

Marcail jerked. "Cara is a *drough*?"

"Nay. Her mother was at least, but they were killed when she was very young. She escaped and was raised by nuns. Cara is a good person. The only way she would become *drough* would be to save Lucan."

"You like her," Marcail said.

Quinn nodded. "I do. She's good for Lucan, good for all of us actually. It was Cara's idea for Galen to come to the castle."

"You didn't fear he was a spy for Deirdre?"

"At first, of course. There are some people who are honest and their word is their bond. Galen is such a man. It was easy to trust him. And when he left signs in the forest for others to find him, we welcomed them as well."

Marcail settled back on his shoulder. Despite where they were, she was content to be held by Quinn and hear him talk. "Tell me about them."

"There is Hayden, who is taller than most men with arms as big around as a tree trunk. I'm not sure what happened to him in his past, but he has a hatred for anything *drough*. When I left, we were still making sure Hayden wasn't left alone with Cara."

"But Cara isn't *drough*."

"I know, but to Hayden she has *drough* blood, so it's the same difference."

"I see," she murmured. "And the others?"

"Ramsey is the quiet one, the listener. You almost forget he's even there until he makes a comment or suggestion. He has an uncanny ability to sum up everything in one or two words, but he can also work through dilemmas."

Marcail smiled. "A level head, he has."

"And it comes in handy to be sure."

"The other Warrior?"

"Logan. He's the youngest of us and always smiling.

He eases tensions with jests and quips that will leave everyone laughing."

Marcail ran her hand down Quinn's taut stomach and rippling muscles. "Do you think more will come to your castle?"

"I hope they do. It will take more than seven of us to defeat Deirdre."

"But you have Duncan, Ian, and Arran," she said. Her hand stopped at his hip. She wanted to wrap her hand around his now flaccid rod, but she wasn't quite brave enough.

"Ten is better than seven."

Then she remembered her desire to take chances she wouldn't normally take since she could die on the morrow. She skimmed her nails down the side of Quinn's hip to his thigh before she moved her hand to his cock.

He sucked in a breath when she wrapped her hands around him. She watched in amazement as his rod grew hard before her very eyes.

"Marcail," he murmured.

She smiled and kissed his chest. "You feel wonderful inside me, but I wanted to know what you felt like in my hand."

His hand at her back flexed and pulled her tighter against him. Marcail slowly moved her hand up and down his length, marveling at how hot he was, and hard. It was as if steel had been forged beneath his skin, he was so rigid. Yet his skin was as soft as velvet.

A bead of liquid formed at his tip. She ran her thumb over the head of his cock and smoothed the liquid over him. Her stomach fluttered when she heard Quinn's low moan.

Up and down her hand moved, learning the feel of

him. She loved watching the way his hips rose in response to her touch.

"Nay more," Quinn said as he shifted to his side and kissed her. He turned her over until her back was against his chest.

"I liked touching you."

He pressed his lips against her neck and moaned. The vibration against her skin was heavenly.

"I know," he said thickly. "But I want to touch you as well."

Marcail couldn't stroke him the way he had her positioned, but before she could complain, his hand shifted to her sex and parted her folds. He then sank a finger deep inside her.

"Hm. I think I like this position. I have you just where I want you."

She bit her lip as his cock ground into her from behind. His other hand had found her breasts and now rolled a nipple between his fingers.

"Quinn," she murmured. The desire pulsing through her was so great she couldn't get another word out.

As if he knew just what she needed, he lifted her leg and guided his rod to her entrance. With one shift of his hips, he was inside her, the feel of him from behind new and exciting.

Marcail moaned as pleasure rippled through her. Taking Quinn as she did, he went deeper, touched more of her. And it was wonderful.

He took his time, moving slowly in and out of her, heightening her pleasure with each thrust, each shift of his hips. When he began to move faster, harder, Marcail was powerless to do anything about the climax that moved quickly toward her.

The first waves of her orgasm engulfed her before she knew it. Quinn jerked behind her, her name on his lips as his hot seed poured into her. Knowing they peaked together prolonged her pleasure.

Long minutes passed before either of them could speak as they lay wrapped together. She had thought the first time they had made love was magnificent, but this second time had been extraordinary.

"Sleep, wee Druid," Quinn whispered in her ear.

Marcail let her eyes close as he tucked her more firmly against him. As she drifted off to sleep she realized he was still inside her.

FIFTEEN

Isla stood at the entrance of the doorway, but could go no farther. She had already descended deep into the mountain, far below the Pit and the other various dungeons.

But more stairs awaited her. These led to only one place, a place she put off visiting until she had no choice. Now was one of those times.

Isla saw the first two steps and then the blackness ate everything. Darkness and silence. Sounds surrounded her and drifted from above. She heard the screams of the tortured, the wails of the dying, and the growls of the Warriors.

But down the stairs was a different story.

Already she had put off descending to the point that Deirdre would mete out punishment. Not that Isla cared. There wasn't a punishment Deirdre had that hadn't already been inflicted on Isla.

Isla picked up her skirt with one hand and took the first stair. She didn't bother with a light. She knew the way, but it was more than that. If she tripped and tumbled down the stairs, it was nothing more than she deserved.

She made her feet move down each step. There were nearly a thousand more to go before she reached her destination. She counted the steps each time, but it never came easier.

All too soon she reached the bottom landing. Isla paused one heartbeat, two, before she turned to her left and started toward the prison in the back. As always her heart bled for the man held there, because it was her fault he was imprisoned.

He bared his long fangs as she approached. He couldn't harm her, though. Not only was he held at both wrists by thick chains that kept his arms out to his sides, but Deirdre had used her magic to prevent him from harming himself or others.

"Hello, Phelan," Isla said.

He growled and jerked at the chains, causing them to rattle against the stones.

At one time Isla had tried talking to him, but it had become apparent that it was useless. The little boy with dark hair and trusting hazel eyes was no more. Before her was a Warrior who wanted nothing but her death by his hands.

She hoped one day that he would take her life. It was the least she could do to help him.

Isla lifted her hand to reveal the gold goblet she had kept hidden in her skirts. If her being there made him angry, seeing the goblet pushed him to the edge of insanity.

He jerked so hard on the chains that she feared they might rip from the stones, but no amount of strength or magic could free those chains, not unless Deirdre wanted it.

"Please, Phelan," Isla begged. "Do not make this more difficult than it already is."

She took a step toward his outstretched arm and unsheathed the dagger at her waist. There was something about Phelan's blood that could cure anything. Though most Warriors' blood could heal other Warriors, Phelan's could heal anyone and anything.

And Deirdre had acquired a taste for it.

It was bad enough they kept Phelan chained in the bowels of the mountain, but to also take his blood seemed more than cruel. Deirdre knew Isla felt this way, which is why she sent Isla to him each time.

"I will kill you one day," Phelan said between clenched teeth.

Isla raised the dagger over his wrist. As a Warrior, his coloring was that of gold skin and eyes. She met his gaze and nodded. "I know."

"You doona fear death?"

It would be a blessing actually. "I do not."

"I trusted you."

Isla swallowed and lowered the dagger. This was the most Phelan had spoken to her since she had brought him to the mountain.

She thought back to that awful day so long ago. Deirdre had already begun using Isla's sister as her seer. Lavena helped Deirdre locate potential Warriors, which is how they found Phelan.

Isla had refused Deirdre's order to bring the child to the mountain. Lavena was lost to Isla already, but Isla had foolishly thought her niece was safe. That's when Deirdre gave her the option of Grania's death or Phelan's imprisonment. There was no way Isla was going to watch her beloved niece die, so she had gone after Phelan.

"I trusted you!"

Isla flinched at Phelan's bellow. She opened her mouth

to respond when a blinding headache sliced through her. Isla dropped the goblet and dagger and held her head between her hands as she stumbled backward until she hit the wall. She slid to the ground as the pain grew and grew.

She knew what this was, knew it and loathed it. Because it was Deirdre.

"You test my patience, Isla," Deirdre said in her mind. *"I do not like to be kept waiting. I need that blood!"*

"I'm talking to him. Just as you ordered," she ground out through the pain.

Deirdre's laugh echoed in her head. *"I know you just went down there so do not think to lie to me! You will be punished when you return. Now do your duty."*

Isla doubled over until her head rested on the stone floor. To her horror, tears she had not shed in hundreds of years began to trail down her cheeks.

Everything she had fought so hard to protect, Lavena and Grania, were lost to her. And even if she wanted to escape Deirdre, she was as chained as Phelan was.

"Isla?"

She blinked at Phelan's quiet voice and raised her head. He was crouched down watching her with his brow furrowed. It was bad enough to cry, but to be seen crying was worst of all.

Isla turned her head and wiped the tears away with the back of her hand. She rose on unsteady legs, the pain still throbbing in her head. With her hand on the stones for balance she turned toward Phelan. The chamber swam around her; the vestiges of the headache would last for days, as she well knew.

"Tell me what just happened," Phelan demanded.

Somewhere over time the innocent little boy had

become a man—and a Warrior. She bent to retrieve the goblet and dagger, breathing through her mouth to dispel the nausea that simple movement had caused.

"It doesn't matter."

"It does," he insisted. His gold Warrior eyes impaled her. "You were in great pain."

Isla didn't want to talk about it, but more than that, she was cautious of Phelan's change in attitude. A moment before Deirdre had invaded her head he had wanted to kill her. Now, his tone had softened and he no longer growled.

She licked her dry lips and swallowed. "May I come take your blood?"

Phelan sighed and gave a quick jerk of his head. Isla wasted no time in moving to the Warrior and slicing his wrist. Dark red blood welled out of the cut and poured into the goblet.

Isla held the cup carefully. She had made the mistake of spilling it once, which had meant she'd had to cut Phelan again. There was no way she could return to Deirdre without a goblet full of the Warrior's blood.

"It was Deirdre, wasn't it?" Phelan asked.

Isla glanced at his face. "Why do you want to know?"

"All I know is what I hear through the stones of this cursed mountain. I know Deirdre is as wicked as a person can get, but what I doona know is who she has caged and who is willingly working with her."

His wound healed before the goblet could fill completely with blood, but Isla refused to slice him again. She was already going to be punished. What was a little more?

Isla set aside the goblet and dagger near the entrance of his prison and faced Phelan. Deirdre had told her to talk to him, so she would. If only Isla could remove his chains or go back and change the past.

"Deirdre is an evil Druid called a *drough*. She is amassing powers that will enable her to take over the world."

Phelan clenched his jaw. "Is no one fighting against her?"

She opened her mouth to tell him of the MacLeods, but that would give him hope, a hope he couldn't have. "Some are trying, but it is futile."

"There are others . . . like me, aren't there?"

She nodded. "You've seen a few who have come down here."

"I've seen one. His skin is royal blue."

"That's William. He will do anything for Deirdre."

Phelan rolled his shoulders and shifted his feet as he took her words in. "The other Warriors, are they like me?"

Isla leaned against the rock wall and shrugged. "In a way. All Warriors change as you have. Each of you is a different color because of each god within you. The Warriors not on Deirdre's side only allow their god to show when they are fighting her. How is it you don't know this after all these years?"

"I didn't ask, and no one spoke of it."

If Isla had felt awful before speaking with him, she felt worse now. She had intentionally kept her distance from him because seeing him always made her remember the day he had gone from looking at her as a friend, to being chained and glaring at her with murder in his eyes.

"There are things you need to know," she said. "Each Warrior holds a different power depending on their god."

As soon as the words left her mouth the dark, gloomy

chamber disappeared and she was surrounded by sunlight. She stood on the side of a hill, the tall grass swaying in the wind, and the smell of heather and thistle filled her senses. Her gaze drifted upward to see a cloudless bright blue sky as the sun warmed her.

She knew that somehow Phelan had done this. She didn't know how, and she was enjoying it too much to question him.

"Can other Warriors do this?" he asked.

She turned her head and blinked. Gone were the chains that held him. Gone were the gold skin, fangs, and claws of his Warrior form. She saw a glimpse of the lad he had been in the hazel eyes that watched her.

The man that stood before her with dark hair that hung past his shoulders was so handsome she couldn't look at him. His body was lean and well-developed. She could see the definition of his muscles in his upper body, and though he wasn't as muscular as some of the Warriors, she could sense the strength within him.

"How are you doing this?" she asked.

"This," he said and held out his arms, "is my power."

Isla closed her eyes. "Please stop."

"Why? Do you prefer the darkness?"

She preferred the sunlight, and being in it for even small amounts of time made her long for it more and more. "I'm begging you," she pleaded.

"Open your eyes, Isla."

When she dared to peek, the darkness once more surrounded her. She blew out a shaky breath, not realizing until her fingers began to ache that she gripped the rocks behind her.

"So, each Warrior has a different power," Phelan said. "How many are there?"

"There are many. Some have sided with Deirdre. The ones that are holding out against her are being held in dungeons."

Phelan smiled, revealing his fangs. "But not all are held here, are they? There are some who have managed to escape and elude Deirdre and her wyrran."

It was true, and though she didn't wish to lie to him, she wasn't sure she could tell him the truth.

"Your silence is answer enough," he said. "Why do you pledge yourself to Deirdre?"

"Because I have no choice."

"There is always a choice."

Isla laughed and shook her head. "If only things were that easy. I suspect you will begin to receive more visitors soon. Watch yourself, Phelan. Deirdre has plans to use you in her scheme to dominate the world."

She retrieved the goblet and dagger and walked to the stairs.

"Guard yourself as well," Phelan called after her.

SIXTEEN

Quinn knew he was in trouble when he woke up and couldn't stop looking at Marcail. He had managed to rise without waking her, but now, all he could do was stand and look at her while images of their night together replayed in his head.

How he wished he had met her differently, but he realized, as the man he was before, he wouldn't have given in to the desire to have her. He had changed since being captured, changed in ways he thought he never would.

He still missed his son, but he had come to understand that bad things happen to innocents. Even if his son had somehow survived, Quinn wouldn't have stayed near him for fear of hurting him.

The need for vengeance for his son's and wife's deaths had not left Quinn, however. He would kill Deirdre, or die trying.

A muted curse made Quinn turn away from Marcail's sleeping form to find Duncan leaning an arm against the wall while the other held his stomach.

Quinn went to his friend. "Duncan? What is it?"

"Not feeling well," the Warrior ground out.

Quinn knew he lied. "Were you attacked last night?"

"Nay," Duncan said with a brittle laugh.

"Then what is it?"

Duncan turned his pale blue Warrior eyes on Quinn. "Nothing I canna handle."

Quinn inclined his head and turned on his heel to find Arran on the other side of the entrance. He walked to the white Warrior who stood with his arms crossed over his chest watching Duncan.

"He's not well," Arran said when Quinn reached him.

"Nay, he isna, but he willna tell me what's wrong."

Arran rubbed his eyes with his thumb and forefinger. "I doona like this situation."

"I've never liked it. I have promised Duncan I will set things right, and I will. I need something from you, though."

Arran snorted and shook his head angrily. "I willna bother arguing with you again but know that I think you handing yourself to Deirdre is horse shite. I've already promised to take care of Marcail."

"Aye, and I appreciate it. However, this is more important."

That got Arran's attention. He narrowed his eyes and took a step closer to Quinn. "What is it?"

"I have no doubt Lucan and Fallon will eventually come. No matter what I say, no matter what I do to them, you must leave whenever they escape, because they will escape. I will see to that. Take as many Warriors as you can, but you follow my brothers."

"I'd rather have you at my side."

Quinn wanted to be there, but Broc had been right, his time had run out. "Tell my brothers . . ."

"I will," Arran promised. "I will tell them everything."

Quinn inhaled deeply, feeling better after having Arran's vow. He didn't know how much time he had left with Marcail, but he imagined it wouldn't be long. Deirdre had made her point yesterday, but she wanted Quinn badly enough to grant his audience before too long.

The sounds from the Pit door told him their morning meal had arrived. Quinn transformed and strode from the chamber. When he reached the door he found Isla standing beyond it.

"Have you come for me?" he asked the *drough*.

She raised a black brow and regarded him with her ice-blue eyes. She was as petite as Marcail, but her cool demeanor made her seem taller, deadlier. "I have not."

"Shite," Quinn murmured and curled his claws into his palms.

"What is it you want, Quinn MacLeod?"

He leaned his face into the open square and growled. "You know I want to stop her torture of Ian."

"Her anger is slow to cool."

"Why are you here?" Quinn demanded.

She lifted a slender shoulder. "I've come to watch them hand out the bread and see if any have realized they would rather serve Deirdre than spend another moment in the Pit."

"I have," a voice called from behind Quinn.

He turned to find a Warrior with yellow-orange skin move out of the shadows. Quinn remembered battling the Warrior his first day there, but he hadn't seen the Warrior in weeks.

"Come," Isla said and bade a guard to open the door. She waited for the yellow-orange Warrior to move past her before she glanced at Quinn once more and walked away.

Quinn grabbed his bread and let his claws cut all the

way through it. He was torn between anger at Deirdre for making him wait and fury at having another Warrior turn to her side.

When he reached his cave, Marcail awaited him. She touched his arm and said, "She still won't see you?"

"Nay." Quinn gave Marcail her share of bread. "I didna expect her to make me wait. Isla said she is very angry, and if that's the case, she will take it out on Ian repeatedly."

"She's liable to do the same to you."

Quinn doubted it. "She wants a child by me too much to risk me saying nay. She won't torture me, not in the way she's torturing Ian at least."

"Do you think she will capture your brothers?"

"How do I know she hasn't already?"

Marcail's brow furrowed as she chewed. "Wouldn't you have heard it from Deirdre herself? I would think she would want to gloat and use them as pawns to get you to do whatever it is she has planned for you."

"You could be right. As much as I fear my brothers not coming for me, I know in my heart they will. I've gotten Arran's vow to go with them when they escape. I want that same vow from you."

"What about you?"

He fingered a braid that had fallen over her eyes. "I'm going to be the one who ensures you all get away."

"You're staying behind?"

"I am."

Her beautiful turquoise eyes grew troubled. "You cannot stay."

"I've thought about it all night, Marcail. Someone needs to stay and make sure Deirdre doesn't get all that she covets. I will be that someone. I canna do that if

I'm worried about my brothers, you, or the Warriors who have given me their allegiance."

Her gaze dropped to her lap where she stared at her half-eaten bread. "You ask too much, Quinn. I don't think I will be able to leave you here with her."

"You have to. My brothers will keep you safe. You will be with another Druid and surrounded by Warriors who want nothing more than Deirdre's death."

When Marcail didn't respond, Quinn put a finger beneath her chin and lifted her face to his. "Please. You have the spell somewhere in your mind to end all of this. You are needed."

Marcail didn't like the feeling churning in her stomach. The thought of Quinn not only going of his own free will to Deirdre, but staying behind and appearing to align himself with her made Marcail ill. He was chancing so much, but then again, she understood why.

"Fallon and Lucan won't be happy about your decision. They'll most likely return for you."

Quinn nodded and set aside his bread to grip her shoulders. "That's why I need you to make them understand. You and Arran need to tell them everything I willna be able to. Tell them I'm doing it for our parents, our clan. Tell them I'm doing it for them. I owe them so much."

"I will tell them," she said.

He dropped his arms and took a deep breath. "There's something else you need to know. I believe there is a spy in the Pit."

"Who?"

"My suspicion is that it's Charon. He's always watching me and everything I do. I don't trust him. He hasna fought against me or with me."

She nodded. "Charon does watch you constantly."

The door to the Pit creaked open. "MacLeod!"

Marcail jerked. She couldn't believe Quinn was leaving her. He was the one thing she had begun to trust, and now, she would have nothing.

Before she could beg him not to go, he pulled her into his arms and kissed her with passion and longing that matched her own. She held onto him with all her might. Drowning. Sinking. Yielding.

His hands spread along her back, holding her firm against his rock-hard body. His lips were soft, insistent and unrelenting as they took hers. He plundered her mouth, taking her breath, as well as part of her soul, with one heart-stopping kiss.

A kiss that showed her all the passion, all the longing Quinn had. It was a kiss that Marcail would never forget.

All too soon he pulled away from her. "Stay hidden," he said as he let his god loose. "And for God's sake, doona trust anyone but Arran, the twins, and my brothers."

Then he was gone.

Marcail stumbled to her feet and raced to the entrance of the cave. Just before she turned the corner in hopes of catching another glimpse of Quinn, Arran pulled her back into the shadows.

"Doona," Arran said in her ear. "This is more difficult for him than he is letting on. If he hears you, sees you, he's liable to change his mind."

"Isn't that what we want?" she asked, tears stinging her eyes.

"With all my heart, aye. As much as I hate watching a friend go to his doom, I've given Quinn my vow. I will keep it, regardless of how much I hate it. His sacrifice will save many lives."

Marcail flinched when the door banged shut and the bolt slid into the place. Already the Pit seemed different without Quinn. His mere presence had filled the Pit. Now, the darkness was never-ending.

She pulled out of Arran's arms and walked to where she and Quinn had just sat. Their meal lay forgotten on the stones. She had been starving when she'd first bitten into the bread, but now, she couldn't stand the thought of food.

Marcail sank onto the large slab of rock and let her head drop into her hands. She had known her time with Quinn would be short, she just never expected him to be gone so soon. Too soon.

Quinn followed William from the Pit through small corridors and up countless steps. He didn't need to try to memorize his way. There was only one way to the Pit through the stairwells, and that was found easily enough.

What Quinn found odd was the way William watched him with such open hostility. They'd had their share of battles, true, but this seemed different. As if Quinn was somehow encroaching on William's territory.

And that's when Quinn realized what it was.

"I gather you doona want to share Deirdre."

William whirled around and slammed Quinn against the wall. Quinn laughed even when William used a claw to cut a long gash in his throat.

"You willna be laughing when I'm done with you," William taunted.

Quinn lifted a brow. "Is she too much for you to handle, William? Is that why she needs me?"

"Shut your mouth," William bellowed.

"Try and stop me."

For a moment Quinn thought he would get the brawl he wanted, but William suddenly released him.

"As much as I want to kill you, I canna. One day, though, MacLeod, Deirdre will grow tired of you. When she does, I'll be there to end your life."

"Why wait? Let's take care of this now." Quinn bared his fangs and widened his stance. He needed to take some anger out on the Warrior, and if it was a fight to the death, all the better.

William growled low in his throat as he grinned. "Not just yet. I'm going to enjoy what's coming your way next."

Quinn didn't like the sound of that. He had no choice but to follow William. By the time they stopped, Quinn guessed they were well above the Pit.

When William halted next to a door and opened it, Quinn expected to find Deirdre when he stepped inside the chamber. Instead, it was empty. The sound of the door closing behind him had Quinn turning around. To find William standing there with a cocky smile.

"I think you're going to like this," William said.

Quinn readied himself for anything as he let his gaze wander the chamber. It was small with no weapons or even chairs. The one thing it did have besides the door was a large opening that looked into the next chamber.

"Where is Deirdre?" Quinn demanded.

"She's not yet ready to talk to you."

Quinn narrowed his gaze on the Warrior. The need to feel his blood on his hands, to kill, was overwhelming. "Then why am I here?"

"Watch and find out."

Quinn turned back to the opening when sounds from the next room drifted to him. It took everything he had to remain standing still when he caught sight of Ian. He was still in his Warrior form, but his face was mottled with blood and bruises.

The Warriors on either side of Ian were the only things that kept him standing. When they shackled him in the center of the chamber so that he hung from his arms with his toes dragging on the floor, Quinn knew things were only going to get worse.

"You shouldna have denied her, MacLeod," William said as he moved to stand next to Quinn. "You and your brothers have always thought yourselves better than the rest of us."

"Not true. We just thought we were better than you."

Quinn needed an outlet for his fury, and William was that outlet.

William didn't take the bait, though. "Watch your friend suffer for your arrogance, MacLeod."

The two Warriors who had brought Ian into the chamber each held a lash in their hands. At the end of the whips dangled metal points with jagged edges.

"Ian," Quinn called, but his friend acted as though he hadn't heard.

"Doona bother," William said. "He canna hear or see you thanks to Deirdre's magic."

Quinn gripped the edge of the opening as the Warriors lifted their arms, the whips moving on the floor. He would do anything to stop this, even take the punishment for his own if he could.

Each strike that landed on Ian's back was like a dagger to Quinn's heart. Ian held steady through it all, and when he passed out, they revived him only to do it all over again.

Ian's back was a mass of blood and skin when they were finished, but they weren't done with him. The Warriors dropped the whips and began to beat Ian with their fists and claws.

Quinn wanted to beg them to stop, but he had to be strong. Deirdre wanted him, and he would make her pay dearly for hurting Ian. As long Ian stayed alive he would heal, and Quinn could set everything right.

Until then, Quinn would have to stand solid and not give in to his desire to rush into a fight as he normally did.

"I have much more in store for your friend," William said. "I wanted to bring the other twin, but Deirdre hasn't allowed that. Yet."

Quinn faced his enemy and bared his fangs. "You know as well as I that Deirdre wants me. I've already told her I will be hers."

William threw back his head and laughed. "Actually, MacLeod, the message never reached Deirdre. It stopped with me."

Cold fury poured through Quinn. He lunged for William and had his hand wrapped around the bright blue Warrior's throat in a heartbeat.

"Kill me, and Ian dies."

Quinn let his claws puncture William's skin and blood ran in five rivulets down the Warrior's bare chest. Quinn could kill William and take on the other two Warriors with Ian, but getting Ian and the others out of the mountain without alerting Deirdre would be impossible. And he wasn't leaving Ian behind.

"Why am I here?"

William jerked against Quinn's hand, but Quinn

didn't release him. "I've been ordered to torture Ian until tomorrow. Deirdre has refused to speak to anyone until that time. Even you, MacLeod."

Quinn released William with a growl. He paced the small chamber and glanced at Ian who was helpless to shield his body from the brutal hits.

"I will kill you for this," Quinn told William.

William rubbed his throat. "You can try. Until then, you can either watch your friend being beaten or watch him be killed."

"Deirdre didn't order his death."

"Maybe not, but accidents do happen."

Quinn took a step toward him. "I will tell her what you've done."

"And I have two Warriors who will say differently," William replied. "What will it be, MacLeod?"

Not wanting to chance his friend's death, Quinn turned to the opening. As he watched the torture continue, Quinn planned out how he would leisurely and painfully kill William.

SEVENTEEN

Marcail was lost as she never had been before. She still couldn't believe Quinn was really gone. As much as she wanted to believe that he would return, she knew he wouldn't. Once Deirdre had him, she would never release him.

She huddled in the shadows with her arms wrapped around herself. Though she longed to hide and pretend she wasn't in the worst place in Scotland, she kept herself near the entrance so she could see any movement.

Many times before she had seen Charon take more than just a curious interest in Quinn and his men. Now, that interest had shifted to Arran.

Arran was in the next cave with Duncan, who hadn't been seen since Quinn was taken from the Pit. The more she watched Charon, though, the more interested the copper Warrior seemed to be in whatever Arran and Duncan were doing.

She thought over Quinn's words about Charon being a spy. All she had were her suspicions, and she didn't even know what to do with them.

Marcail grasped the end of a braid and ran her fingers over the gold that bound her hair. If only there were some way to help Quinn.

If she wanted to help Quinn she was going to have to

take risks she normally wouldn't, and that meant leaving the safety of Quinn's cave. Before she changed her mind, she rose to her feet and walked to Charon.

The copper Warrior raised a brow when he caught sight of her. "Have you lost your way, wee Druid?"

She hated being smaller than others because someone always used that against her. She looked up at the tall Warrior and the thick copper horns. "I know my way."

"Do you? Since you've come to me, I gather you want something now that MacLeod is gone?"

"I do want something from you."

He pushed off the wall and smiled down at her. "Protection? Have you come to realize Arran and Duncan are lacking?"

"What I've come to realize is that you are Deirdre's spy."

He blinked, taken aback by her words. Marcail liked that she had surprised him.

"Have you nothing to say?" she asked.

"If you were a Warrior, I would kill you for even speaking those words."

Marcail knew enough to be afraid, but she knew in her gut her suspicions were correct. "Because they are true perhaps?"

"God's teeth, you are bold, woman. Is that what Quinn found so appealing about you?"

She refused to allow the discussion to turn. "Why are you spying for Deirdre?"

He took a step toward her and peeled back his lips to show his fangs. "If I were you, I would forget we ever had this conversation and focus your attention on staying alive."

A low, tortured moan filled the Pit. She knew instantly it was Duncan. Marcail forgot about Charon and rushed into Duncan's lair to find him lying on his side, his arms wrapped around his waist as he curled into himself.

"Marcail," Arran snapped. "Get back to Quinn's cave."

A trickle of blood ran from the corner of Duncan's mouth. Whatever he was suffering was bad. She needed her magic to help, and she'd do whatever was needed to ensure her magic worked. "I can help him."

Arran shook his head. "No one can help him."

She didn't bother arguing. Instead, she shoved Arran out of the way and knelt beside Duncan. She put her hand to his head and felt the heat of his skin. He trembled uncontrollably, and his eyes were squeezed tight.

Marcail licked her lips and prayed her magic would come to her easily. She concentrated on her magic deep inside her just as her grandmother had taught her. The musical chanting began again, just a whisper that floated around her. It took a moment, but her magic shifted inside her as the chanting faded.

She wasted no time in celebrating such a feat but pushed her magic through her hands into Duncan. With the contact she instantly felt the pain and agony writhing inside the Warrior. As soon as she began to pull the emotions out of Duncan, Marcail became dizzy and nauseous.

Duncan's suffering was so great that it took her longer than she expected to take his feelings into herself. By the time she was finished, her body ached so, she couldn't lift her hand to brush away the hair in her eyes. At least Duncan rested comfortably now.

"What did you do?" Arran asked, his voice tight.

"I took his emotions. It's what my magic can do. He was suffering, and I knew I could help."

Arran glanced from her to Duncan and back to her. "Where do the emotions go?"

Marcail tried to shrug but only ended up losing her balance. Arran's hands gripped her shoulders as he cursed.

"Quinn is going to kill me," he murmured.

"Nay. Quinn will never know."

Arran mumbled something under his breath and pulled her to her feet. "Come, Marcail. You need to rest."

She tried to walk, but no matter how many times she told her feet to move, they wouldn't budge. Arran ended up lifting her in his arms. As they left Duncan's cave she spotted Charon watching them, his copper gaze centered on her.

Marcail wanted to tell Arran her suspicions about Charon, but her stomach rolled viciously. She scrambled out of Arran's arms just as he reached Quinn's cave and emptied her stomach.

With the help of Arran she lay down on the slab. The amount of feelings she had taken from Duncan was more than she had ever pulled from a person before. She wasn't sure how the Warrior had stood the emotions, and the longer they were inside her, the more they made her ill.

Tremors racked her body as her strength melted away. It hurt to breathe, and she flashed from hot to cold with each heartbeat.

"Marcail, tell me what you need?" Arran asked.

"She needs time."

Marcail cracked open her eyes to find Charon standing at the entrance to the cave.

Arran growled at the intrusion. "Get out."

"Heed me, Arran," Charon said in a low voice. "She may get worse. Doona leave her side and give her plenty of water."

Marcail had to close her eyes again when the room began to spin. Even lying down she felt as if she were adrift on the sea.

She must have dozed because when she opened her eyes the next time she felt better, but any small movement sent quivers through her stomach.

"What did you do to me?"

She turned her head to see Duncan walk toward her. She licked her lips and said, "I used magic."

He went down on his haunches beside her. "You felt what was inside me, didn't you?"

She nodded. "I don't know how long the emotions will be gone."

"I will be prepared for them next time."

She didn't know how anyone prepared for pain the like of which had been inside Duncan. "I didn't know you were sick."

"I wasn't."

And then she knew. "Ian," she whispered.

Duncan gave a slow nod of his head.

"I'm so sorry, Duncan."

"I would trade places with him if I could."

She covered his hand with hers. "I will be there next time to take the pain away again."

"Nay," Duncan said. "You have made yourself terribly ill. I appreciate what you have done, but you canna do it again."

Arguing with him was pointless, so she let the matter go. For now. She would help him again, and he wouldn't be able to do anything about it because he would be gripped by the agony of his brother's torture.

"Rest, Marcail. Arran and I are guarding you."

"Have you heard from Quinn?"

Duncan shook his head. "There has been nothing, and it has been hours."

He didn't say the words they all knew in their hearts, that they might never see Quinn again.

Cara stood on the battlements of MacLeod Castle, her gaze to the north where her beloved Lucan had traveled with the others. She missed her husband, the ache in her chest from his absence growing each day. But worse than that was the worry that Deirdre would capture him as she had Quinn.

Everything Lucan and Fallon had begun with the castle had ground to a halt. No longer did Cara hear the laughter and banter of the Warriors as they worked to reconstruct the towers and rebuild the cottages from the village.

The castle seemed more deserted than it had the day she had gazed at it before Lucan had saved her life. Cara was sure she would go daft if she were alone.

But she wasn't. Lucan had asked Camdyn to stay behind. The Warrior hadn't seemed to mind, but she had seen him looking into the distance as she did now. There was also Sonya, the other Druid. Sonya had wanted to accompany the group to Cairn Toul Mountain, but she had stayed behind to help Malcolm recover from his wounds.

Cara sighed as she thought of Larena's cousin. He was the only man at the castle who wasn't a Warrior. Malcolm had risked much to help Larena stay hidden from Deirdre.

If only Malcolm hadn't been attacked by Warriors and left for dead. As it was, he was scarred and his right arm almost useless. Sonya used magic daily to try and help his recovery, but he had long since stopped getting better.

Malcolm's discontent had grown each day. Despite his useless right arm, he was still able to wield a sword with his left as he had proven when he and Camdyn sparred. But Malcolm called himself worthless.

Cara could understand. She was a Druid who could help the herbs in her garden grow and aid Sonya in her healing but could do nothing else. Sonya worked with Cara on the spells all Druids should know.

Yet nothing Cara did worked. Even growing up alone in the nunnery she had never felt so lonely as she did at that moment.

The sound of boots on the stones drew her attention, and she looked up to find Malcolm. He stopped beside her and sighed.

"They will return," he said.

Cara stared at the man who was next in line to be laird of the Monroe clan. "Do you say that to ease my mind or your own?"

Malcolm snorted and rubbed his right shoulder where the constant pain never left him. The Warriors who had beaten him had ripped his arm from his socket, tearing muscle and tendons in the process. "For both of us, I think. I've seen Larena battle and know she is capable of defending herself."

"She is your cousin."

"And my friend. I know Fallon will watch her, but I canna help but worry."

"Fallon would die before he let anything happen to his wife."

Malcolm scratched his jaw where a shadow of a beard grew. "I've never liked being left behind."

"They have powers neither of us have. We would only be in their way."

"Ah, but you are a Druid, Cara. You have magic."

She reached up to touch the Demon's Kiss around her neck. The small vial held her mother's blood, blood given in the *drough* sacrifice to bind a Druid to black magic. It was the only thing she had left of her mother, but it was also a reminder of all that she had lost.

"Sometimes I wonder, Malcolm."

"Do you feel your magic?"

"I . . ." She looked down at her hands, hands she had felt her magic pulse through into the seeds she had planted. "Aye."

"Then you are a Druid. Doona doubt yourself. Lucan doesn't."

She smiled and turned to Malcolm. "And what of you?"

"What about me?"

"Will you allow Sonya to continue her magic on your arm?"

Malcolm frowned and turned his face away. "She is wasting her healing on me. I knew my arm would never work again the moment I felt it wrenched from its socket. They broke every bone in my hand, Cara. It's not just using my arm, but my hand as well. Most of the time I don't even feel my fingers."

"I didn't know."

He signed and shook his head. "You couldn't have. I asked Sonya not to tell anyone. Larena was so worried about me I feared she wouldn't go with Fallon, and they need her to rescue Quinn."

Cara returned her gaze to the distant mountains. "God help Deirdre if Lucan doesn't return to me."

"Aye," Malcolm murmured. "God help her."

EIGHTEEN

Broc flew high above the trees, soaring with the clouds. Thanks to Poraxus, the god inside him, he had the eyes of a falcon to go along with his wings. He closed his eyes and lost himself in the wind and sun.

Below him wyrran ran though the countryside like a quick-moving army. Broc tried to keep them as far away from villages and homes as he could. Superstition ran high in the Highlands, so if anyone saw the small yellow creatures, they would attribute them to one of the many demons they claimed roamed the land.

Broc opened his eyes to look ahead of him where Fallon and Lucan MacLeod were. His power to be able to track anyone anywhere had allowed him to find the MacLeods easily enough. He hadn't expected to find they had split into two groups, though.

With a wave of his hand Broc sent half the wyrran in one direction while the other half stayed with him. His silent command would push the MacLeods back into one group, as he needed them.

Broc whistled down at the remaining wyrran, telling them to halt and wait for him. He folded his smooth wings behind him and dove to the ground. Just before he hit the trees, he spread his wings and glided atop them.

With his keen eyesight he spotted Ramsey well before his old friend saw him. Ramsey's black head jerked up and their gazes clashed.

Broc flew up and back around to land in a small clearing in the forest where the MacLeods and their group traveled. Broc folded his wings behind him once his feet touched the earth and paused.

He need only wait for the wyrran to push Lucan and his group together with Fallon and the others. The wyrran wouldn't attack until Broc gave the signal.

Lucan was the first to break through the trees. His green eyes narrowed on Broc as Ramsey, Hayden, and Logan moved to either side of Lucan.

"Broc," Ramsey said.

Broc shifted his gaze to the man he had come to call his friend. They had made a decision while both were locked in Deirdre's prison that one would escape and the other would spy. Ramsey had gotten out. Broc was supposed to spy. But that had been over a hundred years ago. Many things had changed.

Before Broc could answer, Fallon, Larena, and Galen emerged into the clearing. Fallon glanced at his brother before stalking to Broc.

"What is going on?" Fallon demanded.

Broc raised a brow. Had he ever gotten so angry? Made decisions as rashly as the MacLeods? He couldn't remember, and it really didn't matter.

"You are surrounded by wyrran," Broc said.

Lucan transformed into a Warrior in a blink. "You came to tell us that? We've been battling those nasty creatures for days now."

Broc looked from Fallon and Lucan to Ramsey. He

was going to have to choose a side sooner rather than later. When, though, was the question.

"Deirdre has captured a Druid who holds the spell to bind our gods deep in her mind," he told the small group.

Larena gasped. Logan cursed and Hayden just stared.

"Is the Druid dead?" Fallon asked.

"Nay," Broc answered. "For some reason Deirdre didn't kill her. Instead, she threw the Druid into the Pit. Where Quinn is being held. Deirdre wanted the Warriors in the Pit to kill Marcail."

"Ah, hell," Lucan mumbled as he ran a hand down his face. "So the Druid is dead."

"Deirdre thinks so."

Ramsey took a step toward him, his gray eyes intense as they stared at Broc. "But you do not?"

"Nay."

"Why are you telling us this?" Fallon asked.

Broc debated on what to tell the brothers. "Quinn took over the Pit the first day Deirdre threw him down there. The more he proves his strength, the more she wants him. She's no longer content to wait for Quinn to break."

"That's why you're here," Ramsey guessed. "She wants you to capture us."

Hayden growled, his skin turning the red of his god. "I'll die before I allow her to hold me prisoner again."

"I'm to see that you are slowed in your attempt to reach the mountain. She does want all of you back under her control, but her attention is on breaking Quinn at the moment. There is a prophecy she was told that she thinks Quinn will fulfill," Broc said.

"And what is that?" Fallon asked.

"She wants Quinn to give her a child. That child will house all the evil of the world. Once she has Quinn under her control, she will come for each of you."

Ramsey strode toward Broc, stopping only when he stood in front of him. "I need to know whose side you're on. Why are you warning us?"

"For amusement, maybe."

Ramsey shook his head. "You forget, Broc, I know you better than anyone."

"You knew me. It's been a long time. Things have changed."

"Has your hatred for Deirdre changed?"

Broc couldn't answer him, but his silence was good enough for Ramsey.

"I didn't think so," Ramsey said. "Tell me the real reason Deirdre isn't trying to capture us now."

Broc looked past Ramsey to the other Warriors waiting for his answer. The real reason he hadn't already sided with the MacLeods was because Deirdre had a way of learning things, and Broc wanted to be able to glean as much information from her as he could.

"I convinced her to keep her attention on Quinn," Broc finally answered.

The next thing Broc knew, he was surrounded by Warriors. Lucan and Fallon stood on either side of Ramsey. Broc held up his hands before anyone spoke.

"Don't," he warned. "Deirdre's power is immense, and she uses a seer to gain most of her information. She learns things she shouldn't know. If you want my help, if you want Quinn freed, I cannot tell you much more."

Fallon sighed and exchanged glances with his wife. "Then tell us what you can."

"There are two hundred wyrran with me."

Hayden snorted. "They're easily killed."

"Aye, but they will slow your progress."

"We have no choice but to fight them," Lucan said. He turned to Broc and asked, "Can you keep an eye on Quinn?"

Broc nodded. "When I left, Deirdre was ready to do anything to have Quinn. While in the Pit, he not only took control, but three Warriors have sided with him. She had taken one of those Warriors to torture until Quinn agreed to be hers."

"Shite," Fallon said. "We doona have a lot of time."

"I will do what I can," Broc vowed. "Until then, get to the mountain as quick as you can."

He didn't wait for them to respond as he flew into the air. As soon as the wyrran saw him leave, they attacked. Broc wanted to stay and help the Warriors, but he couldn't. Deirdre had ordered him to lead the wyrran to the MacLeods and then return to her.

If he dallied too long, Deirdre would suspect something. And if he was going to help the MacLeods free Quinn, he had to be near her instead of in a dungeon.

Marcail cautiously sat up. When her stomach didn't rebel, she slowly crawled to the basin of water and cupped her hand in the cool liquid. She was thirsty, but she was careful not to drink too much lest she upset her stomach once again.

The pounding of her head, however, wasn't going to go away any time soon. It was an aftereffect of using her magic for as long as she had, but it had been worth it to see Duncan hale and hearty again.

Marcail used the wall to help herself stand. She looked around to make sure Arran and Duncan were occupied before she walked across the way to Charon's cave.

As soon as she emerged from Quinn's lair, Charon moved from the shadows. She didn't want Arran and Duncan to know what she planned, so she moved deep into Charon's cave.

"I'm surprised to see you up so soon," he said.

She shrugged. "I will be all right."

"You doona look well. You should be lying down."

"I cannot," she said. "We weren't able to finish our discussion earlier."

His lips flattened in annoyance. "There's nothing left to say, Druid."

"There is. I want you to tell Deirdre that I'm alive. Let her know I'm here."

"Why?" he asked, his voice laced with disbelief. "She'll kill you."

"I'm sure she will try. But I want you to have her bring Quinn back in exchange for me."

Charon shook his head. "It willna work."

"It will if you tell her I've remembered the spell to bind the gods."

The Warrior went utterly still. His fists clenched and unclenched several times before he spoke. "What did you just say?"

"Buried in my mind is the spell passed down from my grandmother that will once more bind your gods."

"I would no longer be immortal? Or have the power of my god?"

She shook her head. "Nay, you will have none of it."

"Did Quinn know of this?"

"He did."

Charon blew out a breath. "Now I understand why he protected you so. Tell me, Druid, why didn't Deirdre kill you?"

"Quinn thinks my grandmother protected me somehow. None of that matters now. Will you tell Deirdre I've remembered the spell?"

"Nay."

She blinked at him. "Why?"

"What you have inside your mind could save us all."

"Possibly. If I ever remember it. That's a chance I'm not willing to take. If you want out of this place and away from Deirdre, then you should have aligned yourself with Quinn."

He sliced his hand through the air to stop her. "You've been in the Pit for a matter of days. You have no idea what any of us have gone through at Deirdre's hands. There is only one person I care about in all of this and that's me. Quinn didna give me a reason to side with him. Deirdre did."

Marcail could only stare at him, amazed anyone could be so selfish. "I feel sorry for you."

"I doona want your sympathy, Druid."

"What do I have that I can give you so that you will tell Deirdre what I want?"

He turned his back to her. "There is nothing you have that could tempt me."

Marcail, feeling more defeated than when Dunmore had captured her, turned to leave. There was a loud, vicious growl near her. The next thing she knew, Charon had her against the wall as he used his body to shield her from the attack.

His arms were braced on either side of her head, and his big body prevented her from seeing who had attacked. She winced when Charon threw his head back and bellowed as he was hit from behind. Again and again she heard the claws ripping through his copper flesh, but not once did he budge from protecting her.

If anyone had asked her a moment before if she thought Charon would save her life, she would have said nay.

Marcail chanced a glance around Charon's thick shoulder and saw the white skin of Arran. "Stop it," she yelled, but Arran and Charon's growls drowned her out.

"Arran, stop," she tried again.

Charon turned around as Arran leapt at him. The two Warriors met with a bonecrushing thud. They fell to the ground and rolled around, their claws leaving trails of blood in their wake.

All Marcail could do was watch in horror.

Suddenly, Arran jumped to his feet. He stood in a crouched position, his white Warrior eyes trained on Charon. Once Charon gained his feet they began to circle each other.

Arran was the first to attack. He sunk his claws deep into Charon's chest as his fangs flashed. Charon gripped Arran's arms in an effort to pull the claws out.

Marcail wasted no time in rushing to Arran and laying her hand on his arm. "Arran, halt."

She never saw his arm come at her. It landed in her chest with such force that it knocked the air from her lungs and sent her flying backward. A cry wrenched from her lips as she hit the wall and slid to the ground.

"By all that's holy," Arran said as he knelt in front of her.

No sooner had the words left his mouth than he doubled over in pain. After a few moments, he raised his head. "Marcail, I'm sorry. I didna know it was you."

She tried to talk, but she couldn't put the breath back in her lungs.

Charon lifted her hand and peered into her eyes. "Calm down and allow your lungs to fill."

It took a moment, but finally she could breathe. She nodded her thanks to Charon who released her hand and move away.

"How badly are you injured?" Arran asked, his face a mask of regret.

"I will be fine. What happened to you after I was hit?"

Arran shrugged. "I'm not sure. It was magic, magic I think came from you."

"Quinn was right," she murmured. "My grandmother did protect me with spells."

"I've never felt anything so painful," Arran confessed. "If that's what I got just from striking you, I canna imagine the pain one would experience if you were killed."

Marcail nodded. "I know now why Deirdre didn't kill me. Now tell me why you attacked Charon?"

"I thought he had taken you for his own."

She gave him a smile and patted his hand. "Nay, I had to talk to him."

"Talk to him?" Arran repeated. "About what?"

"To see if he could help trade me for Quinn."

Arran's eyes widened in horror. "Doona try it, Marcail. Quinn is ready to sacrifice himself, but if he returns and you're not here, he's liable to kill all of us."

As much as she would like to think Quinn cared about her and that was the reason Arran looked so taken aback, she knew it was because of the spell she had and nothing more.

But how she wished differently.

NINETEEN

Quinn thought the torture to Ian would never end. Ian had never begged and never cried out, and Quinn knew the pain had been excruciating.

Not only did they whip and beat Ian, but they had pulled his claws out.

Several times Quinn had tried to free Ian, and each time Ian was beaten more until Quinn stopped trying. If he lived forever, Quinn would never forget seeing his friend tormented so. And to make matters worse, Quinn knew it was his fault. He'd never felt so helpless in his life, helpless and useless. So much for being one of the great MacLeods.

"Doona worry for your friend," William said with a smug grin. "His claws will grow back."

Quinn fisted his hands and let his claws puncture his palms. It was the only thing that kept him from attacking and killing William.

He faced the royal blue Warrior. "One day I'm going to get the battle I want between us. Know that when I do, I will take great pleasure in killing you."

"Ah, MacLeod, you can certainly try. As much as Deirdre might enjoy seeing us spar, she willna let either of us die."

Quinn would make sure William died, regardless of what it cost him later.

"I think it's time to return you to the Pit," William said.

As Quinn was ushered from the chamber he spotted Isla being led toward him by four black-veiled women. Blood dripped from Isla's hands onto the floor. The *drough*'s face was pale and dark circles could be seen under her eyes.

William halted in front of Isla. "Well, well, well. I see Deirdre was thorough with your punishment."

"Get out of my way," Isla demanded of the Warrior.

"Or what?"

Isla's ice-blue eyes bore holes in William's forehead. "Do you really care to find out?"

William laughed and stepped aside to let her pass. Just as she drew even with him, William slapped her on the back. Isla hissed and stumbled, but she didn't stop and never looked back.

Quinn watched Isla long after William had turned his attention away, so the royal blue Warrior missed the way Isla had to hold onto the wall to help support herself and the way she limped. Quinn found himself wondering what the Druid had done to be punished.

"MacLeod!" William bellowed.

Quinn turned from Isla and started toward William, but his thoughts were on the *drough*. If Deirdre had tortured her as William had suggested, then perhaps Quinn could turn Isla to his side. The question was, how much of a hold did Deirdre have on Isla?

The closer Quinn came to the Pit, the more his thoughts turned to Marcail. He had no idea how long he had been gone since the hours had blurred, but he prayed she was still safe.

He was anxious to see her, hold her . . . kiss her.

Just thinking of having her soft curves against him made his balls tighten in anticipation.

His ears strained to catch her voice as he waited for the door to be opened. He inhaled and tried to catch her scent of sunshine and rain.

But all he smelled was blood and death.

His heart quickened as fear took root. Had Marcail been hurt, or worse, killed? Had Deirdre somehow learned of her presence while Quinn had been away?

As soon as the door cracked open, he shoved it aside and strode into the Pit. The first person he saw was Charon lounging against the stones as if he had all the time in the world.

"MacLeod," Charon said as Quinn walked past.

Quinn gave a nod of his head. "Charon."

When Quinn came to the entrance to his cave, he paused. Arran and Duncan weren't guarding it, and there was no sign of Marcail either.

"Thank God," Arran said as he walked to Quinn.

Quinn clasped his forearm in greeting. "How were things?"

Arran's gaze dropped to the ground. "You need to come inside."

Instantly, worry for Marcail filled Quinn. He pushed past Arran only to stop a few steps into the cave when he spotted Marcail.

She slowly rose to her feet, her lips parted and tilting into a smile. He had never been so happy to see anyone in his life. The horror from the past hours faded away as he gazed at her beauty.

"You've returned," she said.

"Aye." He couldn't get anything else past his lips, not when he wanted to kiss her as desperately as he did. He tamped down his god, not wanting to harm her with his claws and fangs.

Uncaring of who was around, he pulled her into his arms as his lips took hers. He kissed her deeply, passionately, the hunger inside only increasing with the sweet taste of her mouth and the feel of her hands on him.

He took her mouth, letting the desire that pulsed within him grow until he shook with it. He remembered vividly what it was like to be inside her, and he wanted her slick walls to surround him once more.

"I could kiss you for eternity," he said as he nipped her ear lobe.

She smiled against his cheek and hugged him. "That sounds heavenly."

He rubbed his hands up her back and felt her stiffen. Quinn took her by the shoulders and looked into her turquoise eyes. "What has happened?"

"It was nothing," she said.

"I didn't mean it," Arran said at the same time.

Quinn looked from one to the other. "Someone better explain."

"I went to speak to Charon," Marcail began and tucked a strand of sable hair and a small braid behind her ear.

"Charon?" Quinn repeated. "Why?"

She lifted a slim shoulder. "I wanted to know if he could help you."

Arran rubbed his jaw. "I saw her over there and thought Charon had taken her. I attacked."

"And I made the mistake of trying to stop it," Marcail said. "I should have known better."

"I shouldna have struck you."

Quinn turned his gaze to Arran and began to shake with rage. "You struck her?"

Marcail grabbed Quinn's hand. "Only because he didn't realize it was me. And he didn't really hit me. It was more of a shove."

"Holy hell," Quinn murmured.

"It was an accident," Marcail repeated. "Please do not be angry at Arran."

Quinn glanced at the white Warrior.

"You were correct in thinking she had protection spells around her," Arran said.

Quinn frowned. "You were harmed?"

"It was pain unlike anything I'd felt. It's no wonder Deirdre didna want to chance hurting Marcail herself. I never meant to harm her."

"I believe you, my friend. Is that all that happened?"

Quinn didn't miss the look that passed between them. He opened his mouth to ask what was going on when Arran spoke.

"Duncan is . . . doing better. He's still not himself."

"I doona expect him to be." In fact, Quinn was surprised Duncan hadn't tried to claw his way through the stones to get to his twin. And if Duncan had any idea just what they were doing to Ian, Quinn knew Duncan would do whatever he had to in order to reach Ian.

Marcail entwined her fingers with his, bringing Quinn's attention back to her. The frown marring her forehead told him something bothered her.

"What is it?" he urged.

She glanced at Arran before she said, "There seems to be a very tight bond between Duncan and Ian."

"Of course there is. Not only are they brothers, but they are twins."

"It's much more than that."

Quinn moved so that he could lower himself onto a large boulder. "I think you better explain."

"It began after you were taken," Arran said. "Duncan hadna left his cave, so I had gone to check on him. That's when I found him on the ground, writhing in agony."

Marcail sat beside Quinn. "I don't know how much time passed before I heard his tormented moan. I raced to Duncan to find blood trickling out of his mouth and his body wracked with pain."

Quinn closed his eyes not wanting to hear any more, but knowing he had to. "You used your power, didna you?"

"Aye," Marcail whispered. "He looked as if he were dying, Quinn. I had no choice."

He nodded. "I know. Thank you for looking after him."

Arran snorted. "I'd rather her not do it again because it made her so sick."

"Arran," Marcail snapped.

Quinn silenced her by turning her face to his. "How sick?"

"It was nothing I couldn't tolerate."

"That isna what I asked, Marcail. How sick?"

She sighed. "There was much pain and distress inside him. I took as much as my magic would allow me."

Quinn pulled her against his chest and kissed the

top of her head. It scared him that she had done such a thing when he wasn't there to see to her, but he was also grateful she had helped Duncan. "Thank you."

"I don't know how long it will last," Marcail said as she looked up at him. "Duncan could begin again any moment. He told me he could feel the torture that was inflicted on Ian."

Quinn rubbed his eyes as regret and resentment settled in his gut. "Where is Duncan now?"

"Resting," Arran answered. "What happened, Quinn? Did you see Deirdre?"

Quinn briefly thought about not telling them, but they all had a right to know, especially Duncan. Though Quinn would rather cut off his own arm than have to tell Duncan what had been done to his brother.

"I never saw Deirdre," he began. "William took me to a small chamber where I had to watch Ian being tortured hour after hour. I tried to stop it, but William had ordered Ian to be killed should I deliver one blow to William."

"My God," Marcail murmured.

Quinn looked at Arran to find the Warrior with his arms crossed over his chest and his head lowered. He could well imagine what Arran thought of him now.

"I would have traded places with Ian if I could," Quinn said.

Arran shifted his feet. "I never doubted that. I'm just trying to figure out what William is about."

"He hates me almost as much as I despise him. I've vowed to kill him for this, and I will see it done."

"What I don't understand is where was Deirdre? I thought she wanted you to give in?" Marcail asked.

Quinn nodded. "That was my question. It seems that

Deirdre has told William she wants to speak to no one. I assure you she has no idea that William made me watch Ian's torture. She doesna even know I've requested to see her, since my demand got no farther than William."

Arran dropped his arms and lifted his head. "What are we going to do?"

Quinn knew exactly what he was going to do, but he wasn't about to tell Arran or Marcail. They wouldn't understand. But he had no choice now. There was too much he had to set to rights.

"We wait," he answered. "It's all we can do."

TWENTY

Marcail couldn't believe Quinn was really back. She had thought she would need to resign herself to never seeing him again. Yet here he was, his hard body pressed against hers.

She licked her lips, still feeling the kiss he had given her. There had been such desire, such hunger in that kiss that it had shaken her to her core. She didn't need her magic to know that she was becoming attached to Quinn. Despite that knowledge, she couldn't move away from him.

It was as if Quinn had magic of his own that tugged her to his side. They were in the worst place in the world, but all she thought about was Quinn and how he made her feel.

Quinn's revelation about having to watch Ian being beaten made her heart constrict. She couldn't imagine having to endure something so terrible, knowing there was nothing she could do to stop it.

"Are you really all right?" Quinn asked as he tugged gently on one of her braids.

She smiled up at him and nodded. "I'm much better now that you've returned."

His hand stroked through her hair. She closed her eyes and leaned her head into his hand. She reached up to begin releasing her braids so he could move his fingers through her hair when he stopped her.

"Nay," he whispered and kissed her neck. "I love your braids. They are part of what make you *you*."

Marcail stroked his cheek and whiskered jaw before letting her finger trace his lips. The feelings he stirred in her were arousing and glorious. And she never wanted them to end. "Quinn."

No more needed to be said. His arms wound around her tightly, crushing her against his chest, but she didn't mind. She couldn't get close enough to him.

His mouth nipped and nibbled hers, and then his tongue licked along the seam of her lips. She groaned and opened for him. His tongue swept inside her mouth in a rush, swallowing her moan of pleasure.

Marcail was carried away on a tide of ecstasy unlike anything she had ever known. Quinn's mouth conquered hers, seducing and claiming her with just the touch of his tongue.

She didn't stop him when Quinn lifted her and settled her on his lap so that her legs straddled him. Marcail gasped when she felt the rigid length of his arousal against the sensitive flesh of her sex.

She throbbed with a need so deep, so intense that she ground her hips against him, sending spirals of yearning through her each time she came in contact with his cock.

"You're driving me wild," Quinn told her, his breath coming in great gasps.

Marcail wanted to tell him he was doing the same to her, but her voice wouldn't work. She clutched his shoulders as he began to massage her breasts.

One of his fingers grazed her nipple, sending shock

waves of longing to her center. She cried out and arched into him. She had to have more of him, all of him.

She clawed at his tunic, wanting it gone so she could feel his skin under her palms. He released her only long enough to jerk the garment over his head.

Marcail sighed in contentment as she brushed her hands over the muscles in his back and they moved beneath her hands. His mouth was doing wonderful, amazing things to her neck that left her panting and needy.

She threaded her fingers in his light brown locks and tilted her head back.

"Remove your gown before I strip it from your body."

Marcail shivered at the desire that roughened his voice. With shaky hands she tried to remove her clothes. She heard a seam rip when Quinn's hands joined hers and he gave a quick yank. But she didn't care. Not when she was in Quinn's arms.

His lips closed around a nipple and began to tease it with his tongue and teeth. She whimpered when his tongue swirled around the tiny bud. She ground her hips against him seeking the release that was building with each nip of his teeth.

She reached between them and grasped his cock through his breeches. He groaned, the sound ecstasy to her ears. Just like before, she was amazed at the hardness in her hand.

"I want to touch you," she told him.

In the next instant he had unfastened his breeches and pushed them down so his rod sprang free. Marcail took him in hand and marveled at the feel of him. He was spectacular. And for now, he was hers.

"If you doona stop, I will spill."

She wanted to bring him to climax with her hand,

but the need to have him inside her was greater. She rose up on her knees and positioned herself over him.

He looked into her eyes while his fingers pinched one of her nipples, blending pleasure and pain so that she groaned and swayed toward him.

She lowered herself onto his thick, hard shaft. Marcail closed her eyes when she was seated fully. The feel of Quinn deep inside her was one that she would never grow tired of.

Quinn's hand wound in her hair and held her head in place. "Look at me. I want to see your eyes when you come."

A tremor went through her at his words. How he could touch her with his voice alone, she didn't know, but she loved that he could. She opened her eyes. With his free hand, he gripped her hip and began to move her back and forth. Marcail bit her lip as a wave of rapture raced through her.

She never looked away from Quinn's amazing light green eyes, not even when he ground into her, rubbing her clitoris in the process.

It was amazing the control she had being on top of him. She rotated her hips, loving the sound of his moan as she did. She also used her legs and rose up and down on his shaft. But then it became too much. Her release was so close that she couldn't hold back any longer.

Quinn took over then, rocking her back and forth until her world fell apart. Her breath locked in her lungs and white lights blinded her to all but Quinn as her body convulsed around him.

"Marcail," he whispered as he gave a final thrust and she felt him jerk inside her.

She collapsed onto his shoulder while his hands

caressed her back. Now that Quinn had returned, the anxiety that had plagued her vanished, and all she wanted to do was lie in his arms for all of eternity.

Each time she made love to Quinn, it seemed a part of her opened up, as though she felt more, experienced more. Understood more.

The strange musical chanting she had been hearing ever since she had been thrown into the Pit suddenly filled her mind and grew louder than it had before.

She lost herself in the chanting. Though she tried, she could only catch a few words, but she recognized the language as that of the Celts.

What it meant though, she had no idea.

Quinn kissed her neck, reminding her that she was naked and Arran or Duncan could walk in at any moment. She sat upright as the chanting vanished and looked around for her gown.

"They will not bother us yet," Quinn said with a smile.

She winced as she imagined the sounds she had made. "They heard us, then?"

Quinn's laugh was music to her ears. "I doona know, and I doona care. Do you?"

"Aye, I do. What we did is personal."

"True, but we aren't exactly in a private place."

She thought over his words and then shrugged. She would never see the light of day again. Who knew how many days she had left before she was killed? Why should it matter if everyone in the mountain knew she and Quinn had made love?

"You're right," she agreed. "I don't think I do care."

"Liar," he said with a quick kiss on her lips. "I like that you are bashful about our lovemaking. Makes me want to take you again until you scream my name."

Marcail's body throbbed at the idea. "Does it?"

"You know it does."

A laugh escaped her as he toppled them sideways until they were lying face to face on the stone slab.

Charon looked away, unable to watch Quinn and Marcail another moment. He hadn't intended to spy upon them as they made love, but he'd been unable to turn away.

The way they touched each other, looked at each other, was unlike anything he had ever seen before. They had made magic together, something Charon knew he would never in his very long life experience.

He turned from the entrance and retraced his footsteps to his own cave. Ever since Marcail had told him she had the spell to bind his god, his mind had been working.

Given his two-hundred-plus years of life, he knew better than to align himself with a side that was destined to lose. Yet, neither could he go against Deirdre who was so powerful. Marcail's admission, however, gave him just what he needed.

He had planned to speak to Quinn about it, and he was glad he hadn't. Charon's plan was his own. He had never needed anyone before, and he certainly didn't need anyone now.

TWENTY-ONE

After all the evil Quinn had witnessed at William's hand over the past hours, it felt right to hold something so good as Marcail in his arms. She wiped away the stain of evil from him, reminding Quinn that there was good in this world.

"Are you all right?" she asked.

He started to nod his head, then paused. "I could withstand any amount of punishment and torture they could give me except what I saw today. To know that Ian was being tortured because of me was too much."

Marcail intertwined her fingers with his. "I cannot imagine what you went through. Are they done with Ian?"

"I doona think so, not if I know Deirdre."

"That doesn't bode well for us then."

He lifted their hands and kissed the back of hers. "I willna let them take you." And he meant it, whether she believed him or not.

"I know," she answered. "It's strange how your life can alter in the space of a heartbeat. Just the other week I was lamenting the fact that my life was boring. I did the same tasks every day with nothing to look forward to. I was alone, and would likely have been alone for the rest of my days."

"You aren't alone now."

She smiled. "Nay, I'm not. Now, I'm stuck in this mountain wishing I could return to my cottage and pull the same weeds day after day from my garden, collect and dry my herbs, and practice my spells. I didn't realize how good a life I had until I was brought here. Strange, isn't it?"

"Nay. For three centuries I've gone against my brothers in everything they asked because I couldn't let go of my rage and guilt. I should have listened to them."

"Ah, but you'll have plenty of chances for that," she teased.

"Will I? I doubt it." He hated to dampen her mood, but he needed her to understand he wouldn't be with her much longer.

Just the thought made him want to rip out his own eyes, but it was the truth. He needed to make sure no one else was hurt because of him. And he could do that by Deirdre's side.

"Please don't say that," Marcail whispered.

He cupped her cheek. "I wish there was another way, but there isn't."

She blinked rapidly. "I had a cat when I was a little girl. A great big tom, black as midnight. He had the most unusual green eyes, and he was fiercely protective of me."

Quinn listened to her, understanding her need to change the subject. "Was he?"

"Aye. I found him when he was just a kitten. He would wander off as male cats do, but he always returned. Sometimes he would be so cut up that I wondered if he would live. Thankfully, Grandmother would use her magic to make him better."

"What happened to him?"

"He died two years ago one winter's night in my arms. As he had gotten older, he wandered less and less. He got into the habit of sleeping with me every night curled at my feet." She smiled suddenly. "I would fall asleep listening to him purr."

Quinn ached to hear the sadness in Marcail's voice for her beloved pet. She had lost so many people in her life that he didn't want her to lose any more.

"One morning I woke to hear him wheezing when he breathed. I knew his time was short. He had lived a long life, but I wasn't ready to let him go. He was in so much pain for days. No matter what I did, I couldn't call my magic to me to ease him. Three days later he died."

Quinn didn't know what to say or even why she had told him that moving story.

Marcail's turquoise eyes were filled with tears. "I have no control over my magic, Quinn. I want nothing more than to help you, to give you the spell to bind your god, but I cannot."

He tucked her head into his neck and sighed. He understood all too well the need to help, to control some aspect of what was happening. The only one who had control was Deirdre, and she wouldn't relinquish that easily.

"My father used to tell us that as men, we should be able to look back over our lives and know we've done the best we could on everything. I couldn't say that before, but I will be able to say it soon."

Marcail lifted her head to meet his eyes. "You're the best man I've ever known."

He was humbled by her words, even though he knew

they weren't remotely true. There were many men better than him. "Thank you."

"When do you think Deirdre will come for you?"

"William will hold off telling her as long as he can. He has become attached to Deirdre and doesna wish to share."

Marcail giggled. "Attached? Are you telling me he has feelings for her?"

"I'm not sure if it's genuine feeling or if he just enjoys the power being near her gives him. She's granted him much command while she's been angry with me."

Marcail shifted, her brow furrowed. "That doesn't give us much time."

"Much time for what?"

"To convince the others to side with you."

Quinn loved how her mind worked, but sometimes things weren't as easy as she made them. "It willna happen. We've only got Duncan and Arran. That's not nearly enough."

"Do you remember when you told me you thought Charon was a spy?"

He got a sick feeling in his gut as he stared into her eyes. "That's the real reason you went to speak to him, isn't it?"

"It is. He didn't outright admit it, but he didn't deny it either. I do think he's the spy, Quinn."

"Then what made you think he would help?"

She scrunched her face. "I thought maybe whatever Deirdre used to make him spy we could either get back or help him with."

"And . . ." Quinn prompted. He had thought to confront Charon that way himself, and was surprised Marcail had done it alone. She had risked much in taking such a chance.

"He refused. Apparently, whatever Deirdre is using to make him spy is too great for him to even consider going against her."

"Shite," Quinn murmured. He was short one man with Ian gone. It would help greatly to have Charon on their side.

Any words Marcail might have spoken were drowned out by the unmistakable sound of the trapdoor over the Pit opening. Quinn leapt to his feet and jerked up his breeches.

"Stay in the shadows," Quinn said as he glanced at Marcail over his shoulder.

He transformed. Quinn reached the cave entrance a moment before something large landed with a heavy thud on the ground. He wasn't surprised to see the orange skin of a Warrior on the ground.

"Friend or foe?" Arran asked as he stepped beside Quinn.

Quinn didn't take his eyes from the newcomer. "We'll find out in a moment."

Duncan moved to Quinn's other side. "I'm in need of a fight."

At that moment the orange-skinned Warrior leapt to his feet, blood running down the side of his face and his kilt ragged and stained. He growled, showing one of his fangs missing.

"I think he's looking for a fight as well, Duncan," Quinn said.

But it wasn't Duncan the Warrior wanted to fight. Quinn lowered his shoulder the moment he saw the orange Warrior come at him. The force propelled the Warrior backward, and Quinn slammed him into the rocks.

"Why did she throw you down here?" Quinn asked.

The newcomer laughed. "She told me you would try to trick me."

Quinn was so taken aback by his words that he didn't put his arm up in time to stop his chest from being sliced. He groaned and punched the Warrior on the jaw.

"I willna listen," the orange Warrior bellowed. "I will die if I listen to you."

Quinn wrapped his hand around the Warrior's throat. "If you doona listen to me, you'll die. Deirdre only sends Warriors down here that she wants to break."

"We are the evil ones," the Warrior said as he clawed at Quinn's fingers. "She is trying to stop us from being made. She tried to stop my god from taking control, but she was too late."

Quinn tossed the Warrior aside and threw back his head as he roared. Deirdre had sensed the weak soul of the new Warrior, had sensed it and made sure he wouldn't believe a word Quinn said.

The orange Warrior scrambled to his feet, wary and waiting.

"When were you turned?" Quinn asked.

Frantic orange eyes looked around the Pit at the other Warriors who stood and watched. "Two days ago."

Quinn raked a hand down his face. "In time you will learn that what Deirdre says is all lies. She's the one who unbound your god, friend. She's the one who is evil."

No sooner were the words out of Quinn's mouth than

the Warrior attacked. More gashes appeared on Quinn's chest as he fought the frenzied Warrior.

There was no talking, not now. Time, however, was Quinn's friend.

"Quinn," Arran yelled in warning.

Quinn spotted the bottle in the orange Warrior's fingers. He rolled over until he held the newcomer on the ground, but somehow the Warrior had uncorked the bottle. Quinn managed to pin the Warrior's arm out to the side as something dark and red spilled out of the bottle.

He didn't need to sniff the liquid to know it was blood, but why would the Warrior want to pour blood on him?

"Cease or you will die," Quinn warned. He wouldn't kill the Warrior, but he knew Arran or Duncan would.

"I will be redeemed if I kill you," the orange Warrior shouted.

Quinn didn't know what Deirdre was playing at, but he would be sure to find out.

The Warrior tossed the bottle at Quinn, aimed at his chest and his multiple wounds. Quinn managed to duck the vial, but Duncan had already removed the orange Warrior's head from his body by the time Quinn looked up.

"I willna see you harmed," Duncan said by way of explanation.

Quinn nodded and rose from the Warrior's dead body. The only way they could be killed was by decapitation, and though Quinn hadn't wanted the Warrior dead, it was probably for the best.

Overhead there was laughter as Quinn remembered

too late that he was being observed. He looked up and found Deirdre watching him with a cruel smile on her lips.

"I abhor her," he mumbled. A good man had died for her benefit.

"Does she have so many Warriors that she can have them killed so easily now?" Arran asked the question that had been going through Quinn's mind.

Quinn refused to move until the trapdoor was closed. He turned to his men, but a banging on the Pit entrance took his attention. Did it mean another attack? His wounds were healing, but he needed a little more time to be completely restored.

He spotted Broc through the square in the door. At the winged Warrior's nod, Quinn walked to him.

"What was that all about?" Quinn demanded. "A Warrior died for nothing."

Broc raised a brow. "The man is dead. The god is not."

"Explain."

Isla stepped beside Broc and trained her ice-blue eyes on Quinn. "Just as the god passed through the bloodlines, finding the best Warrior, he will continue to do so until the bloodline runs out."

"Are you telling me the god of the Warrior back there has left his body and now traveled to another of his bloodline?"

"That is exactly what I'm telling you," Isla replied. "Look for yourself."

Quinn looked over his shoulder to find the orange skin of the Warrior gone. In its place was that of a young lad who had barely reached manhood. He ground his teeth together and faced Broc and Isla.

"So what now?" he asked. "Does Deirdre want to

gloat? I've spent too many hours watching Ian being tortured for her to want more."

"What did you say?" Broc asked.

Isla turned her head slightly to Broc. "Deirdre has been in a rage. She put William in command for a few hours."

Broc let out a measured breath. "Did William touch you?"

Quinn found his question odd, especially for one who worked for Deirdre. "Does it matter?"

"Aye," Isla said. "Answer the question."

Quinn looked from one to the other. "Nay," he finally answered. "He didna. He seemed to know better."

"The Warrior thrown into the Pit was Deirdre's way of telling you she can do whatever she wants," Isla said.

Quinn chuckled. "The bitch has always been able to do what she wants, except when it comes to my body. I find it odd that she doesn't try to use magic on me. It must be because she canna. And the child of prophecy willna be born unless I give her my body willingly."

Isla gave a slight nod of her head. "You are correct, MacLeod."

"What do you want?" Broc asked. "In exchange. What do you want for willingly going to Deirdre?"

Quinn thought back to the lovemaking he and Marcail had experienced, how with one touch she brought light into his world. As much as he wanted to free her now, he couldn't. He had to keep his brothers away from Deirdre. Marcail he would liberate as quickly as he could.

"My brothers," Quinn said. "I want them left alone."

Isla lifted her hand and Quinn saw the slight wince

that passed quickly over her schooled features. "That she will not grant. She has need of your brothers."

If Quinn spoke of Marcail now, Deirdre would likely have her killed immediately regardless of the protection spells. Quinn couldn't ask for the release of Arran and Duncan because no one would be there to guard Marcail.

"Ian. I want Ian released not just from the torture but from the mountain. Send him on his way."

Isla's mouth pinched in what appeared to be fury. "Ian is a Warrior, MacLeod. He can withstand much."

"He's withstood more than anyone should have to."

"Is this really what you would have me trade your . . . seed for?" Isla asked.

Quinn frowned. There seemed to be more in Isla's words than what she was speaking. Even Broc looked at her strangely. If only they were alone, then Quinn could speak to her.

"What would you have me ask for?" Quinn asked.

Isla's ice-blue eyes seemed to flame with emotion. "That is not for me to say."

Quinn was so tired of the riddles and evasive answers. He just wanted to do the right thing and protect the people he cared about. It was becoming more and more difficult, though.

Isla stepped closer to the door. "It is said, MacLeod, that your brothers are headed this way."

"It is also said that Deirdre has sent an army of wyrran to stop them while Warriors set a trap to capture them," Broc said.

Quinn's hope had risen only to be dashed as quickly. "If she takes my brothers, I will never give her my body."

"Don't say never," Isla cautioned. "You don't know how powerful she's become."

Broc nodded. "Isla isna speaking false. Be cautious, MacLeod. Deirdre always gets what she wants in the end. You need to decide how you plan to come out when all this is over."

Quinn watched Isla walk away. He knew how he would come out in the end. He would bed a great evil only to spawn the greatest wickedness to ever walk the earth. If that happened, any good that might still be in the world would be gone forever.

"Think carefully, MacLeod," Broc said. "Whatever you choose in bargaining for your body canna be undone. Deirdre is granting you this one gift. Do not waste it."

"She willna give me what I really want, which is my brother's freedom."

"Is that all you really want?"

Quinn thought of Marcail, of her exotic turquoise eyes and braids that framed her beautiful face. "There is too much I want."

"Then I will return on the morrow for your decision."

Quinn turned and leaned against the door. Now he knew how much time he had with Marcail. And it didn't seem near enough. He feared eternity wouldn't be enough.

TWENTY-TWO

Fallon broke the neck of a wyrran and tossed the creature to the ground. He glanced to his wife to find Larena finishing off one of the last wyrran. She winked at him to let him know she was all right.

He walked to her, eyeing the blood that covered her. "Is any of it yours?"

"Nay," she answered with a shake of her golden head. "It's all wyrran."

Fallon looked at the ground that was littered with the small creatures. They had been battling for hours. He was hungry and tired. He was just moving to find Larena some water when he heard a roar. His head jerked around to look for the source.

"I believe Hayden is enjoying this," Larena said, her smoky blue eyes brimming with mischief.

"Hmm. I think you're correct." Fallon watched as Hayden and Logan finished off the last dozen wyrran.

Fallon took Larena's hand and walked her to the tree line where the others sat. She blew out a breath as she slid down the tree to rest against it.

"Will there be more?" Lucan asked.

Fallon shrugged. His hair had fallen from the queue at his neck. He pulled out the strip of leather and retied the queue. "I imagine there will be."

"Nay," Galen said. "The next time Deirdre will send Warriors to capture us."

Ramsey looked at Fallon with cool gray eyes, his black hair stuck to the side of his face with sweat. "Then I suggest we aren't here."

Fallon knew they wanted him to jump them to the mountain. He'd gladly do it himself, despite the fact he didn't remember its exact location, but he refused to endanger anyone else, especially Larena.

"Hold," Ramsey said as Fallon parted his lips to speak. "We all want to go forward, but what if we do the opposite?"

Logan snorted as he and Hayden joined them. "You mean return to the castle?"

Ramsey shook his head. "Nay. Not all the way to the castle, but far enough back."

"It could work." Fallon scratched his chin. "Broc found us easily enough the first time, though."

Larena smoothed her golden locks from her face. "I thought Broc was now on our side?"

"He is, but he's still trying to deceive Deirdre," Ramsey said. "That's not an easy thing to do. He'll have to be verra careful lest he's caught."

Fallon nodded, his decision made. "I know the spot I can take us to. It's secluded, and it will give us a few hours to rest and eat before we return here."

Lucan jumped to his feet. "Want to take a look around before we leave? I'd rather return farther ahead if we can."

"Be safe," Larena called after them.

With their speed, Lucan and Fallon covered a great distance in a short amount of time. Fallon pulled to a stop and looked at the forbidding mountains ahead of them. Their brother was in there suffering who knew what kinds of torture and pain.

"We could have been at Cairn Toul already had we not had to fight the wyrran," Lucan said as he too gazed at the huge mound of rock.

"I agree. I feel better knowing Broc is with Quinn." Lucan rubbed his jaw and frowned.

"What is it?" Fallon asked.

"Deirdre could set a trap for us anywhere."

Fallon had already thought of that. "It's a chance we have to take. Hopefully, she'll be occupied with Quinn."

"Which will allow us to get in," Lucan finished. He clapped Fallon on the shoulder. "I hope you're right, brother."

"Me, too," Fallon murmured before he jumped them back to the group.

Marcail opened her eyes to find herself back in her cottage, or rather her grandmother's cottage. She blinked and sat up. Everything was in order and as it should be. Not at all as it had been when the wyrran attacked it looking for her.

She frowned and swung her legs over the bed. Something wasn't right.

Marcail clutched her skirts as her grandmother walked into the cottage. It had been so long since she had seen the woman who had raised her and taught her the Druid ways that, for a moment, Marcail couldn't breathe.

"There is much to be done, Marcail. You must get up now," her grandmother said in the same wise and loving tone she had always used.

"Grandmother?" Marcail could scarcely believe what

she was seeing, and even though she knew she was dreaming, it was so good to see her grandmother again.

Her grandmother set the basket of herbs on the table and turned to Marcail with a warm smile on her wrinkled face. She had always been a petite woman with shoulders that hunched forward, but she had strength within her that Marcail envied.

"What is it, my child?"

Marcail rose on legs that shook. She didn't want the dream to end. "You're dead."

Her grandmother tossed back her head of silver hair and laughed. "Of course I am. Listen carefully because there isn't a lot of time. I kept much from you, more than I probably should have. Do you remember the one thing I told you to follow above any other?"

"Aye. My heart."

"Exactly." Her grandmother nodded in approval. "Follow your heart, my precious child. It will help you to make the decisions that will alter your life."

Marcail shook her head. "I don't understand. What did you keep from me?"

"That doesn't matter now. You are already in Deirdre's hands. It wouldn't help you."

"How can I escape?"

Her grandmother's smile died. "I'm afraid you cannot."

Marcail released a shaky breath and squared her shoulders. "What must I do?"

"Remember the spell to bind the gods."

"I cannot. You've buried it too deep."

Her grandmother's thin arm sliced through the air. "You aren't listening to your magic, my child. Listen and allow your magic to flow through you. Once you have, you'll discover the spell."

The cottage began to fade. Marcail winced as her grandmother's nails bit into her hands.

"Listen, my child."

"Grandmother," Marcail screamed as the cottage disappeared completely.

Marcail's eyes flew open to stare into the darkness and gloom of the Pit. Her lungs burned from her rapid breathing. Why had she dreamed about her grandmother now, and what had the vision meant?

Somehow, there was a message in the dream that her grandmother was trying to tell her. Marcail turned onto her side and replayed the dream through her mind once more. It had been so comforting to see her grandmother. It was too bad the old, powerful woman wasn't with her now. Marcail would have liked to see her grandmother show Deirdre a thing or two.

Quinn could tell by the way Marcail woke that she had been dreaming. He wondered what filled her dreams. And as selfish as it was, he hoped she dreamed of him after he was gone.

He leaned his shoulder against the rocks at the entrance to his cave. As much as he wanted to sleep with Marcail, to hold her body against his, he knew he had to keep watch.

The Warrior Duncan had killed no longer lay in the middle of the Pit. Several of Deirdre's guards tried to come and take him, but others in the Pit had made quick work of slicing the dead man to pieces.

It was obvious to Quinn that many of the Warriors locked in the Pit had lost their minds and their humanity. Their gods had taken control of them, and Quinn feared he would share their fate eventually. He just prayed he got the ones he cared about out of the mountain first.

"Quinn?"

"I am here, Arran," he answered. "What is it?"

Arran paused. "It's Duncan."

"I'm fine," Duncan ground as he walked out of his cave. He glared at Arran as he moved past him to stand beside Quinn. "I'm all right, Quinn."

Quinn looked from Arran's white eyes to Duncan's pale blue ones. "Tell me."

"The . . . pain is returning."

Quinn lowered his gaze and sighed. He'd been dreading telling his friend what had occurred with Ian, but Quinn could no longer put it off. "You feel Ian's pain."

"I do," Duncan agreed. "Did you see him?"

"I wasna able to speak to him, and he had no idea I was there, but I did see him." He told Duncan all that had happened the day before with William and Ian. When he was done, Duncan stood with his fists clenched and death in his eyes.

"I will kill William for this."

Quinn nodded. "I plan on doing the same. Ian is holding up well, my friend."

"How much more can he withstand?" Arran asked.

Duncan moved until he was nose to nose with Arran. "He will withstand it all."

"Easy," Quinn said and pushed the two men apart. "Arran wasna casting doubts on Ian's strength. He's worried, just as I am, about Deirdre turning Ian to her will."

Duncan peeled back his lips to reveal his long fangs. "Never. Ian will never surrender to her."

Quinn wanted to believe Duncan, but Duncan hadn't seen the torture. "Be that as it may, we should be prepared either way."

"I know my brother. He willna submit to her," Duncan repeated.

Arran crossed his arms over his chest and jerked his chin to the Pit entrance. "What happened with Broc earlier?"

"It was Broc and Isla," Quinn said. "The orange Warrior was to prove to me that Deirdre dictates everything."

"But she let a Warrior be killed," Duncan said.

Quinn sighed. "She killed the man who housed the god. She didna kill the god."

"Shite," Arran murmured. "Even with the gods unbound they canna be killed?"

Quinn shook his head. "The gods will descend upon the strongest in the bloodline."

"Except for your bloodline," Duncan pointed out. "You, Fallon, and Lucan are the last of the MacLeods."

"I know," Quinn said. "Regardless, Deirdre proved a point. If we doona submit, she will find those that will."

Arran blew out a breath. "Is that all Broc had to say?"

"Deirdre has granted me a boon in exchange for going to her. Broc will return in the morn for my decision."

Duncan turned and glanced at Marcail. "You havena told her, have you?"

"Nay," Quinn admitted. "Once I'm with Deirdre, I will do my best to free everyone here. I doubt she will allow me to return and speak to either of you, so be on the lookout for any opportunities to escape."

Quinn saw that both Duncan and Arran were about

to argue the point. He caught sight of Charon and made for the copper Warrior.

"What brings you to my side of the Pit, MacLeod," Charon said as he rubbed one of his horns. "Did Arran confess to hitting your woman?"

Quinn didn't believe the nonchalant attitude Charon tried to pass off. The Warrior's eyes saw everything.

"Aye," Quinn finally answered. "Arran and Marcail told me what happened."

Charon's dark brow rose. "Interesting."

"What I find interesting, Charon, is that you would willingly spy for Deirdre."

Instantly, the copper Warrior's demeanor changed. He pushed from the wall and glared at Quinn. "You dare much speaking to me in such a way."

"I'll speak to you however I wish. I'll admit Deirdre is powerful. Her magic is fierce and swift, and she doesna tolerate betrayal. But these are your people being killed in her mountain."

"Not my people," Charon growled.

"You're a Highlander. Every man, woman, and child brought to this mountain, whether they be Druid or Warrior, is a Highlander. So, aye, your people. Deny it all you want, but it's the truth."

Charon turned his head away.

"I took you for a strong Warrior," Quinn continued. "I've seen the way you watch everyone down here. You use your charm when you can and your brawn when you have to. What I doona understand is how you could be so weak as to not fight against Deirdre."

In a blink Charon was in his face. "You know nothing of what you speak."

"I know much more than you ever will." Quinn

shoved Charon away from him. "We all have sad stories, and we've all had someone we love taken from us. You should know the difference between good and evil."

"I know the difference."

There was something in the Warrior's eyes, something haunted, that stopped Quinn from saying more. "Maybe you do."

Charon turned and strode into his cave without another word.

"Eventually, Charon, you are going to have to choose sides."

A harsh laughed followed Quinn's words. "I already have, MacLeod."

TWENTY-THREE

Isla's gut churned with bile, but she dared not move. She stood still as stone in the chamber Deirdre used to kill Druids and take their magic.

It was a room Isla hated with every fiber of her being. Just being inside it made her skin crawl, but having to watch a Druid die made her want to vomit.

"Dunmore did well, didn't he?" Deirdre asked her.

Isla nodded, unable to speak. She swallowed and tried not to look at the frightened young Druid strapped to the stone table in the center of the chamber.

Deirdre cocked her head to the side as she regarded the young girl. "Thanks to your sister's magic, Isla, I no longer have to wait until the spring equinox to find those that I search for. It was so tedious having to wait, especially when I am building an army."

Isla parted her lips and breathed in through her mouth to stop the nausea that rolled in her stomach.

"It took me too long to realize you, Isla, are stronger than your sister. Aye, Lavena is a seer, but you, you are almost as perfect as the Warriors."

Isla had heard enough, and though she knew she would be punished again, she didn't care. "You know I don't do your bidding willingly."

"Ah, but you willingly submitted to my command once upon a time. I told you then you would always be mine, Isla. I meant it."

"Why keep Grania? She was nothing to you, just a little girl."

Deirdre's smile vanished as she sneered down at Isla. "I suppose your torture wasn't enough yesterday. Should I take the lash to you once again for being so insolent?"

Isla turned to face the Druid about to die. "Do as you wish, Deirdre. I care not."

And that was the truth. Isla had stopped caring. Lavena was no longer her sister, and Grania, dear precious Grania, was no longer the adorable little girl she had loved so dearly. Both her sister and her niece had been corrupted by Deirdre.

Isla understood then what she hadn't so long ago: that she couldn't save Lavena or Grania. If only she had known before, she might have saved her own soul. But it was too late now. She was damned to an eternity in Hell, and after suffering under Deidre's wrath, there was nothing in Hell that could frighten her.

"Now," Deirdre said as she walked to the Druid on the table. She placed a hand over the girl's chest and smiled. "For one so young, I sense much magic in you."

"Please," the young Druid begged. "Let me go."

Deidre tucked a strand of her white hair behind her ear. "I'm afraid that's not possible. I need your magic, and in order for me to get your magic, you have to die."

Isla clasped her hands behind her back as the girl began to cry silent tears. She didn't beg Deirdre again, however.

"If you want my magic, you're going to have to force

it out of me," the girl said. "You don't deserve the magic you were gifted with."

Deirdre drew in a tired breath. "Enough."

"Nay, you vicious hag. You will pay for the sins you have committed, and . . ."

The girl's words were cut off as Deirdre's hair wrapped around her neck. "I told you that was enough. I will not listen to your incessant rambling because you are too afraid to die."

Isla blinked as the Druid began to laugh. No one laughed at Deirdre.

Deirdre's eyes had lost their blue color and turned white with her black magic narrowed on the young Druid. "I can make this as painful for you as I want."

"Do it," the girl rasped.

Isla knew better than to turn away. She had seen too many of her fellow Druids, both *drough* and *mie* alike, die on Deirdre's table. And even though Isla knew what was going to happen, she still flinched when the blade cut into the girl's wrists.

The slashes were deep and long, and the blood drained quickly from the girl's veins into the hollowed parts of the table where the blood then spilled into goblets on the floor.

While the blood flowed, Deirdre stood beside the Druid and began to recite the ancient spell. Isla knew the words by heart, the black magic that called up Satan and all his evil.

But every time she saw the black cloud that rose from the center of the table, Isla still had to fight to keep still and not bolt from the room.

The girl screamed, weak though she was from loss of blood. The cloud, an evil spirit from Hell, descended on the Druid. The girl thrashed, her screams echoing around the high-ceilinged chamber as the apparition took her soul.

"I am yours!" Deirdre screamed and plunged the dagger through the spirit into the girl's stomach.

The ghoul vanished, and the girl's lifeless eyes stared above her. But the ceremony was far from over.

The two black-veiled servants moved from their corners and collected the goblets that were filled with the Druid's blood. They carried them to Deirdre where she drained each goblet, licking her lips stained red with blood.

The servants hastily moved back as wind began to howl and swirl around Deirdre as the new magic mixed with hers. She threw back her head, her long white hair lifting above and around her.

"I am unstoppable!" Deirdre yelled.

Deirdre pinned Isla with a look as the wind began to lessen. Without moving a muscle Deirdre had Isla restrained against the wall, her feet dangling off the floor.

Isla wanted to claw at the invisible hand that held her throat, but she kept her hands in her skirts. Fighting Deirdre only made the pain worse.

And no matter how much suffering Deirdre put her through, Isla knew Deirdre wouldn't kill her. Not yet, anyway. Deirdre had a hold over Isla that she hadn't been able to duplicate with another since. There was no way she would chance harming Isla.

"I've sent the MacClures a message through Dunmore," Deirdre said.

Isla waited, wondering what Deirdre could possibly want with the MacClures. Isla had no desire to return to that clan. She'd had enough dealings with them when the wyrran had destroyed their village looking for the Druid Cara, who was now mated to Lucan MacLeod.

Of course, it was the MacClures who had taken a large piece of the MacLeod land, land that included the castle the MacLeods claimed as their own.

"I think Fallon and Lucan need something to occupy their time," Deirdre said.

Isla knew she should keep silent, but she couldn't help it. "I thought you wanted to capture the MacLeods?"

"Oh, I do. And I will. I want them to suffer first. The MacLeods might have scared the MacClures from their lands, but I will ensure the MacClures have what they need to get their lands back. Once they have what they require, you will stand with the MacClures."

Isla bit her tongue to keep from speaking again.

Deirdre released the magical hold. Isla's knees buckled when she hit the floor, but she managed to stay upright by grabbing onto the stones in the wall.

"You have gotten quite audacious recently, Isla. I received information just this morning, and I think I'm going to need you to take a trip."

Isla's blood went cold in her veins. She knew what that meant, but she was powerless to fight Deirdre.

Lightning split the room, but it was only Deirdre's magic. Isla grabbed her head and bit back a scream of pain as Deirdre's voice boomed in her mind giving her instructions she would be helpless to reject.

No matter how hard Marcail tried, sleep eluded her after the dream about her grandmother. And to make matters worse, Quinn hadn't come to her.

When she had seen him walk from the cave, she had sat up and leaned to the side. She hadn't been prepared to see him and Charon speaking, but whatever they were talking about wasn't good because it was obvious by the way Charon's face went hard that he was angry.

Marcail watched them for long moments until Quinn returned to stand beside Duncan and Arran. She was curious as to what Quinn had to say to Charon.

She pulled her legs against her chest and wrapped her arms around them. She was bored and anxious. Quinn wanted her to stay in the shadows, and though she understood why, she was used to moving about and doing her daily chores. She wasn't used to sitting for hours upon hours in the dark.

Marcail blew a braid that had fallen into her eyes. Quinn had made her stay in the Pit tolerable, but once he was gone, then what?

I'm liable to go daft.

And that was the truth. As a Druid, the sun, air, and water sustained her. In the darkness and gloom of a mountain filled with the evil and dark magic, it would only be a matter of time before what little magic Marcail had was gone.

Out of the darkness, the strange musical chanting began again. It was so faint she could barely hear it. Marcail cocked her head to the side and closed her eyes.

She concentrated on the chanting, on hearing the words. The more she focused, the louder the music became. She lost herself in the soft, lyrical music, the words washing over her like a summer storm and infusing her soul with magic.

"Marcail?"

Her eyes flew open to find Quinn standing before her, a frown on his face.

"Are you all right?" he asked.

She swallowed, missing the strange chanting. "I am."

"I've been calling your name for some time."

"I must have fallen asleep." Even as she said the words, she didn't believe she had been dreaming. What she experienced was something else entirely.

Quinn squatted down in front of her and took her hands in his. "Charon is Deirdre's spy, just as you suspected."

"Is that why you went to speak to him?"

"One of the reasons. He will likely stay away from you for the most part, but doona expect him to aid you in any way no matter what he might say to you."

"You mean when you've gone." Just saying the words caused a lump to form in her throat. How she wished she didn't care for Quinn as much as she did. She had lost too many people in her life already. To know she would lose Quinn—again—was just too much.

Quinn sighed and nodded. "I wish I could guarantee that you would be safe, but down here, no one is safe."

"I know," she whispered.

"Duncan and Arran will be with you always. I've told them, and I will tell you, Deirdre willna allow me to return, but be on the lookout for any signs you could escape. It will be quick, and you'll have to be ready at a moment's notice."

She brushed aside a lock of his light brown hair from his eyes. "And you? While we escape, you still think to stay here?"

"Aye."

The way he said it was so final.

"I know what you would say, and I ask that you doona," Quinn said. "This is hard enough as it is, and the thought of leaving you here . . . I don't like it, Marcail."

"Whenever I was indecisive about something, my grandmother used to tell me to follow my heart, that it would guide me to do the right thing."

"That's what I'm trying to do. For you, for my brothers, for everyone."

The knot of fear and dread grew in Marcail's chest until she found it difficult to breath. "And you think by giving Deirdre a child you will be helping us?"

Quinn smiled then and fingered one of her braids. "I never said I would give her a child."

"But . . ." Marcail shook her head. "If you go to her, that's exactly what she will expect."

"No doubt that's exactly what she will expect, but I plan to make things interesting. I will try and give you and the others time to flee this god-awful mountain and find my brothers."

Marcail threw her arms around him and buried her face in his neck. "You are risking so much."

"Someone has to, and I'm the perfect one." His hands rubbed up and down her back.

And that was the problem. He was too perfect.

TWENTY-FOUR

Broc had survived another meeting with Deirdre. Every time he was with her he expected her to reveal that she knew of his duplicity. It was a dangerous game he played, but one he had no choice but to take part in.

He had hoped to speak to Quinn privately the day before, but Isla had demanded to go along with him. The petite *drough* was one of Deirdre's favorite tools in her bid for dominance of the world.

From what he had seen, Isla was a force to be reckoned with, which was why he didn't try to dissuade her from accompanying him to the Pit. Deirdre may very well have sent Isla to spy on him as Deirdre was wont to do.

Broc had seen the careful way Isla had moved as she made her way down to the Pit. She had been punished by Deirdre, as they all had at one time or another. Deirdre liked to make sure everyone knew she could kill them any time she wanted.

As Broc walked through the corridors, his wings scraped the top of the ceiling. He hated being in the mountain. The freedom of an open sky, the taste of the air upon his body, that's what he craved.

And Sonya.

His hands fisted as he thought of the Druid. Ramsey

had told him Sonya was at MacLeod Castle, but Broc hadn't been able to see for himself. He worried endlessly for her, and until he was free of Deirdre, both Sonya and her sister, Anice, would have to stay hidden.

Broc ignored the black-veiled servants who stood aside to let him pass. His mind, like always, was on Sonya. She didn't know of him, didn't know he had been the one to save her and her sister from slaughter when they were but infants. And he didn't want her to know.

He forced Sonya to the back of his mind and focused on the task at hand. Broc was on his way to see Quinn again. He had hoped Deirdre was still too angry to speak to Quinn, but she had heard of Quinn's request to see her.

If there was time, Broc planned to let Quinn know his brothers were on their way. How soon they'd arrive, though, was the question. Broc had no doubt the MacLeod brothers would think of a way to get to the mountain without being captured. At least he hoped they did.

Broc paused in mid stride as he reached the stairway that veered off into different directions. He could turn to his right and go up the stairs toward Deirdre's chambers, or he could go forward and take the steps that would lead to the Pit. However, it was the flight of stairs on his left that led deep into the bottom of the mountain from which he heard the unmistakable roar of a Warrior.

As far as Broc knew, there was no one being kept below, had never been anyone kept below. But it was obvious by the angry, lonesome roar he heard that someone had been put down there.

Broc decided he'd look for himself later. The more he knew what Deirdre had going on, the better for the MacLeods.

With a sigh, Broc took the stairs in front of him and proceeded to the Pit. There were always at least two guards posted outside the door. Broc always thought it was useless. The door was locked with black magic. It didn't matter how strong a Warrior was, he wasn't getting out of the Pit unless Deirdre wanted him out.

Broc greeted the guards and peered through the window of the door. The torches Deirdre allowed were scarce, but their red-orange flames helped to beat back the darkness. He found it amusing Deirdre had need of the torches to see when she was as powerful as she claimed to be.

Broc took a deep breath because things were about to get very interesting.

Quinn let his fingers run though the sable length of Marcail's hair as he held her against his chest. He could feel her unease, knew that she was more scared than she wanted him to see. She was such a brave lass, a woman he would be proud to call his own. And would call his own if he were able.

Marcail lifted her head so that she looked at him. He gazed into her clear turquoise eyes and tried to memorize every inch of her face.

"I wish I could have met you before," Quinn said. "You would have been good for my soul."

"Just your soul?" she asked with a teasing grin.

He shook his head. "You have been good for me."

"And you have been good for me." Her brow furrowed

for a moment. "Quinn, there is much that I would tell you of how I feel."

He put his finger over her lips. If she told him she cared about him, he wouldn't be able to leave her. Just thinking she had any feelings for him made his heart skip a beat.

Quinn kissed her. He let himself drown in her intoxicating taste. He wished, then, he had made love to her instead of standing guard. There were many ways Quinn wanted to enjoy her body, many ways he wanted to watch as she peaked and screamed his name.

Her arms wound around his neck and her fingers slid into his hair. He groaned and deepened the kiss, intent on having her one last time.

"Quinn!"

Both of their heads swiveled to the side. Quinn closed his eyes with regret. When he opened them, the fear he saw in Marcail's depths ate away at his soul.

"I'll get you out of here," he vowed. "Just promise me you'll stay hidden."

She nodded woodenly. "Quinn, I . . . stay safe."

He wondered what she had been about to say, but decided it was best if he didn't know. "You as well."

The hardest thing he had ever done was lowering his arms from her body and moving away from her. He stood to find Arran and Duncan waiting for him.

"We canna change your mind?" Duncan asked.

"Nay, my friend, you canna."

Arran slapped him on the shoulder. "Doona let her take your soul."

Quinn clasped Arran's forearm before he did the same with Duncan's. "Stay watchful," he warned before he turned on his heel and walked to Broc.

Broc's indigo Warrior eyes were trained on Quinn as he approached the door. When Quinn was a few steps from it, the door swung open and he stepped through it.

Quinn paused as the door banged shut behind him. Every fiber in his body wanted to turn around and take one last look at Marcail, but he didn't dare. Not now, mayhap not ever again.

"Have you changed your mind?" Broc asked.

Was it Quinn's imagination, or did Broc sound hopeful? "I have not."

"Hm," Broc said as his mouth flattened into a thin line. "Have you decided what boon you will ask?"

Quinn had thought of little else. "I have."

"Then I will take you to Deirdre."

He followed Broc through the hallways and up the stairways as they left the Pit behind. And yet, all Quinn could think about was Marcail, not the evil that awaited him. He should be concentrating on how he would fend off Deirdre for a day or two, not worrying if Marcail would be safe or not.

"You are preoccupied," Broc said.

Quinn raised a brow. Broc hadn't turned around once to look at him, so Quinn didn't know how the winged Warrior knew what was going on with him. "I'd rather be taken to my own death than to Deirdre."

"Then why do you go to her?" Broc halted and turned to face Quinn.

"I do it because I must."

Broc lowered his gaze for a moment. "Are you sure about that, Quinn?"

"Why doona you tell me?" Quinn was in no mood for enigmatic words. "Do I have another choice?"

Broc shrugged. "You have insisted that your brothers will come for you."

"And you've told me Deirdre sent wyrran to slow them down. Tell me, Broc, does Deirdre already have my brothers?"

"Nay," Broc answered. "She intends to once you have agreed to give her the child of the prophecy."

Quinn ran a hand through his hair, frustrated with everything. "Why canna she be content with me?"

"Because when the three of you fight as one, you are unstoppable."

And that's when Quinn realized how futile his efforts had been. It wouldn't matter how long he stood against Deirdre. She would have what she wanted no matter how long it took her to gain it.

Quinn thought of Cara and how she and Lucan looked at each other. Just as Quinn's parents had done. He didn't want Lucan to lose the one woman who had captured his heart.

"You have to go to her now," Broc said, his voice lowered.

Quinn looked at the dark blue Warrior with suspicion. "Why?"

"Because you've asked to see her. She expects you to comply. You must, Quinn. Your brothers are coming, but you need to give them some time."

Quinn took a step back from the Warrior. "What are you trying to do?"

Broc cursed under his breath and moved closer to Quinn. "What do you think? I'm risking *everything* just by speaking with you."

"You expect me to believe you've sided with my brothers? I doona believe that any more than I do the absurdity of whatever destiny Deirdre thinks I have."

"Then you are a greater idiot than I thought. Follow me, MacLeod."

Quinn was grateful when Broc continued onward. He couldn't stand to hear another word Broc said, not when it inspired hope to flare in his chest, hope that he knew would be dashed as soon as he realized he'd been played for a fool.

He prayed he could go through with everything. Just looking at Deirdre was a chore, and the thought of bedding her turned his stomach.

Holy Hell. What am I going to do?

He'd do whatever he must for his brothers, Marcail, and the men who relied on him. Even if it meant sacrificing his soul to Deirdre, he would do it.

Broc halted outside a door and motioned for Quinn to proceed. Quinn glanced at the Warrior, but Broc wouldn't look at him. Quinn pushed the door open and found himself once more in Deirdre's chamber.

The last time he had been here he found himself naked in her bed. He wondered what she had done with him while he had been unconscious, but he hadn't allowed his mind to dwell on it too long for fear of discovering what she had done.

Deirdre stood in the doorway to her bedchamber, her white hair touching the floor. She wore her normal black gown with material that hugged her shape.

"I was told you wished to speak with me?" she said with a knowing smile.

He nodded and folded his arms over his chest. "I did. I wonder, Deirdre, if you know all that William has been doing in your name."

In an instant her smile was gone. She took a deep breath and narrowed her white eyes at him. "Explain yourself."

"I asked to see you mere hours after you had taken Ian. William came for me, but refused to allow me to speak to you. Instead, he made me watch as they tortured Ian."

"William wouldn't bring you to me?"

He almost smiled at the anger that shook her voice. "Nay."

"Get me William," she commanded Broc.

Quinn glanced over his shoulder to find Broc watching him, a small smile upon his face, almost as if he approved at what Quinn had just done.

"William tells me you favor him over any other," Quinn said after Broc had left to do Deirdre's bidding.

She waved away his words. "William likes to be in command. I give him a little power every now and again."

"To keep him in line?" Quinn asked. "Is your hold so tenuous that you must resort to such petty methods?"

Her lips thinned in anger. "You dare to question me?"

"I do."

"I will show you just how powerful I am in this game you and I play, Quinn. Afterward, you will realize how fruitless it is to deny me anything."

He snorted. "I doubt it."

She opened her mouth to retort when William strode through the door with all the cocky confidence of one who had gotten all he desired.

"You wanted to see me, mistress," he said. Then he caught sight of Quinn and that confidence faltered.

Quinn slowly smiled. He wanted William to suffer,

because had Quinn been able to talk to Deirdre, Ian wouldn't have been tortured.

Deirdre stepped in front of William and ran her hand down his bare chest to his breeches in an intimate caress. "Tell me, my dear William, did Quinn ask to see me before now?"

William looked from Quinn to Deirdre. "You said you didna want to be disturbed."

"By everyone else, but you knew I was waiting to hear from Quinn. Didn't you?" she said as she reached down and grabbed hold of his balls.

William winced as Deirdre squeezed. "Nay, mistress."

"Don't you dare lie to me," Deirdre said between clenched teeth.

William's chin lowered to his chest. "I doona want to share you."

With a snarl, Deidre shoved William away from her. "Because of you a day has been wasted. You will be punished."

"As you wish," William murmured.

Quinn was surprised when Deirdre turned her unholy white eyes to him.

"How should he be punished?" she asked.

The answer was easy for Quinn. "I want him to suffer just as Ian suffered. Every hit, every cut, every bite of the whip, I want William to feel. And lest we forget, pull out his claws as well."

William growled, his lip curling in anger. Quinn lowered his arms, ready to fight him, but Deirdre stepped between them. Instantly, William calmed.

Quinn rolled his eyes at how easily William did as she bade. He didn't even balk at being dragged away by two guards. Quinn knew that one day he would kill the Warrior, and he would enjoy it immensely.

"Now," Deirdre said, gaining his attention. "It's time you followed me."

As much as Quinn didn't want to be around her, he needed to know everything he could so he could tell his brothers and they could kill the evil bitch.

Deirdre didn't say a word as she led him out of her chamber and down several hallways until they came to an archway that held a set of double doors.

The doors swung open as Deirdre neared. Quinn stepped over the threshold and looked in revulsion and wonder at the woman that hovered over the floor, surrounded by onyx flames.

"Isn't she magnificent?" Deirdre asked.

Quinn wasn't sure what he was looking at. "Who is she?"

"She was a Druid, a *mie*, who had the special gift of being a seer."

"As in seeing into the future?"

Deirdre shrugged. "Of sorts."

"And you are using her ability?"

"Of course."

Quinn moved closer to the woman. Her eyes were open, but they stared unseeing at the opposite wall. Her long, black hair floated around her as if she were in water, and her gown proved that she had been held for several centuries, if not longer.

There was something about the woman that looked familiar, as if he had seen her before. She was young, her skin fair and unblemished. Her arms hung by her sides while the black flames, which almost didn't look real, licked at her skin.

Quinn lifted his hand to touch the fire.

"Don't," Deirdre warned.

Quinn jerked his gaze to Deirdre. "What are the flames?"

"My magic, Quinn. Strong magic. It holds her in a state of being so that I may use her seer abilities to my advantage while keeping her alive as long as I want."

He was disgusted with how little Deirdre valued life. "How long have you had her?"

Deirdre smiled. "Not nearly long enough. Does she look familiar to you?"

"She does," he admitted carefully.

"She is Lavena, Isla's sister. I imprisoned both of them as well as Lavena's daughter years ago."

Quinn ground his teeth at the mention of the child. "And what has become of the child?"

A door opened suddenly and in walked a child with hair so black it shone blue, just as Isla's and her mother's did. Ice-cold blue eyes stared at Quinn.

"I thought you said you took them years ago," Quinn said as he stared at the child of no more than eight.

Deirdre nodded. "I did. Grania will stay this age forever."

Quinn glanced at the child and saw the same malice in her that he did in Deirdre. He was going to have to use the cunning his father had always commended him on very carefully if he was going to survive the evil around him.

TWENTY-FIVE

The slamming of the door still echoed in the Pit long after Quinn had departed. The distress and melancholy that had taken Marcail was hard to break through. Quinn was gone from her again. This time she knew it was for good.

Deep in her heart, she understood the reasons Quinn had given himself to Deirdre were good ones born of love and devotion to the people he cared about. Yet she found herself angry at his brothers for not coming for Quinn before now so he wouldn't have to give in to Deirdre.

But his brothers weren't there.

Arran and Duncan had not left Quinn's cave since he left. Marcail knew they were guarding her, but she didn't care anymore. Nothing mattered without Quinn.

Enough! Stop feeling sorry for yourself!

Marcail blew out a breath and focused on doing the one thing she could to help Quinn and all the Warriors— remembering the spell to bind their gods.

But no matter how long she searched her mind, how many times she thought back over all her grandmother had taught her, Marcail couldn't find the spell.

She rose from her place on the slab and began to pace the width of the cave, anything to keep from going insane. Her mind was on Quinn, on the sacrifice he had made for all of them, and how she pined for him. It stunned her to realize she missed him more than she missed her family or her grandmother.

"You care for him very much, doona you?" Duncan asked.

Marcail swung her head around to find the pale blue Warrior watching her. "I do. Very much." More than she ever imagined possible.

Duncan nodded. "It is obvious he cares for you as well."

"Quinn feels protective of me, aye," Marcail said. "He cares because he needs to keep me safe so I may help end all of this."

Duncan snorted and shook his head slowly. "Believe that if you will, Druid, but I've seen Quinn and how he watches you. He cares."

Marcail wanted it to be true, to the very depths of her soul she prayed it was true, but she knew the reality. She was nothing more than someone who had given Quinn comfort in a dark, evil place.

Quinn had awakened something within her she hadn't known she had. She craved his touch, his kisses, his body. She loved the way his pale green eyes looked at her. She loved the way his brown hair was too long and tended to land in his face. She loved the way he commanded such power and authority that every other man near him knew Quinn could best them. She loved the way he put himself in harm's way just to protect her and the ones he loved.

She loved . . . him.

Marcail grabbed the wall as the truth hit her. Love? She had never thought to know what it meant to fall in love with a man, and it had happened without her even knowing it.

"Marcail?" Arran said as he came toward her. "You've gone pale."

"I love him," she whispered. "I . . . love him. And I've lost him."

Duncan's large hand took her arm as he was careful to keep his claws from cutting her gown. "You need to sit."

"I've been doing too much sitting," she said and pulled her arm from his grasp. "I need to do something. Anything."

"Then remember the spell," Arran said. "It's the only thing that will help Quinn now."

Marcail shook her head. "I've been trying, Arran. I don't know what my grandmother did, but it's buried deep. Too deep, I'm afraid."

Quinn searched Grania's face for any of the innocence that always surrounded children, but all he saw was the taint of malevolence. "Were you so desperate for a child that you had to keep her this way?" he asked Deirdre as he pointed to Grania.

Deirdre laughed. "Now come, Quinn. You know I only do things that benefit me. I had my reasons for keeping Grania this age, and those reasons haven't changed. In fact, I doubt they ever will. Grania is . . . well, let's just say she keeps certain people doing as they should."

He knew she meant Isla. It was the only explanation. "Have her leave." He couldn't stand to look at the child any longer.

"I will come to you later," Deirdre told Grania.

One of the veiled servants came forward to escort

the child out of the chamber. Quinn glanced at each of the other three servants. All wore the black veils that covered their faces, and even their hair, completely.

"Why do you have them wear the veils?"

Deirdre smiled and lifted a white brow. "These are the ones who dared to defy me, the Druids who thought they had more magic than I."

"So you enslaved them."

"In a way," she said with a shrug. "I made them see the error of their ways."

"In other words, you tortured them until they begged for death and you then offered to make them slaves."

She laughed and tilted her head. "You understand me better than most."

"Doona flatter yourself. You're evil. It isna difficult to decipher the things you've done in order to gain what you want. Now, tell me why the veils."

She motioned a servant to her and removed the veil. "Would you like to look at this?"

Quinn hid his wince as he stared at the scarred and burned face of the servant. She had once been a proud Druid, but now she kept her eyes downcast and her face hidden. Even her dark red hair had been shorn from her head.

Deirdre tossed the veil to the servant and waved her away. "Don't think to try and turn my servants against me. All of their magic is mine."

"How did you manage that without killing them?"

A sly smile pulled at her thin lips. "There is much I am capable of doing with my power, Quinn. More than you could ever imagine."

"Then why has it taken you this long to capture me?"

She sighed. "You're growing tiresome."

He looked down at her with disdain. "I don't think you have the power you want everyone to think you have."

"Shall I prove it to you then? Maybe another of your men from the Pit as an example?"

Quinn closed his mouth. He didn't want to see anyone else hurt from his actions. "Leave them alone."

She laughed, the sound harsh and hollow. "It doesn't take much to halt that tongue of yours."

Quinn turned to Lavena once more. The black flames devoured her, yet her body remained unscathed. But by Deirdre's reaction when he tried to touch it, it would harm him.

He wondered if Isla knew how her sister was being used, and he guessed she did. Quinn tried to imagine what he'd feel if Lucan or Fallon was in Lavena's place. One thing was for certain, he wouldn't allow Deirdre to harm them. He'd kill them himself before Deirdre could put them in such a state.

"Do you not see how far my magic reaches, Quinn?"

He stiffened as Deirdre came to stand beside him. "I see that you will use and kill people however you want."

"To show my good faith, I have offered you a boon as I'm sure Broc told you. What would you have me give you in return for freely granting me your seed?"

"My brothers," he said, even though he knew she would refuse.

She shook her head and looked at him as if he were a child. "Broc has already told you I will not grant that. I need your brothers."

Quinn didn't think he could ever despise anyone as he did Deirdre. He knew Fallon and Lucan were the answer to whatever Deirdre had planned, and he knew it couldn't be good.

"If you doona give me my brothers, I'll return to the Pit." He knew he was pushing Deirdre, but he didn't care. As long as his brothers were free of Deirdre, Quinn could concentrate on getting his men and Marcail free.

"I said I refuse," Deirdre answered, her tone hard.

Quinn shrugged. "Then I had better return to the Pit."

He turned on his heel and started for the door. He wondered how long it would take her before she gave in, because he intended to make her give in or she would get nothing.

"Halt," she said as he reached the doorway.

Quinn turned around with an exaggerated sigh. "What is it?"

"You know I need your seed."

"As much as it revolts me, aye, I do."

She narrowed her unusual white eyes and strode toward him. "I also need your brothers."

"You canna have everything."

"I can. And I will."

"Not this time," he said.

"A compromise then?"

Quinn regarded her silently for a moment. He would have to be careful and use all the cunning his father told him he had to ensure Lucan and Fallon were never caught by Deirdre. "I'm listening."

"I will leave your brothers alone until our child is born. Once the child is born, I will have your brothers."

Quinn considered his options, few that they were, and knew this was as good as he was going to get. "Tell me, why haven't you used magic to get me to your bed?"

"If the child of the prophecy is to come into this world, it has to be done without magic."

"And if I canna . . . perform with you?"

Deirdre's nostrils flared in anger. "Oh, Quinn, I will ensure that you do."

"Without magic?"

"Aye."

There was no way he could bed her. She was everything he hated in the world.

"Do we have an arrangement?" she asked.

Since Quinn knew there was no way, without magic, that he could get hard and mount her, he nodded. "We have an arrangement."

With a snap of Deirdre's fingers a Warrior entered the chamber. "Call the others away from the MacLeods."

"Mistress?" he asked.

"Do it. Now," she demanded.

The Warrior rushed from the chamber to carry out her orders, and when Deirdre turned back to Quinn, he knew she would want him much sooner than he had prepared himself.

"I need to bathe," he said before she could open her mouth. "And I need new clothes."

She grinned, her gaze between his legs. "A kilt, perhaps?"

"I prefer the tunic and breeches I've always worn."

"A pity," she said with a sigh. "I will see it done. Come with me."

They returned to her chambers where food had been set out. The smell of roasted pheasant, fish, and lamb made his mouth water and his stomach growl. It had been so long since he had had more than bread and water that he wanted to dive into the food and stuff his mouth with all of it at once.

"Help yourself," Deirdre said as she sat to watch.

Quinn ignored her and reached for the lamb first. He tore off a piece of meat and stuffed it in his mouth. An explosion of taste had him almost moaning in satisfaction.

He soon had a trencher of food and sat to enjoy the small feast. A servant poured him a goblet of wine that only added to the enjoyment. The more he ate, the more he wanted, and he filled his trencher three times before he was full.

Quinn rested his elbows on the table and thought how much better the meal would have been if he'd been surrounded by his brothers, his men, and Marcail. Then, it truly would have been magnificent.

Instead, he was in Deirdre's private chambers as she salivated, waiting for him to climb into her bed.

"Your bath is ready," Deirdre's voice broke into his thoughts.

Quinn rose without looking at her and followed the servant waiting to take him to the bath. A large wooden tub had been brought to the chamber and filled with steaming water. Heat rose from the bath, and Quinn couldn't wait to get in.

He shed his clothes and quickly stepped into the water. He closed his eyes for only a moment before he began to scrub away the grime of the Pit from his skin and hair; then he shaved off his beard.

Thankfully, Deirdre had left him alone, though the bed that sat before him was a constant reminder of what awaited him.

Quinn didn't tarry long in the bath. He rose from the water and dried off. He wasn't surprised to find a set of clothes on a chair and hurried to put them on. Then he climbed onto the bed and shut his eyes.

He was going to be asleep when Deirdre found him, and too exhausted to wake and perform his "duty" to her. It wasn't much of a plan, but it was a start.

TWENTY-SIX

Lucan scanned the area, and though he could see nothing, he knew something was out there. And that something was Warriors.

"The plan didna work," Fallon whispered from beside him.

"It got us farther than we were before, and it gave us some time to rest and heal our wounds."

Fallon grunted in response. They looked over the surrounding land from behind a clump trees. Nothing had moved in the thirty minutes they had been searching, but their Warrior senses told them more than their eyes ever could.

"How long do you want to wait?" Lucan asked.

Fallon sighed. "I doona want to wait another moment, but we will be outnumbered. We'll be captured if we rush in."

"I agree. I want in the mountain, but not like that. We'll be no good to Quinn then."

"Maybe we send two or three out there and see what happens?"

Lucan nodded. "I like that idea. I'll go."

"Nay," Fallon said. "The point is for neither of us to be taken."

Lucan rested his forehead on the tree and blew out a breath of frustration. "You'll be watching. If it looks as though I'm to be taken, you can help."

Fallon's silence told Lucan he didn't like the plan, but Fallon was thinking on it.

"All right," Fallon finally agreed. "Stay so that I can see you, brother. I've already lost one of you, I canna lose another."

Lucan nodded, and they turned to make their way slowly back to the others.

"What did you see?" Larena asked when she caught sight of Fallon.

Fallon's face was set in grim lines. "The Warriors are there. We didna see how many there are, but they are waiting for us to make a move."

"I'm ready for them," Hayden said as he bit into an apple.

Lucan was ready as well, but he knew Fallon would be extra careful with this battle. He watched how Fallon took Larena's hand and brought her close to him.

Lucan missed Cara, and though he would like to have her by his side, Cara wasn't a Warrior as Larena was. Cara was safer at the castle, but he couldn't wait to get to her, to hold her, to kiss her.

"Three of us are going to go out and see what greeting we get from the Warriors," Lucan said. "I'm going. Who wants to go with me?"

Hayden stepped forward and tossed aside his half-eaten apple. "I'm ready."

"Let's not keep them waiting," Logan said as he moved to stand beside Hayden.

Lucan nodded and then turned to Fallon. "The rest of you stay hidden."

As one they turned and started back to where Lucan had first sensed the other Warriors. Fallon, Larena, Ramsey, and Galen took up posts in trees and on the ground to keep watch while Lucan, Hayden, and Logan kept walking.

Lucan flexed his claws, eager to rid Scotland of the evil Warriors who had aligned themselves with Deirdre. He glanced to his right to see Hayden's red skin as the big blond showed his fangs in a smile.

When Lucan looked to his left he spotted Logan's silver skin. Logan grinned at him, ready—and eager—as any of them for the coming battle.

And just as Lucan expected, ten Warriors poured out of the trees ahead of them. Hayden stretched out his arm as a fireball formed in his hand. He threw it at the oncoming Warriors and quickly formed another.

Lucan crouched low and was about to launch himself at the four Warriors coming toward him when all of a sudden they stopped. After a moment the Warriors turned and raced back into the trees.

"What in the name of all that is holy just happened?" Logan asked.

Lucan shrugged. "I doona know. Could be a trap. They know we'll follow."

"Shite," Hayden growled and clenched his fists. "I was just getting started."

Lucan looked over his shoulder at Fallon, who sat on a limb high in a tree. After a brief nod from his brother, Lucan motioned for Hayden and Logan to follow him.

"We're going to see where the bastards are going."

But when they crested the hill and saw the Warriors continuing on toward the mountain, Lucan drew to a halt. Something odd was definitely going on.

"What's happened?" Fallon asked as he raced up beside them.

Lucan shook his head. "They're running away."

"I can see that. What I want to know is why?"

"They were afraid of me," Hayden said and slapped Lucan on the shoulder. "Let's enjoy our victory and free Quinn."

Lucan turned to Fallon. "What do you think?"

"I have no idea," Fallon said. "It could be anything. Deirdre had to have called them off, and the only reason for her doing that is . . ."

"Quinn," Lucan finished for his brother. "Quinn has to have given in to her."

"But she wants all of us," Fallon said.

"Now that she has Quinn on her side, she knows we'll do anything for him."

Fallon raked a hand through his hair and blew out a ragged breath. "I think we need to get into the mountain. Now."

"I think you're right."

Deirdre waited as long as she could to give Quinn some time to himself. She knew he didn't want her now, but by the time she was done with him, he would think of her and only her for the rest of his days.

She smiled as her anticipation grew. She had even enjoyed watching him eat; how she longed to see him bathe, but that would come later.

Now that he was hers.

She rubbed her hands together and smiled. He was really hers. After all these centuries, she had the one man she had always wanted.

Deirdre rose from her chair and moved to the table where the food had been laid out. She poured some wine into Quinn's goblet and drank where his lips had been a short while ago.

She closed her eyes and groaned as she tasted him mixed with the wine. Her sex throbbed with need, and just imagining him sliding his cock inside her made her wet and achy.

Deirdre paced the chamber until she could stand it no more. She opened the door and peered inside to find the tub empty. With a slight push, she cracked the door wider and searched the chamber for Quinn.

It wasn't until she looked to the bed that she saw him stretched on his back, an arm thrown over his eyes. Anger filled her at finding him asleep. He should have come to her when he was finished bathing, but instead he had gone to bed.

Waiting for you perhaps?

She considered this. It could be, but Quinn hadn't seemed intent on bedding her.

Unless it's a ruse.

Deirdre liked it the more she thought of it.

She walked to the bed and trailed her hands from Quinn's feet to his chest. He was snoring slightly so she tugged off his boots and placed them by the bed. She then straightened and gazed down at him.

She knew firsthand what the Warriors experienced in the Pit and sleep hadn't been something Quinn did often. A strange new emotion filled her, one of almost . . . kindness as she considered allowing him to rest.

Deirdre moved to the other side of the bed and crawled in beside him. She touched his jaw for a moment before she turned on her side to sleep. They had eternity together now. What was a few more hours?

Quinn's eyes slid open as Deirdre turned away from him. He couldn't believe his deception had worked, but he had been desperate for anything so he wouldn't have to touch her. It was bad enough that she was in the same bed with him.

It had been a long time since he had lain in a bed. Waking from being beaten in Deirdre's bed didn't count in his mind.

Even once he and his brothers had returned to the castle he had been unable to sleep in the bed of his old chamber. The night had been his hunting ground. He would race across the land he loved so much, uncaring of what animals saw him.

When his loneliness got too terrible and the need to relieve his cock grew too much, he would find a town and make quick use of a woman.

Then he would roam the castle and the cliffs. Sometimes he would doze for an hour or two, but he was always awake to see the sun crest the horizon.

But it was the softness of the bed that pulled at him now, reminding him how nice it would be to have Marcail beside him. He had made love to her several times, but not once in a bed with fresh linen sheets beneath her beautiful body.

He wanted to see her in the sunlight, to feast upon her curves in the light of day. He wanted to see her spread upon his bed, the MacLeod plaid beneath her with candlelight and firelight burnishing her skin in a golden glow.

There was so much he wanted to do with Marcail. Too much.

Quinn's chest ached as he imagined Marcail huddled in his cave in the cold darkness. It was no place for a Druid, especially one that meant so much to him.

He knew he cared for Marcail, but the caring went much deeper than the responsibility he ought to feel. Quinn wasn't sure when his feelings had changed, he just knew they had.

And now he wouldn't ever be able to touch her, kiss her again.

He didn't want Marcail to see what he would become with Deirdre. Quinn wouldn't be able to carry out his plan if he knew Marcail looked at him with shame and revulsion.

Maybe he should have told Marcail what he intended to do, but he hadn't wanted to give her a chance to talk him out of anything. As it was, he wanted to rush back to her and let Deirdre torture him however she wanted.

Except the torture would be on anyone but him, and that's what kept him in her bed instead of returning to Marcail.

The next few days were going to be the hardest. He could hold Deirdre off for only so long before she demanded the use of his body.

At least his brothers were safe for the time being, and would continue to be so until the child came.

Quinn shuddered thinking of such a child being created. The conception of a baby was supposed to be a joyous occasion. He had to steel himself with the knowledge that he would have to kill the child the first chance he got. Something so evil couldn't walk upon this earth for even a heartbeat.

But what kind of man was he that plotted to kill his own infant when he mourned the loss of a son so much it nearly destroyed him?

TWENTY-SEVEN

Marcail swayed with the mesmerizing music. She had been ecstatic when she had heard the magical chant once again. For a while, she had thought it was gone from her forever, but one thought of Quinn and the music returned in a rush of sound.

The words grew louder, but she still could only understand a few of them. She sensed they were important, but for what, she didn't know.

She let herself succumb to the melody, let it surround her and pull her into its magic. It sounded as if hundreds of voices chanted, but she could see no one.

The breeze that had moved gently around her began to swirl and grow stronger as the chanting rose. It was as if Marcail stood in the center of everything as the magic moved toward her then retreated only to move forward once again, growing closer and closer each time it came at her.

She felt protected, as if she belonged to the magic. The more it touched her, the stronger she felt. It was a wondrous, beautiful feeling she never wanted to end.

The words of the chanting became clear in a blink, their meaning known. She gasped, her heart skipping a beat when she realized the mantra was the spell to bind the gods.

Marcail couldn't believe she finally was able to find the spell, though in the back of her mind, she knew she hadn't done it alone. Was it her grandmother? Or was it something else?

It didn't matter. She would be able to help Quinn defeat Deirdre. Excitement poured through her at the prospect.

Her concentration was shattered and the beautiful melody vanished as hands gently shook her. Marcail snapped open her eyes to find Arran and Duncan squatting before her.

"Why did you do that?" she cried. Instead of listening and memorizing the chant, she had been thinking of Quinn. She only knew half of the spell, and half wasn't good enough.

"You've been sitting like that for hours, Marcail," Arran said. "We grew worried."

She bit her lip. She didn't want them to know she had been so close to freeing them, at least not yet. If word spread before she learned the rest of the spell, it would do them no good. Plus, she had to worry about Deirdre discovering her and ending all hope.

Marcail rose from her position on the floor and moved to the water to splash her face. "Next time, please do not disturb me. I'm not being harmed in any way."

"You were sitting so ever since Quinn was taken. It's been almost a full day," Duncan said.

Marcail paused. She hadn't realized the chanting had pulled her under so completely. Would she have made it back had the Warriors not woken her? She wasn't sure.

She knew she would have to tell them before she attempted to find the chant again.

"What has happened while I've been . . . resting?" she asked.

Arran shook his head, his face grim. "Nothing, and that's what bothers me."

"It's only been a day," Marcail said. "What did you expect to happen?"

"Something," Duncan replied. "It's almost as if the mountain is holding its breath."

Marcail felt the same way. "I know what you mean. It will most likely take Quinn days or weeks before he can manage to help us escape. Until then, we need to stay vigilant as he asked."

Arran glanced at the entrance to the cave. "It's more than that, Marcail."

She looked from Arran to Duncan, then back to Arran. "Tell me."

Duncan looked away.

It was Arran who finally spoke. "We saw Charon speaking with someone earlier."

"So," she said with a smile. That's what they were worried about? That was nothing. "Charon most likely wants to rule the Pit as Quinn did. Charon figures he'll talk to some of the Warriors to get them on his side."

Arran swallowed and scratched his neck with his white claws.

"He wasn't talking to Warriors in the Pit, was he?" she asked as apprehension began to creep up her back.

Arran shook his head. "I'm not sure who he spoke with at the door, but whoever it was, he was there for a while."

Marcail grew sick as realization dawned. "I know what he was doing."

"What?" Duncan asked.

"When Quinn was taken the first time I told Charon to tell Deirdre that I knew the spell, hoping that she would take me in trade for Quinn."

Arran punched the rocks. "Shite!"

Duncan mumbled something underneath his breath.

"Did Quinn know you did that?" Arran asked.

She nodded. "I told him. He wasn't happy. Charon didn't do it, though. I didn't think he would tell Deirdre about me because he was distressed to learn that I had the spell and was in Deirdre's control."

"You canna trust Charon," Duncan growled. "He cares only for himself. No one else matters to him. No one."

She realized that now. Unfortunately, it was too late for her. "They will come for me. Neither of you must stop them from taking me."

"We swore to Quinn we would protect you," Arran said.

"What you'll do is get yourselves beaten or killed," she argued. "Let them take me. The best thing you can do for me and Quinn is to stay alive and unharmed."

Arran sighed loudly, obviously not liking her logic.

She turned to Duncan. "Have you had any more pain that I need to help you with before I'm taken?"

"Nothing I canna handle," he said. "They are no longer beating Ian."

She placed a hand on Duncan's arm, then did the same to Arran. "Both of you are good men. Quinn is counting on you. Don't let him down."

"Never," Duncan swore.

She smiled because she heard the truth in his words. "Deirdre cannot kill me, remember."

"She canna kill you but she can have others do it," Arran said. "Doona forget that, Marcail."

How could she when she would soon be facing that very possibility? And if she knew anything about Deirdre, her death was going to be very, very painful.

"You canna go with her," Duncan said. "If you do, we will never be returned to the men we once were."

Marcail ached for the Warriors. "I don't see how I will have much of a choice. If I could, I would stay with you."

"What if we told the other Warriors in the Pit just what you carry in your mind? They might help us protect you," Arran said.

She shook her head. "You could try, but I don't think it will work. Besides, do you want everyone to know about a spell that I cannot remember?"

"What I want them to know is that we can push the gods away forever."

"Can you really?" she asked. "Deirdre can once more unbind your gods, and I imagine there are Warriors with her that don't wish to be mortal again."

Arran cursed and turned away. She understood his disappointment because she felt the same way.

"What choice do we have?" Duncan asked. "You need to be protected from Deirdre."

Marcail felt the sadness weigh heavily on her shoulders. "I'm afraid that's impossible."

Quinn made sure he appeared to sleep well past the time Deirdre rose from the bed. When she stood beside him and ran her hands over his body, it was everything he could do not to throw her hands away from him.

It wasn't until she finally left the chamber that he rose from the bed. He found a ewer of water and splashed some on his face.

He was sitting to pull on his boots when the door flew open and Deirdre stood in the doorway, fury flashing from her evil white eyes.

"Did you not sleep well?" he asked, uncaring about what had riled her so early in the morn.

"My sleep does not concern you at this moment."

"Is that so?" He pulled on his second boot and stood. "Then what should concern me?"

"Marcail."

Quinn felt as if someone had reached into his chest and yanked out his heart. He couldn't manage to take air into his lungs. The world ground to a halt as he raged between fury and confusion on how Marcail had been discovered.

Deirdre walked to him. "I was told you gave her shelter in the Pit. Why didn't you kill her?"

"Why didna you?" The more Deirdre spoke about Marcail the angrier he got. Deirdre wasn't worthy to speak Marcail's name.

"I had my reasons," Deirdre replied. "The Druid is a nuisance, Quinn. I tossed her into the Pit so she would be killed. You should have allowed that to happen."

He crossed his arms over his chest. "And why is that?"

"She probably told you she knows the spell to bind your gods. She lied. She has the spell that will allow your gods to take over completely."

Quinn shook his head and snorted. "Stop with the lies. Marcail does have the spell to bind our gods. You didna kill her yourself because you fear what will happen to you if you harm her. All those protection spells must be an irritation for one so all-powerful as you."

"Then you don't know me at all. I fear nothing."

"Not true. You fear the magic of Marcail's grandmother. I've seen what can happen to someone who harms Marcail. It's not something you want to tangle with, Deirdre."

A single white brow rose on Deirdre's forehead. "You think you know everything, do you?"

"You've killed almost every Druid you've ever captured, *mie* and *drough* alike, so that you can claim their magic. I had to ask myself, why wouldna you want the powerful magic that runs in Marcail's blood? It was easy enough to figure out."

Deirdre slowly walked around Quinn until she stood at his back. "Tell me, Quinn, what is your interest in Marcail?"

He knew he had to choose his words carefully. He didn't want Deirdre to know how deep his feelings went for Marcail, especially since he was still trying to decipher them himself. "I saved her. She's my responsibility."

"Hm. I wonder if your feelings go deeper than that. You've bedded her, so you must have found something to your liking."

Quinn faced her. He didn't want to spoil what had happened between him and Marcail, but he also couldn't let Deirdre suspect anything.

"It had been a long time since I'd lain with a woman. She was grateful that I saved her and repaid me with the use of her body."

"You could have had mine," Deirdre said.

"I'd rather slit my own throat."

Deirdre suddenly smiled. "Ah, but my dear Quinn, you agreed to bed me in exchange for leaving your brothers alone."

"I did. I willna go back on my vows."

"I don't doubt that you will do your part, but I wonder how long you will try to put me off."

Quinn clenched his jaw. He hadn't expected Deirdre to learn of Marcail so quickly. Damn.

"What do you want?" he asked in the most civil voice that he could.

She laughed. "I've always enjoyed having this kind of power. It's exhilarating."

"What. Do. You. Want?"

"How much is Marcail's life worth to you?"

Quinn wanted to punch Deirdre in the face, to rip her heart from her body and toss her into a fire. "I doona want anyone else to die."

"And Marcail? What will you do to ensure I allow her to live?"

"What do you want?"

"You. In my bed immediately."

Quinn ran a hand down his face. He had no other choice. He couldn't live with himself if he was the cause of Marcail's death just because he found Deirdre repulsive.

"On one condition. You allow Marcail to leave the mountain. And I want to see for myself that you release her."

Deirdre lifted a shoulder. "You agree to bed me after she's gone?"

He nodded, unable to say the words. How had things gone so wrong so soon?

TWENTY-EIGHT

"Finally," Fallon said as they stood before Deirdre's mountain.

"It's not going to be easy," Ramsey stated as he eyed the mound of rock before them.

Logan chuckled. "Getting in will be easy, it's the getting out part I'm concerned with."

"Maybe you should stay behind," Hayden said.

"And let you get yourself killed?" Logan snorted. "You need me to watch your back."

Fallon shook his head at the banter between Logan and Hayden. The need to rush in and find Quinn was too much to bear, but for the sake of Larena, Lucan, and the others, Fallon had to be careful.

"You know what has to be done," Larena said.

He frowned, hating that she was right. "I'd rather not."

"It's the reason I came, Fallon."

Lucan nodded. "You need to let her go inside."

Fallon knew Larena's power to become invisible would allow them to find Quinn, but the thought of his wife, the woman who held his heart in her hands, in Deirdre's mountain left him cold.

"I can handle myself," Larena said. "I am a Warrior. I've proven to you countless times that I can take care of myself."

"Aye, love, I know you can. I just like to be beside you just in case."

She leaned in and kissed him. "And I love you for that, but you need to let me go now. We have to find Quinn."

Fallon reluctantly stepped back. "Doona stay longer than you have to. Find him and get out."

"It's the finding him that's going to take the longest," Galen said. "Quinn could be anywhere in that mountain."

Fallon cupped his hands on either side of Larena's face. "Find Deirdre first. If Quinn isna with her, you're likely to discover where he's being held. Then it'll be a matter of finding where he's located after that."

"I'll find him, Fallon," she promised.

"I have no doubt." He pulled her into his arms and hugged her. "Just promise me you willna be caught."

She leaned back to look into his eyes. "I'll return to you. There's nowhere else I belong."

It took all of Fallon's will to release her. In a blink she transformed, her spectacular iridescent skin shining in the sunlight a moment before she became invisible. Larena shed her clothes quickly after that.

There was a soft press on his check before she whispered, "I love you."

"I love you," he said. "Come back to me, Larena."

There wasn't a response, not that he needed one. She would return if she could. She was his life, and if for some reason Deirdre imprisoned Larena, Fallon would move heaven and earth to free his wife.

"She'll be all right," Lucan said.

Ramsey nodded in agreement. "Thank God we have Larena on our side."

"Aye," Fallon said, though he wished he'd been the one that could turn invisible. He'd rather put himself in that kind of danger than his wife.

Marcail knew the moment the Pit door opened they had come for her. At the entrance to the cave stood the tall winged Warrior. Arran and Duncan refused to let him pass, so Marcail went to him.

"You've come for me?" she asked the Warrior.

"I have."

"Broc," Arran said. "Doona take her."

So this was Broc, the one Quinn spoke of often. Marcail glanced at his large wings and couldn't help but wonder how they looked spread. "He has no choice," Marcail said.

"Everyone has a choice," Duncan said.

Marcail put her hands on Duncan and Arran as she walked past them to stand beside Broc. She faced the two Warriors who had guarded her. "Remember what I told you."

"Marcail," Arran warned.

"Leave it," Broc said. "She must come with me now."

Marcail's legs shook so badly they threatened to give out on her. Somehow she managed to follow Broc from the Pit without making a fool of herself. As she passed Charon's cave, she saw the copper Warrior staring at her, his eyes haunted.

He didn't wear the expression of a man who had gotten what he wanted. In fact, he looked almost beaten down.

When she and Broc left the Pit and the door closed behind her, Marcail took a deep breath and tried to remain as steadfast as she had in the cave.

It wasn't easy.

She had no idea where Broc was taking her and if it would lead to imminent death.

"Keep up," Broc said over his shoulder.

Marcail had to lift her skirts and practically run to keep up with his long strides. The dark blue Warrior seemed to be in a great hurry.

"Have you seen Quinn? Is he all right?" She knew she shouldn't ask, but she had to know.

"Keep your thoughts on yourself."

She halted. "Nay."

Broc slowed, then stopped and turned to face her. "What did you say?"

"I said nay. I want to know of Quinn or I'm not moving."

He took a step toward her. "I could toss you over my shoulder."

"You could."

After a moment Broc sighed. "Quinn is fine. Deirdre willna hurt him. Now, come with me, Druid."

Now that Marcail knew Quinn wasn't being harmed she continued after Broc. She knew in her heart Deirdre would plan a painful death for her.

Marcail had never feared dying, but she wished she'd had more time with Quinn. Those few precious hours had been the best of her life, even though they were spent in Deirdre's mountain.

But her one regret was not recalling the spell. She'd almost had it. She had been so close. If she'd only have recognized what the chanting was earlier she could have already had the spell and freed so many men from their gods, as well as thwarting Deirdre.

Marcail stopped just short of running into Broc's

featherless wings as he came to a sudden halt. The Warrior looked at her and pointed to a door that stood open and led to a dark chamber.

"You need to go in there."

Marcail looked into the chamber and took in a calming breath. "Tell me what awaits me."

"Freedom. If you hurry."

She frowned, her lips parting in confusion. "Are you jesting?"

"Nay. Get in," he said and took her by the arm to shove her into the room.

Marcail spun around to find Broc had followed her and pulled the door closed behind him. "What is going on?" she demanded.

"I'm trying to help you and Quinn."

She wanted to believe Broc, but since she couldn't see his face, she couldn't look into his eyes and see his emotions. "Is there a light?"

No sooner had she said the words than a candle flared to life. Broc lit two more before he folded his arms over his chest.

"Tell me why you are helping me," she urged.

Broc gave a slow shake of his head. "Does it matter? I have my reasons."

Marcail wanted to know those reasons, but she could tell by the stubborn set of his jaw that she would get no more out of him. She had to decide whether to trust him or not, and with her life on the line, she didn't have much of a choice.

"All right."

"Good. Now, I'm going to help get Quinn out, but first, I need to get you away from Deirdre. She learned you were in the Pit."

Somehow, that didn't surprise her. "Did Charon tell her?"

"Aye," Broc mumbled. "Doona blame the Warrior, though. Deirdre has ways of extracting information whether a person wants to give it or not. I'm surprised you were able to stay in the Pit as long as you have."

"It was Quinn. He kept me safe."

Broc nodded. "Everyone knows that."

"Deirdre won't be happy with him."

"She ordered me to bring you to her. I doona know her plans for you, but they canna be good. I heard that she has used you to get Quinn into her bed faster."

Marcail leaned against the wall and squeezed her eyes shut. "Dear God. That cannot happen. Quinn cannot give her the baby she wants."

"I agree. I'm going to tell Deirdre that you escaped."

"Won't she punish you?"

One side of Broc's mouth lifted in a half smile. "I can withstand it. The important thing is for you to get out of the mountain. Take this," he said and handed her what looked like a black veil.

"What is it?"

"The servants wear them. It will cover your face and keep you unnoticed. Watch your hair though. All of the women have had their hair shorn off. Nothing of yours can show."

"Does my gown matter?" she said as she looked down to find it stained.

"Aye. I've procured one of the servants' gowns for you as well."

She prayed Broc was truly helping her and not setting her up for Deirdre's amusement. "Thank you."

"The servants keep their heads down and doona

speak unless spoken to. You should be able to move freely. To depart the mountain, you need to leave this chamber and turn right. The corridor is long, but stay on it. Doona venture down any of the stairwells. If you stay on the main corridor it will lead you to the upper level."

She stared at him, absorbing everything he said. "I understand."

"There is a doorway on the top level. You'll have to walk past Deirdre's chambers. Her doors are always shut and Warriors are standing guard. Once you pass them, you'll take the next hallway to the left. It will take you up a flight of stairs to the door. The door isna easily seen by mortals. You'll have to search for the handle."

"First hallway on the left after Deirdre's chamber," she repeated.

"I'm not going to be able to be with you. When I leave, I'll have to raise the alarm immediately lest Deirdre become suspicious. Get changed and out of here as soon as you can."

Marcail licked her lips and swallowed. "I will."

He paused at the door and turned to look at her. "Good luck."

"Thank you, Broc. If you ever need anything, all you need to do is ask."

He gave her a curt nod, and then he was gone.

Marcail jerked off her gown and hurried to pull on the one given to her. It was coarse and bleached of all color, but it would help her blend in.

She left her hair tucked into the back of the gown and pulled the veil over her head, making sure her face was covered.

The veil was long and hung past her shoulders, and it wasn't easy to see through the dark material. Anything, however, was better than what awaited her with Deirdre.

Marcail blew out the candles and opened the door. She glanced first one way, then the other before she stepped into the corridor. She kept her head down as Broc had advised her.

Broc hadn't lied about spreading the alarm right away. Several Warriors came running toward her. Marcail's heart pounded so loudly in her chest she was sure they would hear it.

She stopped and put her back to the wall to allow the Warriors to pass. They didn't look her way as they rushed down the hall.

Marcail smiled to herself as relief poured through her. Thanks to Broc, she would make it out of the mountain for sure.

TWENTY-NINE

Quinn stared at the stone wall in front of him. He hadn't risen from the foot of Deirdre's bed since he'd learned she knew of Marcail.

All he could think about was Marcail and her extraordinary, striking turquoise eyes and her small braids that framed her face and were held together by gold bands. He could still taste the sweet innocence of her kiss, still feel the way her arms locked around him, and how he was the first to awaken the desires in her body.

He had thought she would be safe in the Pit until he could free her and his men. How had he been so wrong? Who had told Deirdre?

And then he knew. Charon.

The copper-skinned bastard would pay for putting Marcail's life in danger, of that Quinn vowed. He would enjoy making Charon suffer long and repeatedly.

Quinn raked his hands through his hair as he hung his head to his chest. Deirdre had left him in her chambers, locked he was sure. She hadn't said anything, just turned and left when one of the wyrran whispered something in her ear. He wasn't sure if Deirdre would release Marcail as he'd asked or not.

Maybe he could talk Deirdre out of killing her. At

least if Marcail was somewhere in the mountain he would be able to reach her somehow.

But he knew Deirdre wouldn't be satisfied until Marcail was dead. Deirdre was too spiteful to do anything else.

Quinn didn't think he could hate Deirdre more, but it seemed he was wrong. He was angry, aye, but the sadness over losing Marcail outweighed the fury.

He looked down at his hands. No claws were visible, and his skin held no hint of blackness at all. It was almost as if the god was no longer inside him.

The door to the chamber flew open. Quinn didn't turn to look at Deirdre. He could feel her black magic and the evil inside her.

"Marcail is waiting," Deirdre said. "She's most insistent upon leaving my mountain. I don't understand how anyone could want to leave this beautiful place."

Quinn didn't bother to reply. He rose and faced Deirdre, thankful that Marcail would be able to leave. "Take me to her."

Deirdre raised a white brow. "Don't try to talk to her, Quinn. I'm allowing you to see her off. That should be good enough."

It wasn't, but if he complained, Deirdre was likely to keep him in the chamber. "Take me to her," he repeated.

Deirdre turned and walked from the room. Quinn followed, uncaring of the stairwells and doorways he passed. His attention was focused all on Marcail.

When he caught sight of her, it was like a burst of sunlight upon his face. She was so beautiful. He simply stared at the petite woman with her full curves that had captured his attention so quickly.

He wanted to walk to Marcail and pick up one of her

braids, which always fell in her face. He wanted to lean down and inhale the sunshine-and-rain scent that was hers alone. But he would have to be content simply to see her.

Marcail's turquoise eyes met his. She gave him a small smile before she followed the wyrran up a set of stairs to a door that stood open.

Quinn stepped back and ran into one of Deirdre's servants. She gasped, and Quinn murmured an apology. He was lost in Marcail's scent, a smell he knew he would never enjoy again.

He didn't look at the servant, not when Marcail was about to be lost to him forever. As soon as Marcail was through the door, Quinn took the stairs three at a time and stood in the doorway.

"I told you I would release her," Deirdre said as she came to stand beside him.

Quinn nodded and watched Marcail pick her way down the treacherous mountain and its snow. "So you did."

"Are you ready to keep your word?"

He sighed and turned his head to her. "I am."

"Good. Return to my chamber and await me. I have some . . . unfinished business I must attend to first."

Quinn walked down the stairs and past the servant he had stepped on. She didn't bow her head as the others did, and he couldn't help but feel as if she stared at him.

Everything in Deirdre's mountain was strange, so he didn't think too much about the servant. He returned to Deirdre's chamber and his seat upon the bed.

He should be elated that Marcail had her freedom, but his chest still felt heavy. His brothers would be left alone, and Marcail was out of the mountain. Was it because his men were still locked away? It had to be, Quinn surmised. He'd gotten almost everything he wanted from Deirdre.

Now, the most difficult part stood in front of him.

Larena ran as fast as she could down the corridor. Ramsey had been right, it was decidedly too easy to get into Cairn Toul Mountain.

Once she had gotten inside at the base of the mountain, Larena had stood and listened to the Warriors. She heard them speak of a Druid that had somehow gotten free of Broc.

Larena wondered if the Druid really had broken free or if Broc had helped her. If this was the same woman Quinn had aided, then it stood to reason Broc was aiding her. Larena just hoped the Druid was able to stay out of Deirdre's path and get free.

As much as Larena wanted to help the woman, her first priority was Quinn. The thought of returning to Fallon and Lucan to tell them she hadn't saved Quinn was something she refused to do. If along the way she was able to help Marcail or anyone else, then Larena would do it.

She slowed and came to a halt as a group of Warriors came toward her. They couldn't see her, but if she didn't get out of the way, they would bump into her.

Larena opened the first door she came to and stepped inside. The chamber was empty, though dried blood littered the stones at her feet.

As the Warriors passed her she heard Quinn's name mentioned. She slipped out of the chamber and followed the Warriors long enough to learn that Deirdre had convinced Quinn to turn to her side.

The news was going to break Fallon's heart. Larena shook her head, still determined to find Quinn and see for herself.

She turned and retraced her steps. Ramsey and Galen had told her she would likely find Quinn in Deirdre's chambers if he was no longer being held as a prisoner. And after hearing the Warriors, it was obvious Quinn wasn't in the dungeons any more.

Once she found Quinn, then the real danger would begin. In order to speak to him, he would have to be alone. Since he didn't know of her, there was a chance he wouldn't believe her. But she had something that would make him believe.

Deirdre tapped her long nails on the rock wall. Quinn had believed he saw Marcail leave the mountain when in fact it was nothing more than magic—black magic. Had he tried to speak to Marcail, he would have realized it wasn't her.

Where the little bitch of a *mie* was, however, was what put Deirdre's anger high and kept her from finding Quinn so she could finally have his body all to herself.

"You've not found her?" Deirdre asked Broc.

The winged Warrior shook his head. "She was beaten down and knew her time of hiding was up. I didna expect her to make a run for it."

"You know I will reprimand you for this. Severely."

Broc bowed his head. "I expected no less."

"Did you use your god, Broc?" Deirdre asked.

He gave a single nod. "She's still in the mountain."

"But you can find anyone."

His indigo Warrior eyes narrowed a fraction. "I've not failed you before. I willna fail you this time."

She wasn't fooled by his humility. Inside Broc simmered a vengeful nature that she had thus far contained. How much longer she would have control over him she didn't know. But she would make sure she held him for as long as she wanted.

"You will help William and the others. I want this mountain searched from top to bottom. She's not made it out, and if I have anything to say about it, she won't."

"Aye, mistress," William said from beside Broc before they left.

William was still recovering from the torture Quinn had demanded, but William was always willing to serve.

Deirdre turned to give orders to the servant she had seen standing near them only to find the female gone.

"Where is the servant that was just here?" she asked the remaining Warriors.

A wyrran tugged on her skirt and pointed toward her chamber.

Deirdre's gaze narrowed. She petted the wyrran's head and started toward her chamber. She spotted the servant paused outside the door to her rooms. Deirdre came up behind her and ripped the veil from her head.

Instead of short hair, Deirdre saw sable hair tucked into the back of a gown. Marcail whirled around, the braids at the top and sides of her head spinning with her.

"You cannot stay away from him, can you?" Deirdre asked her. "You might have gotten away had you forgotten Quinn."

"I could never forget him," Marcail said through clenched teeth.

Deirdre laughed. "And that, my dear, will be your downfall. I have something special planned for you."

With a snap of her fingers Warriors surrounded

Marcail. Deirdre looked the Druid up and down. She didn't know what had caught Quinn's attention, but as far as he knew Marcail was long gone. And she was going to make sure he never thought otherwise.

"Take her to the chamber to prepare," Deirdre commanded them.

As much as Deirdre wanted to go to Quinn, she needed to take care of Marcail first. If Quinn ever discovered she had deceived him, he would never bed her and give her the child she needed.

Deirdre followed her Warriors as they led Marcail farther and farther from Quinn. Deirdre rubbed her hands together. She might not be able to kill Marcail, but she could do the next best thing.

The Warriors shoved Marcail into the chamber so that she fell to her hands and knees. Deirdre smelled her blood and magic and smiled.

"This is where I kill Druids."

Marcail got to her feet and met her gaze. "You cannot kill me."

"What makes you think that?"

"If you could, you would have already done it when I was first brought to the mountain. Instead, you tossed me into the Pit hoping one of the Warriors there would do the deed. And suffer the consequences of my grandmother's spells."

Deirdre shrugged. "I suppose there is no point in denying anything now. Nay, Marcail, I'm not going to kill you. You see, your grandmother was a powerful Druid."

"I know," Marcail said.

Deirdre ignored the interruption. "She knew there was a chance I would capture you, so she made sure to cast protection spells over you. They are many and are powerful enough that if you are killed, the person responsible will die a horrible death."

"It's too bad you learned of the protections then," Marcail said. "My death is nothing if it would bring about your own."

"Ah, but you are a brave one," Deirdre said. "Is it really courage, or fear so great it is either stand up to me or crumple at my feet begging for mercy?"

Marcail rolled her eyes. "I've seen what your black magic can do. I know how effortlessly you take someone's life. At one time I feared you, but you've shown that even with your power, you have a weakness."

"I have no weakness."

A slow smile spread over Marcail's face. "But you do. You want the child of prophecy. How long have you waited, Deirdre? Has your womb grown cold and hollow? Can your body even sustain life?"

Deirdre reached out and slapped Marcail before she could think better of it. The Druid's head jerked to the side with the force of the blow. Deirdre smiled at having put Marcail in her place. Until she heard the Druid laughing.

"Is that the best you can do?" Marcail asked as she touched her lip, which now bled.

Deirdre opened her mouth to respond when a vicious sting sliced through her. It was a pain unlike anything she had ever felt, and she knew in that instant it was the protections guarding Marcail.

Deirdre closed her eyes to battle the throbbing, but Marcail's laughter only grew. For many moments Deirdre could do nothing but stand and combat the agony that filled her body. It was like hundreds of tiny blades piercing and slicing her skin.

And if it wasn't for her magic holding most of it at bay, it would have brought her to her knees. When she was finally able to withstand the pain, Deirdre opened her eyes to see Marcail smirking at her.

"I hope you enjoyed yourself, because where you are going, there will be nothing. Grab her," Deirdre yelled.

THIRTY

Marcail should have known better than to enjoy Deirdre's discomfort, but it had been wonderful to see the *drough* in pain. If that little bit happened from a slap, what would occur if someone killed her? Marcail was almost afraid to find out.

She struggled in vain against the grip the two Warriors had on her arms. They half dragged, half carried her to the center of the chamber where a table stood with straps that would hold her arms and legs.

"Don't worry," Deirdre said in a much too pleasant voice. "That is not for you, though I wish it were."

Marcail had never known such hatred as she did at that moment. "How can you kill your own kind?"

"Easily," Deirdre said. "If you knew the sheer force of the magic I received with every kill you would understand."

"I could never understand evil such as you."

Deirdre tsked. "Such a pity. Shall I tell you what I have planned for you?"

Marcail bit her tongue to keep silent.

"Have nothing to say this time?" Deirdre laughed. "Ah, well, I won't keep you waiting. Do you see Lavena behind you?"

The Warriors turned Marcail so that she was staring

at a woman who appeared to be floating, though there was no water around her, only black flames.

Deirdre came to stand beside Marcail. "Lovely, isn't she? I've held her thus for hundreds of years."

Marcail's blood turned to ice as she realized Deirdre would do the same to her. She had been so close to getting away, but when she had seen Quinn, she'd had to stop and look at him, to try and talk to him. It had taken everything she had not to reach out and touch him, to tell him it was her.

And now, it was too late.

Deirdre began to whisper words that Marcail recognized as Gaelic, the ancient Celt language. As the spell continued, ice-blue flames shot up from the stones on the floor to the ceiling in a swirling mass of magic.

"I hope you like your new home," Deirdre said. "You'll be with me forever, Marcail. No one will ever know the spell to bind the gods now."

Marcail swallowed and blinked back the tears. She wished she could have been the Druid her grandmother had wanted her to be. She wished she could have helped all the Warriors and other Druids who were locked in the mountain. But most of all she wished she could have told Quinn she loved him.

That's when she realized the connection between the chanting she heard in her head and Quinn. Her grandmother had told her to always follow her heart. Quinn had been the first time Marcail had ever done that, and when she had, the chanting had begun.

Her grandmother had made sure that when Marcail fell in love she would learn the spell. But now it was too late. For everyone.

The Warriors jerked Marcail in front of the cylinder of blue flames, halting her thoughts of the spell and Quinn as panic took hold.

"As soon as the flames touch your skin, you will cease to feel anything," Deirdre said.

Marcail lifted her chin. She was a Druid. She would not cower in front Deirdre. "Your reign will end soon. Enjoy the power you have now because it will soon be gone."

"Wishful thinking, little *mie*. Toss her into the flames," Deirdre told the Warriors.

Marcail's last thought was of Quinn as the blue flames engulfed her. There was a moment of icy pain and then . . . nothing.

Broc cursed under his breath as he watched the Warriors drag Marcail away. He had known it was the Druid when Quinn had backed into her while watching the fake Marcail leave the mountain.

If there hadn't been so many wyrran and other Warriors, Broc would have told Quinn what was happening. But Broc had wisely kept his mouth shut or they'd all be feeling Deirdre's wrath.

Broc pushed open the door to Deirdre's chambers and walked inside. He had hoped to hear from Fallon or someone in the group to let Broc know they where there to help Quinn escape, but Broc couldn't wait any longer. Not now that Deirdre had Marcail.

He found Quinn sitting on Deirdre's bed, his head in his hands. Of a sudden Quinn's head jerked up and he looked at Broc.

"What do you want?" Quinn demanded in a flat tone, devoid of any feeling.

Broc wasn't sure how to begin. Quinn had been in Deirdre's chamber for a full day. Deirdre could have done anything to him.

"Broc?" Quinn urged in a wary voice.

Broc glanced over his shoulder to the open door and wondered how long he had before Deirdre returned. "The Marcail you saw leave the mountain wasna real."

Quinn's pale green eyes narrowed and his brows furrowed. "What kind of jest is this?"

"None. The servant you backed into was Marcail."

"You lie!"

Broc inhaled deeply as he struggled for patience. He needed Quinn to believe him, not spend precious moments trying to make Quinn understand.

"I'm not. I helped Marcail to evade the other Warriors. She was to leave the mountain dressed as one of Deirdre's servants and look for your brothers."

"Stop it," Quinn murmured as he rose to his feet and began to pace the chamber. "I doona know what you're trying to do, but just stop. Marcail is safe. My brothers are safe."

Broc glanced down at his dark blue skin and the long claws. He had lived as Deirdre's for so long that Quinn wasn't going to believe him without proof, and since Lucan and Fallon weren't there, Broc had nothing to show Quinn.

"Is it a fight you want?" Quinn asked. "Do you want to see if you can best me?"

Broc shook his head. "I'm not looking to battle you, Quinn. You must believe me."

"Aye, Quinn, you must believe Broc."

The female voice came from beside Broc but there was no body. Yet he recognized the voice. "Larena?"

"Aye," she answered. "I'm here, Broc. Find me something to cover myself, please."

Broc hurried to the bed and jerked a blanket off.

"What the hell is going on?" Quinn commanded.

There was a soft tug and the blanket was taken from Broc's hand. In a blink Larena materialized beside him, the cover wrapped around her to hide her nudity.

"I was beginning to think you werena coming," Broc said.

Larena grimaced. "I saw them take Marcail."

"I know. I've been trying to convince Quinn."

Quinn punched the stone wall as his skin turned black with his anger. "Tell. Me. What. Is. Going. On."

Larena took a step toward Quinn. "It's finally good to meet you, Quinn. I'm Larena, Fallon's wife."

Quinn stood in quiet shock as he stared at the blonde-haired woman before him. She had just appeared out of nowhere. She was pretty with her classical beauty, but she didn't hold a candle to Marcail.

"Fallon's wife?" he repeated, unsure he had heard her correctly.

She smiled. "Aye. I'm also a Warrior. Deirdre tried to take me a few weeks ago, but Fallon and the others helped to keep me out of her hands."

Quinn rubbed his eyes with his thumb and forefinger. He no longer knew what was real and what wasn't. But Fallon married? That, he couldn't—and wouldn't—believe unless Fallon told Quinn himself.

"We haven't much time," Larena said. "Quinn, I doona know what Deirdre is going to do to Marcail, but we need to get to her quickly."

"Deirdre canna kill Marcail," Quinn said. "Though

it's pointless to speak of it. I saw Deirdre release her."

Larena shook her head, her long blonde braid moving back and forth down her back. "You have to know Deirdre is deceiving you. Would she willingly give up a Druid so easily?"

"I doona know what's real anymore," he yelled. Quinn turned away from them, his stomach churning as he imagined Deirdre tricking him and doing God only knew what to Marcail.

If Broc and Larena were speaking the truth . . . Quinn couldn't even complete the thought.

"You've been away from your brothers for a while," Larena said in a soft voice. "They have thought of you every day. Since you were taken, they have done nothing but try to find a way to get you out of here."

He believed that. He and his brothers might fight, but the love they shared was unbreakable. Quinn knew he'd walk through Hell itself to free his brothers.

"Look at me," Larena bade him.

Quinn turned and watched as she moved aside the blanket from her neck to show a gold torc with boars' heads, just like Fallon's.

"Fallon gifted this to me when I agreed to become his wife," Larena said. "We've been married but days, Quinn. Neither Lucan nor Fallon will rest until you are once more at MacLeod Castle with them."

Quinn couldn't take his eyes off the torc. It was proof that Larena was indeed Fallon's wife. Quinn remembered the day his mother had given Fallon the torc. She had told him it would be his gift to the woman who held his heart. They would be bound forever.

Just as Lucan and Cara were bound when Lucan gave her a dagger with the head of his wolf on it.

Quinn looked to Broc. "And you?"

"I've been spying on Deirdre for years. It was a pact Ramsey and I made. I will explain it all once we are free of this mountain."

"Holy Hell. Deirdre really does have Marcail, doesna she?" Quinn asked in disbelief.

Broc and Larena nodded.

Quinn looked down at his hand and watched his black claws lengthen from his fingers. Fury unlike he had ever known roared through him. It clawed at his insides, demanding release and revenge for the taking of his woman. It demanded blood.

"I'm going to kill the bitch."

"Wait," Larena said. "Fallon wants me to get you out of here first."

"I'm not leaving without Marcail."

Broc walked to the door. "I know where Deirdre took Marcail. I'll take Quinn. There is a door just down the hall that opens out of the mountain. Have the others come through there."

"Then what?" Larena asked. "We are outnumbered with the wyrran and Warriors."

Quinn smiled as he looked at Broc. "Not with all the people and Warriors in the dungeons."

"I'll see them released then," Broc said. "Now come. We must go."

Quinn's heart pounded in his chest. For the first time in a long time it felt good to release his god. He would enjoy killing Deirdre, and he would make it slow and excruciating.

THIRTY-ONE

Fallon paced back and forth outside the mountain. Ever since Larena had left, he had been anxious and terrified that something would happen to his wife and he wouldn't be there to help her.

"She'll be all right," Hayden said.

Fallon hoped his friend was correct, because if anything happened to Larena he didn't know what he would do. She was the very life inside him, the only thing that kept him breathing, and the one thing that helped him remember to be the man he always wanted to be.

She had been gone too long, though. Deirdre's mountain was huge, but there were so many places Larena could get caught. It should have been him that went inside. A man didn't put his wife in danger this way. Fallon rubbed the back of his neck, which had begun to ache.

There was a rustle of something behind him. Then he heard the sweetest thing in the world, his wife's voice.

"I need my clothes," she whispered.

"Everyone turn their backs," Fallon told the men.

Once they complied, he watched Larena materialize in front of him and hurriedly put on her clothes.

"All right," she said when she was covered.

Fallon squatted next to her as she pulled on her boots. "Did you find Quinn?"

"I did. It took some time to convince him who I was. It was the torc that did it."

Fallon glanced at Lucan. "Where is Quinn now?"

Larena held out her hand and Fallon pulled her to her feet. "He went after his woman."

"His woman?" Lucan repeated. "The Druid Broc spoke of?"

"Aye," Larena said. "Broc tried to help Marcail escape, but Deirdre caught her. Quinn and Broc have gone to try and stop Deirdre."

Hayden stepped forward. "Then what are we waiting for?"

Fallon fisted his hands and cursed. "I knew I should have gone into the mountain. Then I'd know where to jump us."

"I can help," Galen said.

Fallon raised his brows. "And how is that?"

Galen moved to Larena's side and placed his hand on her head. "Think of the best place for us to be, a place in the mountain that Warriors wouldn't find us. Do you have it?"

"Aye," she answered.

Galen then put his other hand on Fallon's head. In an instant Fallon saw in his mind's eye a place in the mountain. He didn't hesitate, but jumped all three of them into the mountain.

The darkness of the mountain consumed Fallon. He squared his shoulders and looked at Galen. "You're going to have to tell me how you did that."

"As soon as we're back at MacLeod Castle. Now go get the others."

Fallon gave Larena a quick kiss and jumped back to get the rest of the Warriors.

Deirdre stared at the now immobile Marcail. The blue fire had been the perfect magic to hold the irritating Druid. Whereas the black fire that detained Lavena allowed her to speak to Deirdre with her visions, the blue fire that held Marcail kept her body alive but that was all. It also contained all the magic from the protection spells, keeping it from reaching out and harming Deirdre.

She was so excited about having Marcail and her spell locked away that she decided to spend more time looking at her handiwork. Quinn would be waiting for her from now on. After all, he thought his precious Marcail was safely out of the mountain.

What a fool he was, but then again, all men were fools. Deirdre had thought Quinn would be different.

However, once she had Quinn's baby, the child of the prophecy, everything would change.

Deirdre rubbed her hands together in anticipation. She could very well conceive tonight. And the start of a new era would begin.

"Do you know where Ian is being kept?" Quinn asked Broc as they walked down the corridor.

Broc nodded. "He's in no condition to help, though."

"Damn. We still need to free him." Quinn wanted to get to Marcail, but he knew he would need to time everything perfectly. With his brothers and the Warriors loyal to them coming to help along with his men in the Pit, they just might stand a chance in defeating Deirdre.

Broc led him down several hallways and stairwells before he stopped in front of a door.

Quinn unlatched the door to find Ian hanging from the ceiling by his wrists. "Ian," he said as he rushed to his friend.

Ian lifted his head, dried blood coating his face and chest. "Quinn?"

"Aye, it's me. I've come with Broc to get you out of here."

Quinn and Broc released Ian from his chains and helped him to his feet.

"Can you aid Broc in releasing your brother and Arran from the Pit?"

Ian squared his shoulders and weaved on his feet. "Aye."

"Then hurry. There are many in these dungeons that need to be freed. We need total chaos."

"We'll see it done," Broc promised.

Quinn watched them leave before he stepped back into the corridor. Broc had told him how to reach the chamber to which Deirdre had taken Marcail, and he couldn't get there soon enough. The fear that he was already too late propelled him faster down the hallway.

He knew Deirdre wouldn't kill Marcail herself, but that didn't mean Deirdre wouldn't have someone else do it. Her wyrran would do anything for her, as they had proven countless times.

As much as Quinn knew it would be beneficial to wait for the disorder to begin with the release of the prisoners, he couldn't. Marcail needed him, and he wouldn't allow someone else he cared about to die because of Deirdre.

Quinn kept his strides long and quick as he followed Broc's directions. As he turned a corner, he spotted two Warriors. They stopped and stepped aside for him.

When he reached them he halted. "I'm going to give you one chance. Either you fight for me or you die right here."

The Warriors looked at each other and laughed. Quinn released his god and attacked both of them at once. While he used his claws to slice open one Warrior's chest, the other cut the back of Quinn's knee.

When Quinn tried to stand, he couldn't use one leg, but that didn't stop him. He punched the Warrior who had wounded him, knocking him back. Quinn wasted no time before he used his claws to sever the Warrior's head.

Quinn tossed him aside and turned to the second Warrior. Though he was unbalanced with his wounded leg, Quinn wasn't going to give the Warrior any chance to break free.

He leapt atop the Warrior, sinking both sets of claws into his neck. Blood flowed from the Warrior's neck as his eyes bulged. With a twist of Quinn's hands, he cut off the head.

"You should have chosen to fight with me," Quinn said as the dead Warrior fell at his feet.

Quinn continued on his way, determined to convert or kill every Warrior he encountered. He killed another before he heard a commotion and lifted his head to see his brothers.

He forgot about the third dead Warrior at his feet and smiled as he moved toward Lucan and Fallon.

"My God, it's good to see you," Lucan said as he pulled Quinn against him for a hug.

Quinn had never been so happy to see his brothers. Lucan released him and a moment later Fallon's arms enveloped him.

"I thought I'd never see you again," Fallon said.

Quinn chuckled. "I wasna going to give up that easily." He stepped back and glanced at Larena. "I hear you are married."

Fallon frowned. "We should have waited for you."

"Nay," Quinn said. "You take what joy you can find."

Logan cleared his throat. "Are we going to stand around and reminisce all day, or are we going to kill Deirdre?"

Quinn nodded to Logan, Galen, Ramsey, and Hayden. "We're going to kill Deirdre, but first, we're going to save Marcail."

"Where's Broc?" Ramsey asked.

"He and Ian have gone to free my men from the Pit. Then the four of them will begin releasing others from the dungeons."

Lucan laughed. "I like your plan, little brother. Lead on, and we'll save your Marcail."

Quinn hurried down the hallway, Lucan's words echoing in his head. *His Marcail*. Quinn liked the sound of that. He liked it very much.

They managed to climb two levels before they encountered a group of wyrran. The small pale yellow creatures didn't stand a chance against eight Warriors. In a matter of moments, the wyrran were dead.

"I hope there's more," Hayden said.

Quinn wiped the blood from his hands on his tunic.

"There will be. I'm giving all the Warriors I encounter a chance to fight for me. If they decline, they die."

Hayden chuckled and nodded. "I've missed you, Quinn."

Lucan walked beside Quinn with Larena and Fallon behind him. For every moment that kept Quinn from Marcail it was like a knife to his stomach.

It wasn't much further, but it seemed millions of leagues away.

Below them Quinn began to hear shouts and cries from the dungeons. "My men releasing the prisoners."

"Be careful not to kill the wrong Warriors," Fallon cautioned everyone.

Isla slumped against the wall, the rocks digging into her wounded arm and back. She was so tired . . . so weary. When she'd awoken from the trance Deirdre had put her in, it was to find herself fighting for her life with a man three times her size.

It was only with the use of her magic that she had been able to get away, and as hard as she tried not to look, she had seen the dead bodies of a woman, a girl, and a small boy.

Isla had only woken from the trance while in the middle of her "duty" to Deirdre once before. She had tried to run, and paid dearly for it later with a punishment that had her confined to her bed for almost three months.

Yet a small part of her wanted to give it another try. She wanted as far away from Deirdre as she could go. So she ran and didn't look back. Then she thought of her sister and niece. They needed her, even if they didn't know it.

Isla found a horse and quickly returned to the mountain. She hadn't run far, and she arrived at Cairn Toul in less than a day. Once inside, however, she knew something had happened.

And she had an idea it was all because of Quinn.

The MacLeod brothers weren't going to stand by and watch Deirdre take Quinn. Isla had expected Lucan and Fallon weeks ago. Now, it seemed, they had arrived.

Isla made her way to the stairs that would lead her to Phelan. She lost her footing several times on the slick stairs, and once nearly went over the side.

She slowed her steps even though she knew time was of the essence. Her body, however, wouldn't keep up with what she wanted to do. Blood soaked her right sleeve and dripped down to her hand. There was also something running down her back, which she suspected was more blood.

With no idea how many injuries she had or how much longer her body would keep on its feet, Isla trudged down the stairs. As soon as she spotted Phelan from the stairs her legs gave out and she hit the steps with a jarring thud.

Phelan's head jerked in her direction and he growled.

She didn't have the energy to battle words with him today. She would see him freed, though. His chains weren't locked with a key, but with black magic.

Isla lifted her hand and focused her magic on the chains. She repeated the words she had heard Deirdre say only once before, but Isla had memorized them, hoping that one day she could free Phelan.

Phelan's cuffs released and fell from his wrists with

a thunk. Isla inhaled deeply as her vision swam. She closed her eyes to keep her bearings. After a moment she opened them to find Phelan standing over her.

"Why?" he demanded.

She shook her head. "You shouldn't be here. You're free, Phelan. Run as far from this place as you can."

He glanced up the stairs and cocked his head at the sounds drifting down to them. "What is going on up there?"

"I suspect there has been a revolt against Deirdre. She took one of the MacLeod brothers."

"Quinn," Phelan said.

Isla nodded. "His brothers, Lucan and Fallon, have come for him. The noise you're hearing is the prisoners being released."

Phelan leaned close to her and sniffed. "You're injured."

"Leave the mountain. The world has changed much since you were brought here. Be prepared for that."

He studied her for long, quiet moments. "And you? What will you do?"

Isla thought of Lavena and Grania. "I have one other thing I need to do." She just hoped she had the strength to make it back up the stairs and complete her task.

"You are dying."

Isla smiled sadly.

In the next instant, Phelan had lifted her in his arms and bounded up the stairs. He set her gently on her feet when they came to the doorway.

Isla grabbed hold of the wall and forced a smile. "Good luck to you. If you ever need anything, search for the MacLeods. They are good men you can trust."

He didn't bother to respond, just lifted his head and looked around. A moment later he was running down the corridor.

Isla had managed to free one of the people she was responsible for. Two more, and maybe she could find some peace in her nightmares.

THIRTY-TWO

Deirdre couldn't believe how easy it had been to trap Marcail, though she wished she had thought of it earlier instead of putting Marcail in the Pit with Quinn. That hadn't gone according to plan.

In fact, there wasn't anything to do with Quinn that had gone as intended. But that would change now. He was under her control, and it wouldn't take much to have him give in to his god.

Once that happened, she would have the first of the MacLeods with Lucan and Fallon to follow soon after.

She turned to the door to make her way back to Quinn when she heard an inhale of breath. Deirdre paused. She knew that sound. It was Lavena about to have a vision.

Deirdre hurried back to the Druid. Lavena's ice-blue eyes clouded over as the black flames licked at her face. When she spoke, her voice sounded as though it came from deep in a tunnel, soft and airy.

"They are coming," Lavena said. "You took his woman, and you will pay."

Anger pulsed through Deirdre. She knew Lavena spoke of Quinn, and she could assume the "they" was Lucan and Fallon come to help their brother.

"Who told Quinn about Marcail?" Deirdre asked.

Sometimes Lavena responded, sometimes she didn't.

This time the seer chose not to. "Your death is imminent."

Deirdre had never had cause to disbelieve the seer, but she knew she had more than enough magic to battle a thousand Warriors.

"Then let them come," Deirdre said and faced the door.

Quinn released his god. Behind him his brothers and the other Warriors waited for him to open the door that would lead to their greatest battle yet.

"Watch her hair," Galen cautioned.

Larena grinned. "I'll take care of her hair."

Quinn faced the other Warriors and looked into the faces of the men—and woman—who had risked their lives for him. Before him stood powerful Warriors who fought for good over evil and hadn't asked to have a god inside them. "Deirdre's power has grown. Be prepared for anything."

"If she's so powerful how can we defeat her?" Logan asked.

Ramsey smiled slowly. "We attack together and continue attacking. She cannot fight off all of us."

"She won't be alone," Quinn said. "There will be wyrran and Warriors with her. If you encounter William, the royal blue Warrior, hold him for me. I owe him a leisurely death."

"Consider it done," Hayden vowed. "I'll find him myself."

Quinn gave a nod to Hayden. "It's time for Deirdre's reign to end."

"Ready whenever you are, brother," Fallon said.

Quinn found himself praying to God, something he

hadn't done in centuries. The trepidation inside him for Marcail grew with each beat of his heart.

He turned to the door and kicked it open. Deirdre stood in front of a stone table, an evil smile tilting her lips.

"I've been waiting for you, lover," she said.

Broc left Arran and the twins to free the rest of the prisoners. Ever since he had heard the roar down below, he knew a Warrior was probably chained in the darkness. No one was allowed to take the stairs that led below the earth's surface, but Broc no longer served Deirdre and he would make sure all his fellow Warriors were free.

He walked through the door onto the first step and gaped at the large cavern. Though it would be too dark for a mortal to see, with the god inside him, Broc had no problem.

The stairs would take too long to climb down, so he spread his wings and soared to the bottom.

Broc landed, stunned to find whoever had been held down here had already been freed. He was glad to see it, though he would have liked to know who the Warrior was and why Deirdre kept him separate from everyone else.

The sound of battle could be heard echoing through the rocks. Broc's wings lifted him as he flew back to the doorway.

There was an epic battle raging, and his help would be needed.

Quinn bared his fangs at Deirdre. "Did you really think you could deceive me as you did?"

"It would have worked," she said with a sly grin. "Who told you?"

"Does it matter?" Fallon said. "He knows what you've done. Return Marcail to him."

Deirdre threw back her head and laughed. "Oh, I'm afraid that's not possible now."

Quinn followed her finger as she pointed and felt his heart fall to his feet as he caught sight of Marcail. "Nay," he whispered.

"She will never be yours," Deirdre said.

Lucan grabbed his arm. "Quinn."

But Quinn couldn't help his brothers now, not when Marcail stood in blue flames that held her above the floor and immobile. He felt sick to his stomach. Once again he'd been unable to help a woman he cared for. What kind of Highlander and Warrior was he that he couldn't save his women?

"Quinn," Fallon bellowed.

Quinn turned to his brothers, his soul tearing in half. "You know what has to be done."

They nodded and as one, the small group launched themselves at Deirdre. Quinn allowed himself just a moment to watch as Larena went invisible and removed her clothes. Hayden launched huge fireballs at any wyrran that he spotted, and the others surrounded Deirdre.

Quinn stepped close to Marcail. As much as he wanted to be the one to drain the life from Deirdre, Marcail mattered more. He touched the blue flames and ice formed on the tip of his fingers.

"Holy Hell," he murmured.

He didn't know how he would get Marcail out of the flames, but he knew he couldn't do it alone.

Quinn turned back to the battle to find something

pulling Deirdre's hair from behind. Larena most likely. Deirdre screamed as Larena's claws cut off her hair at the neck. A moment later and the hair grew back.

Fallon cheered for his wife before disappearing, only to reappear somewhere else in the chamber. Quinn blinked, unsure of what he saw until Fallon did it over and over again.

"Impressive, isn't it?" Larena's voice said from beside him.

"Aye," Quinn said.

He didn't take time for more words as he closed his eyes and called up his power. *"Come to me,"* he called to every animal inside the mountain.

A few moments later rats, insects, and other animals began to stream into the chamber. Quinn grinned.

"Attack Deirdre," he commanded.

As one, the animals converged on Deirdre. She shifted her power from tossing Warriors aside to killing the animals.

Lucan shifted to shadow and swarmed around Deirdre while Galen, Logan, and Ramsey sliced her with their claws. Fallon would jump in front of her and cut her face, then jump away before she could use her magic on him.

Quinn started forward to join the group in drawing blood from Deirdre when there was a commotion at the door. He turned and found Arran, Ian, and Duncan.

As soon as they saw the attack, they leapt into the fray. A moment later Broc came into the chamber and joined in as well. With so many attacking Deirdre, Quinn could see her weakening. It would only be a matter of time before she was dead.

Hayden continued to kill wyrran he spotted, which

kept Quinn from having to fend the vile creatures off. Quinn was about to join his brothers when a load roar got his attention. He turned to find none other than William coming toward him.

"I've been waiting for this," William said.

Quinn smiled in anticipation. "Stop talking. Start fighting."

He ducked a vicious swing from William's hand that was aimed at his head and drew first blood with a cut to William's stomach.

William staggered backward and growled. "What did she ever see in you?"

"More than she saw in you," Quinn taunted.

William plowed his shoulder into Quinn's abdomen, knocking the breath from Quinn and driving him back against the wall. Quinn elbowed the Warrior in the back of the neck twice before William's hold loosened enough for Quinn to knee him in the face.

As William jerked up from the hit, his claws raked Quinn's side and arm. Before Quinn could deliver another blow, William bit his shoulder, his fangs sinking far into Quinn's skin.

Quinn bellowed and used his claws to tear at William's skin wherever he could. Blood poured down Quinn's arm, but he didn't feel it, not when the need to kill was so strong.

William stepped away, his mouth and teeth covered in blood. "I'm going to enjoy taking you apart piece by piece, MacLeod. You arena fit to be a Warrior, much less rule over us."

"It isna my fault Deirdre didn't want a child from you. Where were you lacking, William?"

Just as Quinn had hoped, William's anger got the

better of him. He grew more reckless each time he attacked, and it gave Quinn the advantage he needed as he moved closer and closer to the black flames where Deirdre kept the seer.

Despite William's fury, he was able to land several blows to Quinn, drawing more blood. Quinn's body ached from the cuts that covered him from his face to his legs, but he wasn't going to stop, not until William was dead.

William's claws sunk into Quinn's stomach before he jerked them out sideways, leaving a gaping wound in Quinn's belly. Quinn glanced down and saw the damage. He felt his body lean to the side as exhaustion took over.

"Quinn."

He blinked. It had been Marcail's voice, of that he had no doubt.

"You can do this," Marcail said in his mind. *"Finish him."*

Quinn jerked his head to clear it and focused once more on William. Marcail was right. He could kill William.

He smiled at the Warrior and took a step toward him. William sneered and tried to bite him again.

"I've had enough of you." With one shove Quinn pushed William into the black flames.

The Warrior screamed and clawed at his face and skin as he thrashed about. He knocked the seer from the flames, but it was too late for William. The black fire had taken him, leaving him in the same sedate, calm state the seer had been in.

"Quinn," Lucan said and grabbed him about the shoulders. "We need to get to the castle."

"I'm not leaving without Marcail."

"Deirdre is almost dead. Let's get out of here," Lucan pleaded.

Quinn looked at his brother. "I couldna protect Elspeth. I willna be responsible for Marcail's death as well."

There was a loud scream that threatened to burst their eardrums. Quinn covered his ears and turned to find Deirdre screaming and Charon holding her by her neck.

The copper Warrior had death in his eyes, and by the way he squeezed, she wouldn't live much longer.

There was a crack as Charon broke her neck with one hand. He removed her head with a yank and let her fall to the ground before tossing her head on top of her body. Hayden then set her on fire.

"It's over," Lucan said.

But for Quinn it wouldn't be over until Marcail was in his arms.

THIRTY-THREE

Isla stood in the shadows and watched the MacLeods triumph over Deirdre, but it was Lavena that Isla focused on. She had come to save her sister from the never-ending life of Deirdre's seer, but it appeared someone had already done it for her.

She didn't need to go to Lavena and check for breath to know her sister was dead. She wanted to mourn the loss of her sister, but she had been doing that for centuries. Finally, Lavena was at peace.

Which only left Grania now.

Isla turned to go in search of her niece. As she expected, Grania was in her chamber. When she saw Isla, Grania rose from her seat and walked toward her.

"What is going on?" Grania demanded.

Isla licked her lips and reached for Grania's hand, forcing back the pain in her body. Her niece stepped away before Isla could touch her.

It wasn't a good start, but Isla was determined to be the aunt her sister would have wanted.

"Grania, I've some bad news," Isla began.

"Is it about Deirdre?" the child asked. "Tell me it isn't about Deirdre."

Isla hesitated a moment. "Nay, it's about your mother. I'm sorry, but she's dead."

"I don't care about Lavena. Deirdre was more of a mother to me."

"You don't know what you're saying."

"I do indeed."

Isla knew in that moment as she looked into the same blue eyes as her own that Grania was lost to her forever. "Please, Grania. Deirdre's time of rule is over. She's gone."

"Nay," Grania screamed and tried to run from the room.

Isla grabbed her arm and swung the child toward her. She didn't see the dagger in Grania's hand until the last moment. It was pure instinct that drove Isla to use her magic to turn the dagger.

Grania grunted and fell to her knees, her eyes filled with pain.

Isla knelt beside her niece as tears fell down her face. "Oh, dear God, what have I done?" she asked as she spotted the dagger in Grania's chest.

She hadn't wanted to kill Grania, only to remove the weapon.

"Deirdre will make you die a thousand deaths for this," Grania murmured. She fell to her side as blood trickled from her mouth and her lifeless eyes stared at Isla.

Isla couldn't believe Grania was gone. She had begun to hate the child, aye, but only because of the evil Deirdre had put into her niece. Isla had hoped time away from Deirdre would turn the child as she had once been, innocent and pure.

But she knew that for the lie that it was.

It took three tries before Isla found her footing. She

no longer cared about anything. She had to get as far away from the mountain and Deirdre as she could.

"What do we do?" Fallon asked Quinn as they stood around Marcail.

Quinn had come up with an idea when William had pushed the seer from her flames. "I have to get Marcail out of the flames, but I'm going to need someone to hold me so they can pull me out as well. Once I'm in, I willna be able to do anything."

Lucan nodded. "I'll hold onto you."

"We better both do it," Ramsey said.

Quinn hid his wince as he moved to Marcail. He was losing blood rapidly, and though he was immortal, with serious wounds it took a little more time to heal. He would have to get help soon, but not yet. Not before Marcail was out of the flames.

"Someone go to the other side to catch her," Quinn said.

Fallon moved opposite Quinn. "I'll take her to Sonya as soon as she's out."

Quinn met his brother's gaze. He didn't need to tell Fallon how important Marcail was to him. His brother knew.

"Wait," Larena said as she ran into the chamber. She had dressed and was no longer in her goddess form.

Quinn figured that was a good thing. The fewer people that knew what she was, the better. "What?" he asked.

"The other woman. She died," Larena said. "Are you sure we should take Marcail out of the flames?"

"I'm sure," Quinn answered. "Deirdre had kept the

seer for several centuries. She's probably been dead for some time and Deirdre kept her body alive for the visions."

Arran swore. "By all that's holy."

Quinn couldn't agree more. He looked down at the finger that had touched the blue flames. There was no color to his skin and it was as cold as death. He didn't think he would survive the blue fire, and though he longed to be with Marcail, he would do anything to save her.

With a nod to Fallon, Quinn stepped into the flames, his hand held out to give Marcail the push she needed to be released.

Instantly, Quinn was overtaken with cold. He tried to draw a breath but couldn't. He fought the cold, but it took over his body in a matter of moments.

He thought of Marcail and how he would never get to hold her again. Of a sudden he recalled a conversation with his father.

"Son," his father said, "it's fairly simple. When you find a woman that occupies your thoughts every hour of every day and you dream about her and a future together, that's a sign. When you canna wait to see her smile, feel her arms about you, and taste her kiss, then you love her. When you know you would gladly give up your own life regardless of the pain in order to save hers, then you love her."

Quinn's heart wanted to burst from his chest as he realized his father had been right about all of it. He loved Marcail, truly loved her as he had always dreamed of loving a woman.

He mourned a future with her that could never be,

but at least his brothers would keep her safe at the castle. There, Marcail would thrive with Cara.

Quinn's last thought before the cold took him under was of Marcail's sweet smile and turquoise eyes.

"Get him out!" Fallon bellowed.

He held Marcail's frigid body in his arms so he was helpless to do anything but watch as Lucan and Ramsey attempted to pull Quinn from the flames.

"Dammit, Quinn," Lucan yelled. "Doona dare give up!"

The two pale blue Warriors who were obviously twins and a white Warrior stepped next to Lucan and Ramsey and added their strength to tug Quinn's body free.

"Thank God," Larena said as she wiped the tears from her eyes.

"Move," Fallon said as he walked to Quinn. He needed to get both of them to Sonya. The gray pallor of their skin and the way ice hung from their lashes and hair didn't give Fallon much hope.

The white Warrior lifted Quinn over his shoulder. "You're going to need help."

Fallon glanced at his wife before he touched the white Warrior and jumped them to the great hall in the castle.

"Shite," a male voice said as Fallon appeared.

"Get Sonya and Cara," he shouted to Malcolm as he raced up the stairs with Marcail still in his arms.

Behind him the white Warrior followed. Fallon thought about putting Quinn and Marcail in different chambers, then thought it would be easier on Sonya if they where together. Without another thought, Fallon strode to Quinn's chamber.

The Warrior moved past him and jerked the covers from the bed so Fallon could lay Marcail down. Once that was done he helped the Warrior lower Quinn.

"I'm Arran," the Warrior said. "I gave Quinn my allegiance in the Pit."

Fallon nodded to him. "I thank you for that."

Sonya and Cara ran into the chamber then. Sonya didn't say a word as she went to the bed and examined the couple. She straightened and turned to Fallon. "I need to know every detail and especially if magic was involved."

"There was magic. Deirdre's magic to be precise." Fallon then went on to tell her what had happened.

Sonya's lips flatted. "This is going to take a lot of my magic. If only we had another Druid."

"Marcail is a Druid," Arran said. "And she has the ability to heal herself. Does that make a difference?

Sonya slowly nodded her head. "Maybe. If I can get her to hear me, I may be able to have her help me."

"And Quinn?" Fallon asked.

"I will do my best," Sonya said.

Cara stepped forward then. "Where are the others?"

"Lucan is safe," Fallon assured her. "I'm going to get them once I know Sonya has all she needs to see to Quinn and Marcail."

"I do," Sonya said, her back to him as she lifted Marcail's hand. "Bring the others."

Fallon looked to Arran. "There is another Warrior here, Camdyn. Find him and fill him in on everything. Oh, and if Malcolm is still here, he'll need to know as well."

"I'll see it done," Arran said before he turned on his heel and left the chamber.

Fallon glanced once more at the lifeless form of his brother before he jumped back to Cairn Toul to retrieve the others.

THIRTY-FOUR

Sonya looked down at Marcail and Quinn and knew it would take every ounce of her magic to save them, and even then it might not be enough.

"Blankets," she said. "We're going to need blankets. And a fire."

Cara hurried to pile blankets on top of the couple before she began to stack wood in the hearth.

"I'll do that," Camdyn said as he entered the chamber. "Arran told me everything. What do you need besides a fire, Sonya?"

Sonya blew out a breath. "Prayers."

She trusted the people around her to ensure she had everything she needed. Cara would stay beside her, adding her magic as much as she could.

This was one of the times Sonya wished they had more Druids at the castle. The more that could add their magic to hers, the better she would be able to heal Quinn and his woman.

Sonya rubbed her hands together before placing one hand over the heart of first Marcail, then Quinn. She should only heal one at a time, but if she did that, one of them would die.

She began to chant, using just the right inflection and softening her tone. Sonya could feel her magic bubble inside her before it poured through her hands into Marcail and Quinn. She concentrated on Marcail, hoping to find the Druid and get her to help with the healing.

"Hear me, Marcail," Sonya whispered in the Druid's mind. *"You are no longer Deirdre's prisoner. I'm trying to heal you, but I need your help. Use your magic."*

Again and again Sonya repeated it, but the Druid never responded.

Sonya took a deep breath and poured more of her magic into the couple. She could feel Quinn's body begin to push aside the effects of Deirdre's black magic, but with Marcail, there was nothing.

Fallon arrived back at the mountain and had to grab hold of a wall as the peak shook and trembled.

"What is going on?" he asked.

Larena rushed to him, her large smoky blue eyes troubled. "It began not long after you left. Deirdre's body disappeared and the mountain began to shake."

"We need to get out of here. Now," Lucan said.

Fallon took hold of Larena and Lucan; at the same time Larena placed her hand on Duncan's arm.

In the next blink Fallon had them back at his castle. "Find Sonya," he told Larena. "She may need help."

Larena nodded and rushed to do his bidding. Fallon jumped back to the mountain. It took two more trips before he had the rest of the group at his home.

After the last trip, Fallon ran a hand down his face. "Make yourselves at home," he told the newcomers. "If you need anything let me know."

Fallon bounded up the stairs to check on Sonya's progress. He felt a presence behind him and found

Broc. It was odd seeing the Warrior without his wings and the indigo skin of his god, and by the way Broc kept rolling his shoulders, Fallon knew Broc wasn't used to being in his human form either.

Fallon rushed into Quinn's chamber to find Sonya and Cara standing together with their hands over Quinn and Marcail. To Fallon's eyes, Quinn's color looked better, but Marcail's had gone unchanged.

"How is it coming?" he whispered to Lucan.

Lucan shook his head, his sea-green eyes telling Fallon what words could not. Things weren't going well.

Fallon walked to Larena and threaded his fingers with hers. Just being beside her gave him strength. Larena smiled sadly and laid her head on his shoulder.

When Fallon looked to the doorway he found it filled with Warriors and Malcolm. They were a family now, and they all had gathered to lend whatever they could to Quinn and Marcail's recovery.

"She's pregnant," Sonya said into the silence. "Marcail is carrying Quinn's child."

"God's blood," Lucan said. "We'll lose him for sure this time if Marcail dies."

Fallon's throat closed with emotion as he looked at Quinn lying so still on the bed. He had risked his own life to save Marcail's. God help them all if Marcail died and Quinn survived.

Sonya swayed on her feet, her lips moving with words Fallon couldn't hear. Larena was the first to reach Sonya and helped to steady the Druid.

Fallon didn't like feeling ineffective, but that's exactly what he was. Everything was in Sonya's hands, and though she was a powerful Druid, did she have enough magic to counter Deirdre's black magic?

There was a loud sigh from everyone when they heard Quinn take a deep breath and slowly let it out. Fallon watched as Sonya shifted all her attention to Marcail, her forehead furrowed and her face lined with worry.

Moments ticked into hours before Sonya finally stepped away from the bed. "I've done all I can do," she said. "The rest is up to Marcail."

Sonya didn't know how she was still standing. Her body was weak from using so much magic. She'd never used so much before, but after she had discovered the baby growing in Marcail's womb, Sonya hadn't wanted to give up. She'd still be there if her magic was endless.

"Thank you," Fallon said as he took one of her hands and bowed his head.

Lucan stepped forward and did the same. "You saved our brother."

Sonya glanced over her shoulder at the bed. "Who is Marcail to Quinn?"

"Everything," Arran said.

"I thought so." She sighed, trying to hold back the weariness that threatened to pull her under. "If Marcail doesn't improve soon, she never will."

A tall man with long brown hair that fell down to the middle of his back stepped forward. He and another man looked identical, other than their hair. "Is there nothing else you can do for Marcail?"

"I've used all my magic, more than I've ever used before."

Sonya had to get out of the chamber and to her own. She needed to rest. Maybe then her magic would build back up and she could return to Marcail.

She walked to the crowd of Warriors at the door.

They no longer showed their god forms, but a Warrior held himself differently than other, mortal men.

Her gaze was drawn to a handsome Warrior who stood at the door behind the others. He had dark, mysterious eyes and wavy blond hair that fell to his shoulders. Strands of the golden locks fell across his features, but he didn't seem to notice.

His face was so perfect it could have been formed by the gods themselves. Sonya forced herself to look away from his bare chest lest she embarrass herself by touching his golden skin, as she longed to do.

She made it out of the chamber and gripped the wall in the corridor to steady herself. By the way her body was reacting, she wouldn't make it to her chamber without collapsing.

She put one foot in front of the other, determined not to let anyone see just how weak she was when suddenly her legs gave out. Before she hit the floor, strong arms locked around her and held her against a chest of steel.

"I've got you," said a deep, sultry voice in her ear.

"I'm all right. I can make it on my own."

He lifted her in his arms despite her words. Sonya somehow wasn't surprised to see it was the Warrior with the golden hair and perfect face that held her.

"You aren't all right. Now, tell me where your chamber is. I take it you doona want the others to see you like this?"

She shook her head. "Nay, I don't. My chamber is down the corridor to the left."

He began to walk, his stride easy and long. He glanced at her once, his dark eyes as fathomless as the night sky.

"Who are you?" she asked.

A frown flitted across his face so quickly she almost didn't see it. "Broc MacLaughlin."

"Broc," she repeated.

She wanted to ask him if he was the same Broc her sister had known, but she knew that couldn't be possible. Could it?

Sonya's eyes began to close and she rested her head on Broc's shoulder, his warm skin against her cheek. She wanted to thank him for helping her when he laid her upon her bed, but sleep pulled her under.

Broc tugged the coverlet over Sonya's shoulders before he allowed himself to touch her fiery braid. "Finally, I find you. Thank God you are safe. Rest well, sweet Sonya."

Quinn huddled beneath the covers. He'd never felt so cold in his life. His hand brushed against a body, and he found himself turning toward the sunshine-and-rain scent he recognized. He was about to drift off to sleep when he heard his name.

"Quinn?"

He'd know that voice anywhere. Quinn cracked open his eyes. "Fallon?"

Fallon's face split into a huge grin filled with relief and a little sadness. "Aye, brother. How do you feel?"

"Cold."

More blankets were suddenly piled on top of him. He looked around to find the chamber filled with Warriors, including his own men. There were a couple of men he didn't recognize, though.

"That's Camdyn," Lucan said. "He's another Warrior and friend to Galen."

Fallon motioned to the other man in the group, a

man who was obviously mortal by the recent scarring on his face. "This is Malcolm Monroe, my wife's cousin. I'll tell you all about how Larena and I met and how Malcolm helped her once you're on your feet."

Quinn frowned. Why was he in bed and not feeling quite right? Then it came back to him in a rush. "Deirdre," he ground out.

"She's dead," Ian said. "Charon killed her."

Quinn looked around for the copper Warrior. "Where is Charon?"

Duncan shrugged. "He disappeared after he killed Deirdre."

Quinn touched Marcail's hand beneath the covers and felt her icy skin. Her breathing was shallow and erratic, and he knew without looking in her face that she was still unconscious.

"Sonya worked long and hard with her magic to heal both of you," Lucan said.

Quinn nodded and leaned up on his elbow to see Marcail. He pulled the covers up to her chin and ran his finger down her cheek.

"I've lost her, havena I?" he asked no one in particular.

"She could heal herself as before," Arran offered.

It was possible. "How long has she been like this?"

The silence was deafening.

Quinn rested his forehead against hers and squeezed his eyes closed. His heart was in pieces, his soul torn to shreds. He had finally found a woman he loved, truly loved, and she had been taken from him before he'd even told her what she meant to him.

Was he destined to spend his life alone?

"God's blood," he said. "I canna do this again."

There was movement and then two hands rested on

his shoulder. His brothers. As always, they were there for him.

"I love her," Quinn said. "The love I had always thought I would never find found me in the darkness of the mountain. For the second time Deirdre has taken it from me."

One of the hands squeezed his shoulder. "Deirdre is dead," Lucan said. "She willna be able to hurt us ever again."

But that didn't matter anymore. Nothing mattered without Marcail.

Quinn threw back the covers and rose from the bed. He didn't move with the ease he usually did. The residual effects of Deirdre's magic most likely, but he would make do.

"What are you doing?" Fallon asked.

Quinn ignored his eldest brother and lifted Marcail in his arms. "She's been in the dark for days. She needs the light."

No one stopped him as he carried his woman from the chamber. He walked out of the castle and into the bailey. Only briefly did he realize they now had a gate.

He continued through the open gate toward the cliffs. He had wanted to show Marcail his home and the cliffs he loved. This was his only chance, and nothing would stop him.

Quinn found a spot and lowered himself to the ground. He looked down into Marcail's face, which was pale and icy to the touch. One of her braids had fallen across her eyes. Quinn gently brushed it away and kissed her forehead.

"I wish you could see this, Marcail," he said. "The sun is sinking into the sky, casting the dark waters of the sea orange and bronze. It's one of my favorite times of the day."

He swallowed past the lump in his throat. "Below us is the beach where my father taught me and my brothers to swim and fish. At night, as I close my eyes, I can hear the waves crash against the cliffs. It is a soothing sound, one I think you would have come to enjoy."

A tear rolled down his face. He sighed and closed his eyes, wishing he had magic to help Marcail himself.

He looked down into her face, now cast in the red-orange glow of the setting sun. "You would have been happy here. I would have made sure of it."

No matter how hard he stared, Marcail didn't move or answer. As much as Quinn's heart screamed in denial he knew Marcail was lost to him. It would only be a matter of hours before her already weakened heart stopped.

THIRTY-FIVE

The first thing Marcail felt was the warmth. She realized she had been taken out of the blue flames, since Deirdre's magic no longer held her frozen. Yet she couldn't wake.

She knew her heart was failing, could feel the strain of her lungs as they struggled to draw breath.

For a time, she had felt something else as well, *mie* magic. Had another Druid tried to help her? Since she couldn't hear anything but silence, Marcail didn't know.

Though she didn't want to die, the one thing she wanted—Quinn—was gone from her. What was there to live for now? But still her lungs drew in air.

She could either die, or she could use her magic and help to heal herself. Her grandmother had told her once that her life would hang in the balance and Marcail had to be able to heal against anything.

Had her grandmother foreseen what Deirdre would do to her?

Marcail searched for her magic but found nothing. She was a *mie*, a Druid who knew only goodness. Her bloodline could be traced back to the ancient Celts, when her ancestors had held great power. Her magic couldn't have been taken from her.

Then . . . she felt a sliver of magic and reached for it with her mind. She held onto that small thread and focused on it, drawing it into her body and through her blood and heart and lungs.

With each breath she fought against the black magic that wanted her death. Several times the black magic almost won, but Marcail refused to give up. Her grandmother had taught her well, and Marcail wouldn't allow her training and magic to go unused.

Her magic began to grow like a glowing white light inside her. The more she concentrated, the more it grew until it overtook the poisonous black magic inside her and killed it.

In a rush, sound filled her ears. Birds cried, wind whistled around her, and waves crashed below her. But, most wonderful of all, were the strong arms that held her, an embrace she would know anywhere.

Quinn.

She opened her eyes to see him staring off into the distance. Around her the sky was alive with color. Clouds varied from lavender to vibrant pink and lustrous orange. She shifted her gaze and found the sun sinking into the horizon.

Marcail was able to glimpse the last bit of the orange globe before it disappeared and night took its hold over the land.

She turned her gaze back to Quinn and smiled. She didn't know how they had gotten away from Deirdre, and it didn't matter. She was in his arms, the only place she wanted to be.

Her heart was about to burst with happiness, but the grief on Quinn's face made her pause.

He inhaled deeply and looked down at her. His eyes went wide with disbelief. "Marcail?" he whispered.

She smiled and reached to touch his face. "Aye, Quinn. I'm here."

"How?"

"Magic. My magic."

His hand shook as he caressed her face. "Holy Hell. I thought I had lost you. Doona do that to me again."

"Never," she vowed.

He crushed her against his chest and she welcomed his warmth. It felt so good to touch him, hold him again, that she never wanted to let go.

"You're at MacLeod Castle," he said as he leaned back. "All the prisoners were freed from Cairn Toul. Duncan, Ian, Arran, and Broc have returned with us."

Marcail bit her lip. "What of Deirdre?"

"She's dead," Quinn said. "She'll never hurt us again."

Marcail was overwhelmed with the news. She wished she could have seen it, but it was enough that Deirdre's evil was no longer part of their world.

Quinn caressed her cheek and she found herself lost in his pale green gaze. "I realized something when I saw what Deirdre had done to you."

"What?"

"I love you."

In all her dreams, she had never thought to hear those words from him. "You love me?"

"Aye. My whole life I've dreamed of finding a woman I loved. I never thought it possible."

She leaned up so that her lips were near his. "It's most definitely possible, Quinn MacLeod. I fear I fell in love with you the moment you saved me in the Pit."

His lips claimed hers in a fiery kiss fueled with

passion, longing, and the promise of a future. "I doona want to be apart again. Ever."

She laughed, her soul filled with so much joy she could barely stand it. "I agree."

Quinn rolled onto his back and pulled her against him. "I cannot wait to show you everything and have you meet my brothers. Once you are settled maybe Sonya and Cara can help you find the spell to bind our gods."

Marcail frowned and looked away from him.

"What is it?" he asked.

"Deirdre almost killed my magic. I brought it back, and though I'm stronger for it, I'm afraid I might have lost the spell forever. You see, I began to remember it while in the Pit. You triggered it."

He raised a brow. "Me?"

"My grandmother had always told me to follow my heart in everything. I think she cloaked the spell until I fell in love. The more I got to know you and love you, the more I heard the strange chanting in my head. It was only after you were taken that I realized what it was. I almost had it when Broc came to help me escape. I've not been able to try since."

Quinn smiled and kissed her. "It will be all right. If you find the spell, we will use it. If not . . ."

"You live forever while I die."

His lips flattened at her words. "I'd rather have eternity with you, but I'll take anything I can get."

And in her heart she agreed with him. "We've lost so much time."

Quinn rolled her onto her back and jumped to his feet. He held out his hands for her and gently pulled her next to him. "I cannot wait for you to meet Lucan and Fallon."

Marcail laughed and turned her head to see the large castle with its gray stones and mighty towers. "It's magnificent."

"A lot of work has been done to restore it," he said. "So much has happened while I've been gone."

"And you've changed."

He nodded and pulled her into his arms. "For the better. I never dreamed I'd say this again, but will you be my wife, Marcail?"

She nodded as happiness overflowed within her. "I wouldn't dream of being with anyone else."

He groaned and bent his head for another kiss, a kiss that was the beginning of a love more glorious than either could have imagined.

EPILOGUE

Quinn couldn't stop smiling. Marcail not only returned his love, but would now be his wife. It felt right, as nothing ever had before. Even knowing that his god might never be bound and Marcail was mortal wasn't enough to dampen his spirits and hope for their future.

"It's good to see you smiling again," Lucan said as he came to stand on Quinn's right.

Quinn nodded and raised his goblet to Marcail who stood with Cara and Sonya at the other end of the great hall. Sonya had told them earlier about Marcail's pregnancy. Quinn was awed and overjoyed, though a thread of fear hadn't left him since the news.

"It feels good to smile," Quinn admitted.

Fallon moved to Quinn's left. "How things have changed around here. I think our parents would approve."

"They would," Quinn agreed. "We've defeated Deirdre, gotten our castle returned thanks to Malcolm's influence with the king, found great women to share our lives with, and we have a new family."

"I can drink to that," Lucan said and raised his goblet.

Fallon laughed and raised his next to Lucan's. It had come as a shock to Quinn to discover Fallon had stopped drinking wine. Water would be found in his goblet now.

"To our future," Quinn said and put his goblet alongside his brothers'.

Lucan smiled and said, "And our women."

They each drank deeply and let out a sigh.

It was Fallon who spoke first. "What do we do now that Deirdre is gone?"

"I've been thinking about that," Quinn said. "There is no need for Warriors. I think we should find the spell to bind our gods. Marcail is willing to try."

Lucan nodded as he lowered his goblet from his mouth. "I agree. I'd like to grow old with my wife."

Quinn happened to concur with Lucan. Not to mention that with the baby on the way, Quinn wanted a normal life for his new family.

"I wonder if we should go back to the mountain," Fallon said.

Quinn looked at his brother to see if Fallon was serious. "Why?"

"There might be those that need our help that couldna get out. Not to mention, I'd like to make sure all the wyrran are dead."

Lucan rubbed his jaw. "Fallon has a point. Maybe we should return. Other Druids could be hurt or trapped."

The thought of returning to that mountain left Quinn in a cold sweat. He knew Deirdre was dead, had seen her body with his own eyes, but he still couldn't shake the feeling she wasn't gone forever as he had told Marcail.

"I'll take Hayden and go in the morn," Fallon said.

Quinn laughed. "Ah, your power to jump from one place to another. That's a nice power."

Fallon shrugged but didn't bother to hide his smile.

"It is, though I canna jump somewhere I've never been before. Speaking of powers, do you have one you never told us about?"

"I can speak to animals."

Lucan whistled. "When did that begin?"

"While in Deirdre's dungeon. I hated the rats. Once I figured out how to keep them away, they never bothered me again."

"Ah," Lucan said. "You were the reason all those animals attacked Deirdre."

"God help any mortal man fool enough to try and take this castle from us," Fallon said.

Larena walked up and put her arms around Fallon. "Are you already plotting a war?"

"They are never content, are they?" Cara said as she joined Lucan.

Quinn smiled and took Marcail's hand in his as he pulled her against his chest so he could wrap an arm around her. He glanced at the cuff around her upper arm with the wolf's head on it, matching his torc and bonding them forever. "We'll do whatever it takes to keep our women safe."

"I expect nothing less from a Warrior," Marcail said before she rose up on her toes to kiss him.

The hall erupted in cheers. Quinn laughed with Marcail. It was going to take some getting used to, having a life so full of love and happiness, but he was ready to find out.

Isla stumbled in the snow and fell to her knees. She had gotten turned around as she tried to walk down the mountain, and now she feared she would never leave it.

Her fingers were frozen and she could no longer feel

her feet, which was why she kept tripping over things. Snow had begun to fall, hampering her vision, but then again, on Cairn Toul, there was always snow.

She pushed off the snow and saw the blood where her hand had been. She needed to see to her wounds soon. Already she had lost so much blood. Anyone looking for her simply had to follow the blood to find her.

A tear fell from her eyes. She wiped it away and tried to push Grania from her mind. It had been an accident killing her niece, but the pain of what she had done would haunt her forever.

If Deirdre didn't find her first.

Read on for an excerpt from

UNTAMED
HIGHLANDER

The next thrilling novel from
Donna Grant and St. Martin's Paperbacks!

Cairn Toul Mountain
Summer 1603

Hayden Campbell swore viciously as he turned over yet another frozen body on the rocky slope.

"This one is dead," Fallon MacLeod yelled from his position farther up the mountain.

"They're all dead." Hayden blew out a breath that puffed around him, ignoring the frigid temperatures and steady snowfall. Though he felt the cold it didn't bother him because he wasn't quite human.

He was a Warrior, an immortal with an archaic god inside him that gave him powers and immeasurable strength—among other things.

Hayden rubbed the ice from his eyelashes as his gaze wandered over the snow-covered slope and the numerous dead Druids. "We should have returned sooner."

Fallon, another Warrior, walked toward him with heavy footsteps, his green eyes grave. "Aye, we should have, but my concern was for Quinn. We scarcely got him and Marcail out of this cursed mountain in time as it was."

"I ken." Hayden gazed at the hated mound of rock.

He had always loved looking at the great mountains, but being locked in Cairn Toul for too many decades and forced to watch the evil that grew there took away the pleasure the mountains had once given him. "Damn Deirdre."

Deirdre, the one who began it all, was finally dead. She was a Druid, but from a sect who gave their blood and souls to *diabhul,* the Devil, for the use of black magic. She was, or had been, a *drough.*

There was another set of Druids, the *mie*, who used the pure magic born in all Druids to bond with nature and harness the natural power that came to all of them. The *mie* used their magic to heal and aid those in need, not to destroy as the *drough* and Deirdre did.

But Hayden and the other Warriors had defeated her. It had cost many lives, however. Too many lives.

Hundreds of Druids had been enslaved in the mountain for Deirdre to drain their blood and harvest their magic to add to her own. No one knew how old Deirdre was, but if Hayden could believe the rumors, she had lived for nearly a thousand years, going back to the time just after Rome was driven from the land by Warriors.

Warriors who had been made thanks to both the *drough* and *mie* in response to the cries of the Celts for help. Though Hayden couldn't fault them. Rome had been slowly suffocating Britain, ending all that made Britain great. And the Celts had been unable to defeat them.

The Druids had done what they could for Britain. They had no idea the primeval gods they called up from Hell would refuse to leave the men they took control of.

The gods were so potent that the Druids couldn't

remove them. The only thing the Druids could do was bind the gods inside the men after Rome had been defeated and departed Britain's shores.

And so the gods moved from generation to generation through the bloodline and into the strongest warriors. Until Deirdre found the MacLeods and unbound their god.

Deirdre's reign of evil had lasted far longer than Hayden liked to think about. Deirdre might have been powerful, but even a *drough* could be killed.

Hayden grinned, reliving the moment Deirdre's neck had been crushed by another Warrior and Hayden had engulfed her in fire.

"What are you smiling at?" Fallon asked, breaking into Hayden's thoughts.

Fallon was leader of their group of Warriors. They had banded together to fight Deirdre and the wickedness she spawned. Though they had expected it would take years, Deirdre had changed everything when she took the youngest MacLeod brother, Quinn, captive. That's when they had taken the fight to Deirdre.

"The fact Deirdre is dead," Hayden explained. "Everything we've been fighting against all these years is over. Gone."

Fallon smiled and slapped him on the shoulder. "It's a wonderful feeling, isna it? Now all we have to worry about is having the Druids find the spell to bind our gods once more. Then we can live as mortal men."

Binding the gods was all Fallon, Lucan, and Quinn spoke about. But the MacLeod brothers had wives, so they yearned to have their gods gone from their lives.

Hayden, on the other hand, wasn't sure he wanted to be mortal again. He was too powerless that way.

"I'm going to look on the other side of the mountain," Fallon said. "Maybe we'll find someone alive."

"I think the ones that could make it out of the mountain did. It was the weather that killed them."

Fallon blew out a ragged breath and clenched his jaw. "We should look inside the mountain then. Some might have been too afraid to leave."

They both turned to the door that stood ajar amid the rock as if waiting for them to enter its wicked domain. All Druids were gifted with a certain power. Deirdre's had been moving stone. She had instructed the mountain to shift and form so that she had a palace inside it, shielded from the world.

Hidden from all.

Countless Druids had died heinously, and many a Highlander had been brought to her to have his god unbound. If he didn't house a god, he was killed.

Even now Hayden could smell the stench of death and iniquity that permeated the mountain, could still feel the helplessness that had weighed heavily on his shoulders while he had been locked in one of the various prisons.

But he had been one of the lucky ones. Hayden had broken free and escaped, determined to fight Deirdre and her bid to rule the world.

"Why would anyone stay inside that place?" Hayden murmured as unease rippled down his spine. He fisted his hands and forced himself to stand still and not give in to the urge to turn away from the malevolent mountain.

Fallon scratched his jaw, his gaze thoughtful. "I doona know, but it's worth a look. We freed these people, and it's our responsibility to make sure they return to their homes."

Hayden considered Fallon's words. "They may not want our help. We are, after all, Warriors. They might not be able to tell the difference between us and the Warriors who allied themselves with Deirdre."

"True. But I must look either way. I wasna held longer than a few days in the mountain so it doesna hold the memories for me it does for you."

Hayden might not want to go into Cairn Toul, but he would. "I'm not afraid."

Fallon put his hand on Hayden's shoulder and looked into his eyes. "I would never think that, my friend. I would not torment you, though." He dropped his arm and smiled. "Besides, I want to return to Larena as quickly as I can. You give a final look over the mountain while I go inside."

Before Hayden could object, Fallon was gone. He used the power his god gave him to "jump" inside the mountain in the blink of an eye. Fallon couldn't jump somewhere he had never been before, but the use of his power had saved them countless times.

They all had different powers. For Hayden, Ouraneon, the god of massacre that was inside him, gave him the ability to call up and control fire. There were other differences as well. Each god favored a color, so every Warrior transformed to that color when they released their god.

Yet, for all their differences, there was a great deal they had in common, like strength, speed, and enhanced senses, as well as deadly claws and sharp fangs. The most disturbing, though, were their eyes, which changed the same color as their god.

It had taken Hayden a long time to get used to that. He hadn't seen his own eyes, but he could imagine how he looked when the whites of his eyes disappeared and his entire eye turned red.

As much as Hayden had rebelled and fought the god within him, that same god allowed him to defeat Deirdre. With Deirdre dead and his family massacred by a *drough* sent by Deirdre, there was nothing in this world for Hayden to do.

For so many years he had roamed Scotland, watching the world change around him while he hunted *drough*. Deirdre had taunted him that she had sent a *drough* to kill his family as she tortured him day after day. So he fought against Deirdre while seeking his vengeance on the *drough*.

Now there was no place for him in this new world. There was no place for him anywhere.

He continued wandering the mountain, looking for anyone who might still be alive, as he thought of what his next move might be. He had stayed in Scotland because of Deirdre and his revenge, but maybe now he would travel and see the different countries others spoke about.

Hayden leaned against a boulder and raked his hand through his damp hair. The snowfall had begun to grow more dense, the flakes thicker and heavier, but it didn't hamper his superior eyesight. They stuck to his eyelashes and covered everything in a blinding white blanket.

Hours went by with Hayden locating nothing but more dead. The fact that they were most likely Druids only made the findings more difficult to bear. Druids might have magic, but they were as susceptible to the elements as any human, and thanks to Deirdre's affin-

ity for killing them, the Druids were becoming more
and more scarce.

A shout from Fallon let Hayden know it was time to
return to MacLeod Castle. As Hayden began to turn
away something caught his eye.

He paused and narrowed his gaze when a gust of
wind lifted a lock of long, black hair in the snow.
Though Hayden knew the woman was most likely dead,
he hurried to her anyway, hopeful he would leave the
mountain with at least one alive. He spotted a pool of
bright red blood in the snow, which gave him hope she
was still alive.

"Fallon," he barked while scraping away the flurries
and ice from around the small, much-too-slim body.

The woman was lying on her stomach, one arm bent
with her hand near her face, and matted ebony hair ob-
scuring her features. Her fingers were slim as they dug
into the snow as if she had tried to crawl away.

Hayden could only imagine the pain she had been
put through, the heartache Deirdre had given her. He
held his breath as he put a finger beneath her nose and
felt a soft stirring of air.

At least they would leave the cursed mountain with
one life. He reached for her and paused again. He didn't
want to hurt her, but it had been so long since he had
been gentle, he wasn't sure he knew how. All he knew
was battle and death.

Maybe he should allow Fallon care for her. But as
soon as the thought went through his mind, Hayden re-
jected it. He had found her, he would see to her. He didn't
know why, he just knew that it was important to him.

Hayden blew out a breath and slowly, firmly placed

his hands on the woman's body before he tenderly turned her over. Her arm fell to the side, lifeless and still. Disquiet settled in his gut like a stone.

He shifted so that he leaned over her, shielding her from the onslaught of snow. Once he had her in his arms, Hayden brushed the hair from her face to see her incredibly long black lashes spiked with frozen snow.

He felt something shift inside him when he saw her face was pale as death, but even beneath the scratches, dried blood, and ice he could see her beauty, her timeless allure.

She had high cheekbones and a small, pert nose. Her brows were as black as the midnight sky and arched over her eyes. Her lips were full, sensual, and her neck long and lean.

But it was her cream-colored skin, so flawless and perfect, that made him reach out and stroke her cheek with the back of his finger.

A shock of something primitive and urgent went through his body like a bolt of lightning. He couldn't take his eyes from her, couldn't stop touching her.

Her body struggled for breath, struggled for life, proving she was a fighter. Even with the elements taking the breath from her one heartbeat at a time, she didn't give up.

Something inside him broke at that moment. He hadn't been able to save his family or the many Druids on Cairn Toul, but he would save this woman, whoever she was.

A feeling of protectiveness wound through him. It had been so long since he'd felt protective of anyone or anything that he almost hadn't recognized the emotion. Now that he did, however, it grew stronger the longer he held her in his arms.

He would make sure she survived. He would ensure she was protected at all times. It wouldn't make up for the lives of his family or the Druids, but he had to do it.

Hayden found himself wishing she'd open her eyes so he could see them. He wanted to give his oath to her right then, for her to know that he would fight with her. Instead, she lay unconscious in his arms.

His vow would have to wait, but nothing could stop him from pledging himself to her.

"Does she live?" Fallon asked.

Hayden glanced up, startled to find Fallon near when he hadn't heard him approach. That wasn't like Hayden, but then again, he had never held such a lovely woman in his arms before, especially one that needed him as she did. "Just. She's bleeding badly, though I cannot tell where she is wounded."

"Judging by the blood on your hand, I would say somewhere on her back."

Hayden looked at the hand holding her and grimaced. He doubted they had much time to save her. For the first time in . . . ages . . . the need to defend, to shield someone consumed him, drove him. "She's shivering."

"Then let's get her out of here," Fallon said.

Hayden lifted her small frame in his arms. She was light, but through her clothes he could feel the sumptuous curves that proclaimed her a woman. He gave a nod to Fallon and waited. Fallon laid his hand on Hayden's arm, and in a blink they were standing in the great hall of MacLeod Castle.

"God's teeth!" someone yelled at their sudden appearance in the castle.

"Sonya!" Fallon bellowed.

The hall swarmed with Warriors, but Hayden only had eyes for the woman. He wanted, nay needed, her to survive, and was surprised to find himself praying—something he hadn't done since before his family's murder. He decided then and there he would protect her with his life.

He felt the warm stickiness of her blood as it traveled from his hand down his arm to his elbow to drip on the stone floor. Her breathing was ragged, her body so still he would think her dead if he didn't see her chest rising and falling, slowly but surely.

"Sonya, hurry!" Hayden shouted. The thought of holding another dead body in his arms made Hayden's heart quicken with dread.

Death surrounded him, always had, most likely always would. But now, he wanted life for this small woman, whoever she was.

There was a whooshing sound as Broc landed in the great hall, Sonya in his arms. Broc folded his large, sleek indigo wings against him as he set Sonya on her feet and pushed his god down to return to normal.

Sonya said not a word as she rushed to Hayden. The single, thick braid holding her fiery hair hung down her back with small tendrils curling about her face.

"Put her on the table," Sonya instructed him.

Hayden didn't want to relinquish his hold on the woman, but he knew he had no choice if he wanted her to survive. He glanced at her, at her parted lips and ethereal face. "She's cold."

"And I'll get her warm as soon as I heal her," Sonya

told him, her amber eyes meeting his gaze. "Let me heal her, Hayden."

Quinn took a step toward the table. "Broc—"

"I know," Broc answered.

Hayden looked between the two Warriors to find their gazes locked on the female in his arms. There was something in their tone, something he should recognize, but he couldn't focus on anything but the woman.

He forced his attention back to Sonya. "I think the wound is on her back."

"Then lay her on her stomach," Sonya said as she pushed up the sleeves of her gown.

"I'll help," said Lucan's wife, Cara.

Hayden glanced down at Cara. They'd had their differences, and in some ways still did, since Cara carried *drough* blood in her veins. She might never have undergone the ritual, but it was enough that Hayden had wanted to see her dead.

It was only out of respect for the MacLeods that Hayden left Cara alone. Still, it rankled him to have her near. Evil bred evil, it was just a matter of time before it took Cara.

The next thing Hayden knew, the other two women of the castle, Marcail and Larena, were also there. All but Larena were Druids. Larena was the only female Warrior, and she had the distinction of being Fallon's wife.

Matter of fact, the only female that wasn't mated to a MacLeod was Sonya, and Hayden had seen the way Broc watched the Druid when he thought no one was looking.

"I need her gown cut," Sonya said.

Hayden didn't hesitate to allow a red claw to lengthen

from his fingertip. He sliced the woman's gown with one swipe, and when the gown fell open to reveal the female's back, the entire hall sucked in a breath. Hayden's gut clenched and his blood turned to ice.

"Holy hell," Quinn murmured and rubbed a hand over his mouth.

There were no words as Hayden stared at the scars that crisscrossed the slender back of the woman on the table. Whoever this female was, she had suffered greatly and horrifically. And often. If he felt protective of her before, it was nothing compared to what arose in him then.

He would find who did this to her, find them and make them suffer as they had made her suffer. Then he would kill them.

However, it was the wound on her shoulder that drew Hayden's gaze. "What happened to her?"

Sonya leaned close and poked at the bleeding injury. "Looks like a blade of some sort. I need to clean it to be sure what happened, but from what I can see, I think the weapon pierced her skin, and then was dragged from her shoulder down her back to her shoulder blade."

In an instant a bowl of water was placed next to Sonya. She wrung out a cloth and began to clean the woman's wound. Agonizing moments later, Sonya lifted her head, her lips compressed in a tight line.

"There's magic involved in this wound. I cannot tell if it caused the wound or only made it fester."

Lucan and Fallon moved to stand on either side of Quinn, who was at the woman's feet. Broc had also shifted closer to Sonya. It was then that Hayden looked around the hall and noticed every Warrior at MacLeod Castle now ogled the female.

Hayden's gaze swung to Quinn to find the youngest MacLeod watching him with sharp, pale green eyes. Before he could ask Quinn why he was staring, the woman let out a low moan full of suffering and agony.

Sonya stilled. A heartbeat later she tossed down the cloth and lifted her hands over the woman's wound, palms down, fingers splayed. Sonya's eyes closed, and Hayden could feel her magic fill the hall as she began to heal the wound.

Cara and Marcail soon joined their magic with Sonya's, but nothing they did seemed to assist the healing. The woman let out a scream and tried to jerk from the table.

Hayden held her down, careful not to touch her wound, but the more magic the Druids used, the worse the woman became. Frustration welled up within Hayden while he watched helplessly as the woman suffered.

"What are you doing to her?" he demanded of Sonya.

The Druid's amber eyes snapped open to glare at him. Sonya reached over and took Cara's and Marcail's arms and lowered them. As soon as they did the woman stopped her movements and lay still and quiet.

It was like she had died. Yet Hayden could still see the breath leaving her body, could still see the blood flowing from the wound.

"Something isn't right," Sonya said.

Marcail shook her head, the rows of tiny, sable braids on the crown of her head moving against her cheek. "It was almost as if she fought against our magic."

"What could possibly do that?" Cara asked. Her mahogany eyes sought out Sonya, but Sonya didn't answer. Instead, Sonya moved aside the tangled mass of ebony locks from the woman's neck. With slow movements, she tugged at the thin leather strap until she found what she was looking for.

Hayden took one look at the Demon's Kiss dangling from Sonya's fingers and felt the same betrayal and fury he had on the night of his family's murder.

Look for the other novels in Donna Grant's
sensational Dark Sword series

DANGEROUS HIGHLANDER
ISBN: 978-0-312-38122-6

FORBIDDEN HIGHLANDER
ISBN: 978-0-312-38123-3

Available from St. Martin's Paperbacks